Welcome to Fortune Bay

Summer of Fortune is *the first full length novel of the Fortune Bay series.*

Years ago I lived in a village in the Pacific Northwest near where I live today that was the inspiration for Fortune Bay. On my walks, I could see, through the trees, a cabin on the lake and in my mind I hung stories on its crumbling chimney.

Gradually the story of the cabin and the people who lived in it took shape and I wrote this book—and then watched in surprise as the community of Fortune Bay came to life.

To find out more about my inspirations for this series, sneak peaks into the other books, and **the free book, Lake of Dreams, that I send to my Reader's Group,** *go to my website,* **www.JudithHudsonAuthor.com**

Thanks for reading,
Judith Hudson

The Fortune Bay Series
Available on Amazon as eBook and paperback.

Lake of Dreams
Get this free prequel e-novella when
you sign up for my readers group at
bit.ly/freeFB-e-book

Summer of Fortune
Book One
Maddie wasn't looking for romance. Could a summer of
freedom change her life forever?

The Good Neighbor
Book Two
Sean hates to see Frankie and her father estranged. He'd give
anything to know where his own daughter is.

Home for Christmas
Book Three
Blue's carried a torch for Louise his whole life, but this time
he's not sure he can wait around to pick up the pieces.

Family Matters
A Sequel Novella
Things are at a low ebb for Frankie and Sean. Be sure to read
The Good Neighbor and *Home for Christmas* first!

Starting Over
Book Four
After a horrific motorcycle accident, Marshall's life seems to
be over—until Lily knocks on his door.

Starlight and Tinsel
A Christmas Novella
Star finally gets her chance to shine in this Christmas novella.

Also by Judith Hudson
Writing as J.M. Hudson

The Rocky and Bernadette Mystery Series

Temple of the Jaguar
A Mayan Murder Mystery
A travel cozy mystery. A travel writer and a
photographer's first job together in the Yucatan quickly
unravels when a body is discovered in the crocodile lagoon.

Summer of Fortune

Book One in the Fortune Bay Series

Judith Hudson

MAY

Chapter 1

When life hands you lemons, you make lemonade.

My motto in life, thought Maddie Tedesco when her ex-husband's name popped up on the caller display. But really, how much lemonade did one woman have to drink?

When she answered the phone, his greeting was brief. "Maddie."

"Mark."

They didn't spend much time on pleasantries anymore. He was Jenny's father though so, when he asked to speak to their daughter, Maddie handed her the phone.

"Hi Dad...Everything's great...No, nothing planned ..." Jenny's voice rose to a shrill crescendo. "I'd love to... Sure, we'll talk." She put down the phone with a satisfied smack.

Listening from her post at the kitchen sink, Maddie's jaw clenched. How many times had Mark disappointed their daughter, making plans and then not showing up? If he did it again, she'd wring his neck.

Plastering the smile on her face that she'd perfected in the ten years she'd been divorced, she turned to her daughter.

"Mom. You'll never guess what. Dad asked me to spend the summer with him and Kate."

Maddie's cheeks stiffened as the smile melted like a chalk drawing in the rain. Jenny would graduate from high school next spring and, thorny as it may be, this could be her last summer at home. By asking Jenny first, Mark had undermined Maddie's veto again, swooped in like a fairy godfather and invited Jenny to Yuppiedom-by-the-sea.

Maddie leaned heavily on the counter. "Do you want to go?" Her voice sounded hoarse.

"Of course I do. Why would I spend the summer in this stifling attic when I can be in a mansion by the beach?"

Hardly a mansion, but Mark's beautiful Seattle Craftsman-style home *was* right across the street from the beach, and a far cry from Maddie's third floor walk-up.

"How about it, can I go?" Jenny asked.

"I don't know. I have to think..."

"Come on. This is my chance to move up in the world. I don't want to end up like you—living in an attic when I'm thirty-five. "

"Hey, it's cozy."

"And working at a job I hate."

"I don't hate my job," Maddie objected. But Jenny had pretty well nailed it. Being a receptionist at an art gallery—or an administrative assistant, as Maddie preferred to call it—wasn't her dream job, but it did pay the rent.

"You could have fooled me." Jenny put her hands on her hips in a perfect imitation of Maddie. "You always say I can achieve whatever I want if I just put my mind to it. 'Go after what you want,' you say. Well, I want this. A chance for something better."

Maddie stared at her daughter. Jenny stared boldly back, her long, straight, reddish-blonde bangs hanging in her eyes. Maddie's hand itched to reach out and brush them aside but she resisted. Instead, she turned away, picked up a scrub pad and began scouring the sink. "We'll see."

As she sensed Jenny watching her from the door, her shoulders stiffened and her hand slowed in the sink.

"It's clean enough Mom," Jenny said softly. Then, like a wraith, she vanished into her room.

Maddie put her hands on the counter, dropped her head and sunk her weight into her arms. It was unnerving when Jenny caught her cleaning. And really, was cleaning so bad? Jenny seemed to think so but Maddie could think of things that were much worse.

She had promised herself she'd be a good role model for her daughter, the best mother ever. Fun yet patient, adventurous yet wise. Her daughter's best friend. And it had worked, at first. But sometime during the last few years, their relationship had gone from BFFs to combatants. Mark could offer Jenny a life Maddie couldn't hope to achieve. What if Jenny didn't want to come back after the summer?

She glanced at the clock, six thirty, time for a family-fix.

In the living room she turned on the TV and the *Family Ties* opening scenes appeared on the screen. As always, the reassuring music was an anchor for her turbulent emotions. Turning up the volume, she went back to the kitchen to start dinner.

These were the families she'd grown up with: The Seavers, the Cosbys and her favorite, the Keatons. Elyse Keaton had been her dream mother, had taught her more about being a mother than her own mom ever had. Despite being an architect, Elyse always had time for the family.

Maddie longed to be part of a family like that and had tried to give Jenny the best home she could. But obviously her best wasn't good enough or Jenny wouldn't be so eager to go and live with her dad.

Elyse's voice echoed in her head. *"Of course Jenny wants to connect with her father. Don't you remember what that was like?"*

She remembered all right. The longing, the wondering, the ache in her chest. At least Jenny knew who her father was.

Maddie let out a sigh that left her hollow. The weight of inevitability settled on her shoulders. Of course Jenny should go to her dad's. It was the right thing to do.

Go after what you want. She *had* said that—and meant it.

Maybe in this case, being a good mother meant letting her daughter go.

Wiping her hands on a dish towel, Maddie called Jenny back into the kitchen. Maddie's heart twinged when she recognized the suspicious look on her daughter's face that pretty well epitomized their past year together.

She tried to smile but her cheeks felt like hard plastic. "I've made a decision. You can go to your dad's for the summer."

Jenny let out a whoop and threw her arms around her mother. The irony wasn't lost on Maddie that this was the first spontaneous hug in so long, and all because she was letting her go.

Jenny rushed to her room to call her friends. Maddie took a deep breath and turned back to her magazine recipe. She'd splayed the chicken on a roasting pan—apparently it baked faster this way—and now crumbled the dried rosemary and thyme between her fingers, sprinkling the herbs over the bird. She added salt and pepper and, as the final notes of the *Family Ties* theme song died, slid the chicken into the oven.

Then she turned off the TV, grabbed a rag and started to scrub.

So bite me, she thought. *It helps me think.*

Jenny was right about her job. What happened to her dream of being a photographer? When she and Mark had first married, she was just starting out. A creative fire had burned in her belly. Some interesting freelance assignments came her way that hinted at a promising career, but once she was married and a mother, Mark wanted her at home. She'd resisted at first, but somehow the jobs petered out until, without even a puff, they completely disappeared.

After the divorce, she'd been happy to get the job at the gallery, but ten years in, it felt like—settling.

The only bright spot that she could see in this whole situation was that now she could spend the summer working on her photography. Maddie's boss Eileen had never supported her work as an artist, but there was another gallery owner, Tori at the Edge, who had expressed interest in her black and white darkroom art.

Maddie threw down the duster and pulled her portfolio out from behind the couch. If she was going to make lemonade, she might as well get started. She'd show Tori her photographs tomorrow.

* * *

The following evening, dusk had fallen and her boss Eileen was long gone when Maddie finally closed the heavy glass gallery door and turned the key in the lock. The neon signs of gallery row reflected in the wet pavement as she fought the stream of people hurrying home from work and headed to Pioneer Square. A historic district popular with tourists, it was a mecca for new galleries like the Edge.

Good name, the Edge. Tori had a knack for marketing. Maddie had never been able to get out there and flog her work. After ten years of putting her dreams on hold, it had only gotten harder as her faith in herself slowly ebbed away.

Time to make a change.

As the downtown hustle fell away and she entered the relative quiet of the streets around the Square, her boots sounded a determined rhythm on the pavement. The rain had eased to a heavy mist that fogged the streetlights and frizzed her hair. The trees showed a faint haze of green and she could smell spring in the air.

In a week the city would be in full bloom. Other years, she would have had her camera out and been snapping atmospheric nighttime shots as she walked. Lately though, the city had lost its magic, and tonight her mind was focused on her meeting with Tori.

Rounding a corner, Maddie's heart lurched at the outline of a hunched figure on a dark storefront step. Tucked in out of the rain, a woman sat with an upturned hat on the ground in front of her.

Time slowed and the ground felt like quick sand beneath Maddie's feet. *Please, no.*

The woman turned to face her. It wasn't her mother. The hand squeezing Maddie's heart loosened its grip and she blew out a sharp breath. Taking a bill from her purse, she dropped it into the hat. "Get yourself something hot to eat," she said gently, even though she knew the chance of that was virtually nil.

As she walked away, her shoulders twitched as she tried to shake off the adrenalin buzz. Now that her mother lived in the city, in the back of her mind Maddie knew that Cindy could pop out anytime, anywhere, and turn Maddie's world upside down.

Suddenly she was standing under Tori's hand-carved gallery sign. Time to get back on track.

She prided herself on being fearless, most of the time. But this one-two punch of her two worst fears, meeting her mother by surprise and showing her photographs to a gallery, had turned her knees to mush. She forced the thoughts of her mother out of her mind—*that wasn't her, just a sad old woman*—and pulled her thoughts back to the job ahead.

Showing her photographs always felt like she was stripped naked and flattened on the gallery wall. She closed her eyes and breathed deeply. *In, one, two. Out, one, two...*

She'd read about this breathing technique in a magazine. It was designed to ease panic attacks and, she discovered while reading the article, apparently she had them.

By the time she reached ten, her heart rate had slowed. Pulling a tube of crimson lipstick out of her shoulder bag, she applied it with a sure hand. The ritual always gave her courage, allowing her to channel the kick-ass, take-no-prisoners femme fatales from the black and white movies she loved.

She rolled her shoulders. *Showtime.* Tugging open the wooden door, she climbed the steep gallery stairs, the envelope with her prints clutched in one clammy hand.

The smell of fresh paint rolled down to greet her and she stopped at the top of the stairs to admire the dark red paint, the color of borsht, that Tori had applied to the walls in preparation for the next show. "Wow."

A muffled voice called out through an open door at the back of the room. "Somebody there?"

Shaking the raindrops off her jacket, Maddie crossed the gallery and peeked into the office. Tori's ample rear end, sheathed in leopard-skin pants, stood in bold relief as she bent over a stack of paintings.

Maddie smiled. "Busy?"

Tori stood up and shook her head, her short pixie-cut hair sticking out in all directions, as usual. "Tuesday night is Art Walk and we're going to be swamped. Not that I'm complaining." Her gaze dropped to the envelope in Maddie's hands and her face lit up. "For me?"

Nerves hit the panic button in Maddie's brain and her fingers instinctively tightened on the envelope. Tori tugged it out of her hands with a wicked grin and spread the gritty eight-by-ten black and whites of the city and its people out on the table.

"These are fantastic. Great contrast. Your darkroom work adds so much drama; I just want to rub my finger over those velvety blacks. People are eager for black and whites again. They're tired of photoshopped specials."

Maddie's shoulders relaxed. It was going to be fine.

Then Tori asked, "Weren't these in your show last year?"

Maddie's chin came up, her eyes widened. "You saw the show?" That venue had been more of a gift shop, not a real gallery at all.

"I read the article in *The Caller* and stopped by."

Maddie nodded, her mind racing. "It brought in a lot of people. I only have a few pieces left. I was hoping you could put them up sometime."

Tori shook her head. "I don't know kiddo." She tapped the prints on the table in front of her. "These are great, but they're old work. I was hoping you'd bring me something new."

Gritting her teeth, Maddie attempted to smile. That was a

problem. She didn't have any new work. Shortly after last winter's show, somehow, somewhere, she'd lost her muse. The urban shots on which she'd built her reputation—such as it was—didn't inspire her any more. The spark had died leaving her a gutted candle, a hollow puddle of wax. She had hoped getting a few pictures into a gallery would give her the push she needed to start moving in a fresh direction. Tori was right though. She couldn't put up old work.

Maddie gathered the prints into a pile. "I understand."

Tori fisted her hands on her sturdy hips. "I don't think you do. You need to get your ass out from behind that counter at Eileen's and get behind the camera where you belong. These are great, but it's time you had your own show. Right here. My October artist just cancelled. Can I pencil you in?"

Maddie's eyes widened. Her own show. *Her* work up on the walls. The chance of a lifetime. The star falls and breaks her leg and Maddie Tedesco steps in.

But October was only six months away. Could she possibly get a new body of work together by then while still working full time? Eileen would hit the ceiling...

But what about her resolution to be a better role model for Jenny? Wasn't the best way to go after what *she* wanted, too?

Although Tori was several inches shorter than Maddie, she managed to put her arm around Maddie's shoulders. "You know, sometimes to get the good things in life you have to take a leap of faith. Like I did last year when I opened this gallery."

Maddie heard Elyse Keaton's voice whisper in her ear. *Time to make lemonade, dear.*

Okay. She grabbed the last lemon and squeezed.

"I'll take the show."

"Good, I'll pencil you in."

"No. You can write it in pen. I'm not sure if I'm jumping or if I've been pushed, but I'm definitely taking the show."

* * *

Elbows on the kitchen table, Maddie rested her head in her hands, the bass rhythm from the floor below beating a backbeat to her thoughts.

What was she thinking, accepting Tori's offer? How could she take the show?

How could she not?

Even after she and Mark had split up, she had continued taking pictures. Preferring the compositional challenge of black and white, she had set up her darkroom in the bathroom, taking Jenny inside when she was too young to be left in the apartment alone.

But Jenny was almost grown now, taken care of for the summer, and this show—*a solo show*—had dropped in her lap. How could she pass it up? Especially with the long, lonely, rest-of-her-life looming ahead of her. This was her chance to get back in the game.

If she was being perfectly honest, she knew why she'd stayed working for Eileen for so long. It was safe. Secure. Didn't demand she put herself on the line. Now, though, she was afraid she had traded that safety for her daughter's respect, and lost her own creative spark along the way.

That was something Mark had never understood, that to her photography was like breathing. It was how she experienced the world and without it, she only felt half alive. She might as well just breathe into the top half of her lungs, never feeling the satisfaction of filling them completely. Without her photography as an outlet, numbness had slowly crept into her extremities.

Outside her tiny kitchen window, the setting sun gilded the snowy mountain tops that peeked up from behind the downtown. She'd never been to the Olympic Peninsula before. Had never had the time or money for any kind of holiday. She needed something to jumpstart her creative juices though. And leaving the city and heading into the mountains? That would be different. That would be new. Surely then she would find her muse.

Take the summer off to work on the show? That was crazy. Wasn't it? Could she afford it? Maybe just barely.

This would be something truly worthwhile to spend her nest egg on. An investment in herself, in her future. A fresh start.

If she was going to make the most of this chance, she couldn't hold back. She had to be all in.

Chapter 2

Three weeks later to the day, Maddie dropped Jenny at Mark's house to finish the school year. Eileen had hit the gallery's vaulted ceiling when Maddie told her she wanted to take the summer off to work on the show, but once Maddie found an art student to fill in for the season, things had tumbled into place. As if the universe was giving her a big thumbs-up. She just crossed her fingers that her job would be waiting for her when she got back.

As she pulled away from Mark's house, father and daughter stood on the stone front steps, waving goodbye, Mark's arm draped casually over Jenny's shoulder. Maddie watched them recede in the rear-view mirror and—*oh, great*—Mark's new wife Kate joined them on the steps. The stone front steps of the beautiful heritage house they had lovingly restored. The perfect family in the perfect house. Maddie shook her head and dragged her eyes back to the road. How could she ever compete with that?

Two hours later, Maddie stood on the deck of the giant car ferry as it plowed across Puget Sound. Her Nikon digital to her eye, she zoomed in on the forested slopes of the Olympic Peninsula as sunlight caught the rugged, snowy peaks. She snapped a shot.

The salt air whipped around her, clearing away all doubt. *This is why I came. This is what I am looking for.* Her new muse was a forest nymph. She just knew it.

But she needed a cheap place to rent for four months, because she planned to be back in the city by Labor Day to work at the gallery and welcome Jenny home. Assuming her daughter wanted to come home after, as Jenny had put it, her "summer in paradise."

That was what worried Maddie most, that Jenny would

decide to live with her father. She had to win back her daughter's respect and that meant making good on the show.

It had been years since she'd been on her own. It felt exhilarating—and weird like she had lost her anchor with no timeline to follow and no one to look after. Adrift and disoriented, she needed a home base and she needed it soon. With high hopes and a few apartment leads in her pocket, she drove her aging station wagon, fondly known as The Beast, off the ferry in Bremerton.

Two days later, still looking but starting worry, Maddie pulled into the lot of a fast food diner. None of the places she'd looked at were at all possible. All lacked any hint of inspiration and, in some cases, even basic hygiene. This was no closer to her forest nymph than Seattle.

Tapping an agitated rhythm on the Arborite tabletop, she studied the map. Roads circled the Olympic Peninsula close to the shore with a few smaller roads heading up the river valleys into the mountains.

Further inland was probably less expensive, an important consideration since in the end, unable to bear the thought of other people using their dishes and sleeping in their beds, she hadn't sub-let the Seattle apartment. Online from home, she hadn't seen any inland rentals but maybe she could find a cottage somewhere. Nothing fancy, just a place to sleep, a small kitchen, and a bathroom where she could set up her darkroom.

She could see it in her mind's eye—nestled in the forest, dripping with atmosphere.

A young waitress stopped at her table, pad in hand. "Road trip?"

"Sort of. If you could go anywhere on the peninsula for a holiday, where would you go?"

The girl chewed the end of her pencil, then stabbed a finger at a lake in the center of the map. "Fortune Bay on Majestic Lake. It's beautiful, right in the mountains. My uncle has a hunting camp there and I go up sometimes in the summer. I love it. He's right on the lake."

Maddie ordered a burger and studied the map. Fortune Bay was a dot on the map at the end of the road running up one side the lake. Isolated, probably rustic and picturesque as all get out. As good a place to start as any.

She ate quickly, then climbed back into the Beast and headed west.

An hour later, she crested a ridge and pulled into a rest stop at the top of the pass. Majestic Lake hugged the curves of the valley below, surrounded by forested mountains, some still tipped in snow, that rolled out to the horizon. Pulse racing, she pulled out her camera, first taking wide-angle shots, then zooming in on the shore.

Goosebumps prickled on her arms. Something down there pulled her like a magnet.

Back in the car, she flew down the mountain and through the town of Majestic, following the signs toward Fortune Bay. Fifteen minutes later, all spent driving through a dark forest worthy of the Brothers Grimm, the lake winked at her again through the trees and, soon after that, a sign welcomed her to Fortune Bay.

Maddie drove slowly though the town; a handful of streets lined with faded, crayon-colored houses and, at the end, a general store. The road continued along the lake from there, in and out of forest and field until, a mile out of town, the trees opened up and a fallow field, bordered by tall evergreens, ran down to the lake.

A cabin peeked through the trees, the crumbling chimney stretching toward the sun as if preening for her attention. Maddie's foot hit the brake and the Beast shuddered to a halt. She inched ahead to the spot where a lane disappeared into the trees, and pulled over to the side of the road. From here, the building was hidden in the forest but a hand-painted sign nailed to the trunk of a massive fir tree announced that the cabin was for rent. Someone had written a phone number across the bottom of the sign but, having been disappointed before, she decided it couldn't hurt to take a peek before she called.

She jumped out of the car, ducked under the rope strung across the drive and headed down the lane. A gusty breeze swirled branches overhead and the air had the faintly medicinal tang of lake water and cedar.

At the end of the drive the cabin was waiting, with weathered white siding, an overgrown flowerbed and a porch facing the lake thirty feet away. The wind blew white caps out on the bay and rocked the limbs of the towering evergreens protecting the cabin. Maddie framed a shot of the porch in the viewfinder and clicked.

It was perfect. Charming and oozing with inspiration. She pressed her lips together in excitement. She had found her muse, but could she afford it?

Up on the porch, a sun-bleached couch stood under a picture window and, cupping her hands to the glass, she peered inside. The room was dark. Dead flies lined the sill. Definitely deserted and possibly right in her price range.

Then something moved at the back of the room. Something big.

Maddie stifled a scream and leaped back off the couch, landing on her butt on the wooden porch floor.

The inner door flew open and a man stood in the doorway.

"Looking for something?" he asked, his voice deep and rumbly. He held a work-gloved hand out to help her, but Maddie was already scrambling to her feet.

"Sorry. I thought the cabin was empty."

"It is." He crossed his arms over his chest, his shoulders taking up most of the doorway. Dark hair hung long on his forehead and his eyes, a startling color as bright as the blue dome over the lake, set off faint warning bells in her head.

For a moment she forgot why she was there. Then he raised an eyebrow.

Right. "Is the cabin for rent?"

"It is now. I was just cleaning up. It's been empty, but some kids got in—were partying inside. We're lucky they didn't burn the place down. That's why we decided to rent."

A gust of wind pushed Maddie like hands on her back towards the door until they were standing face to face. "Can I look inside?"

He stepped out of her way and waved her in.

A tattered doormat *kaflumped* in place sending up a cloud of sun-spangled dust. Looking down, she read the script on the mat, *Welcome Home*, and smiled as she stepped inside.

Most of the cabin could be seen at a glance; one large room with the kitchen on the left and the living room on the right. Through an opening at the back she glimpsed a bedroom, mostly hidden by a flowery curtain hanging in the doorway.

The furniture was old and well used but would do just fine. A calendar, six years out of date, hung on the wall beside a shelf lined with figurines of dancing women. Dust was thick on every surface but the place smelled clean and fresh—she sniffed—almost sweet.

It was perfect.

She returned to the porch but the man had gone down to stand by the water, looking out over the bay with his cell phone to his ear. When he heard her come out, he put the phone in his back pocket and walked up to the cabin.

As Maddie hurried down the steps to meet him, the bottom step rocked and she stumbled. He reached out and grabbed her arm—letting her go almost at once when she regained her balance.

She stood perfectly still, pulse racing, her heart beating double time, the imprint of his hand still warm on her arm. *No harm, no foul.*

"I'll fix that," he said. "So are you interested?"

"How much?"

"Four hundred a month, two months in advance. As is. Water's on. Everything works."

"I'll take it. And I'll pay cash. Could I have a receipt?"

"Sure," he said and went into the cabin.

Maddie spun around, her back to the cabin door, and felt around in the bottom of her shoulder bag until her hand closed on a soft lumpy shape. Her money sock, her nest-egg, all the money she had in the world. She liked to have it close, just in case.

She pulled a roll of bills the size of her fist out of the sock, much of it earned at the show last year, and wincing, peeled sixteen fifties off the roll. It was a big chunk of cash, but compared to sleeping in motel rooms and eating in diners, the cabin was a bargain.

The man came back onto the porch, a pad in his hand, pen at the ready. "My name's Jake Murphy. Phone number's on the receipt. And you are?"

"Maddie Tedesco."

She spelled out her last name and he wrote it on the pad, then they exchanged the money for the receipt.

"Where are you from?"

"Seattle."

"How long are you planning to stay?"

"For the summer."

He handed her a key on a brass chain that pooled cool as water in the palm of her hand.

Her eyes widened and she shrugged. "That's it?" She had expected a lot more red tape. References at the very least.

"I know where you live," he said, one side of his mouth twitching back in a half-smile that popped a dimple on his lean, whiskered cheek.

She pressed her lips firmly together. That dimple could definitely be a problem. But before she could ruminate on that any further, he was gone, raising a hand in salute as he disappeared around the corner of the cabin.

Maddie closed her hand around the key and did a silent fist pump in the air. *Yes.* She'd found her home base.

The Beast was still out on the road, but first things first—

to find the bathroom.

There weren't many places to look. A steep staircase without a railing at the back of the kitchen led to a trap door in the ceiling. She hoped it wasn't up there—the attic was probably full of mice, or worse.

Lifting the flowered curtain, she surveyed the bedroom. Bed, dresser, a time-speckled mirror. Lifting the lid of a large cedar trunk in the corner, she saw it was full of clean linens that smelled sweet, like the rest of the cabin, of vanilla and spice. Surprising considering it looked like the place had been empty for years.

She pulled a quilt out of the trunk. Like something a grandmother would make, the fabric felt soft against her cheek and she inhaled the safe, clean smell of cedar. For a moment her eyes drifted shut. Forcing them open she shook her head. She'd make the bed later but first, the bathroom.

Where could it be? The cabin was small—unless ...

She sucked in a horrified breath. What if she'd rented a place with an outhouse?

Back on the porch, she scanned the woods for a shed with a sickle moon on the door.

Nothing. Then she noticed a shorter than normal door at the end of the porch. Feeling a little like Alice, she turned the knob and stepped into an antiquated laundry room. Another door faced her on the far wall and she opened it cautiously, her mind reeling back to thoughts of mice and worse. To her relief, there was a small but complete bathroom inside. A broken, boarded-up window stood over a claw-foot tub, but otherwise, as advertised, everything worked.

She used the facilities, running her hand longingly along the tub's cool porcelain lip on her way out. A hot soak would have to wait.

Pulling the Beast up beside the cabin, she carried everything inside and shut the door. May was cold in the mountains, and the cabin, surrounded by trees, received little direct sunlight at this time of year. Wrapping her arms around her ribs for warmth, she searched the walls for a thermostat. Instead she came face to face with a woodstove in the corner.

She groaned. *How did I miss that little detail?*

"Unpack first, deal with the woodstove later," she said aloud, then shook her head. "Talking to myself already and only four more months to go."

She put the map of the Peninsula up on the living room wall and plugged in an old TV in a big wooden cabinet that stood in the corner behind the front door. She didn't expect color but was dismayed when all she got was static.

Of course there wasn't cable. Or wifi. She'd have to figure something out if she was going to work on her website because that was the other prong of her new career strategy—to design a website to market the thousands of digital photographs of Seattle she'd taken to magazines and online travel sites.

Carefully, she arranged her framed photographs of Jenny on top of the old TV, wondering if she could stay busy enough to not miss her daughter.

She unpacked her clothes and made the bed, then fished the money sock out of her purse. Getting down on her knees, she stashed it safely at the back of the bottom dresser drawer.

When she returned to the kitchen, the mountains across the lake were a dark silhouette against a fading turquoise sky. Her darkroom equipment still lay in a pile on the living room floor; enlarger, plastic trays, jugs of chemicals and boxes of paper. It would all have to wait until morning.

She switched on the lights and shivered as the cold settled into her bones. Finding a heavy plaid jacket hung behind the door, she tugged it on and turned to the woodstove in the corner.

Should have done this first thing. A roaring blaze would chase out the cold that clung to the walls. She'd seen firewood piled neatly in the driveway, so she marched outside and picked out a round log the diameter of her thigh. Back inside, she scrunched up some paper, put it in the stove, set the log on top and struck a match.

The match flamed, the paper caught, the fire flare brightly—then burned out. The log sat untouched on a bed of ash.

Maddie tried again, using more paper and a pile of wood scraps from the pail behind the stove. A few minutes later smoke poured out the open iron door but this time a faint waft of heat drift up.

Pretty darn proud of herself, she swung the heavy door shut and brushed the soot off her hands. She looked around and nodded. She could do this. Just stick to the plan. She always had a master plan. It was how she kept her life on track. The current plan was: take the pictures, get Jenny back, then mount the show. Definitely do-able. Moving on with her life.

Suddenly exhausted, she made a quick dinner of the bread and peanut butter she'd had in the car. Then she hung the jacket on the back of the bedroom chair, kicked off her shoes and fell into bed, pulling up the soft quilt up under her chin.

Sometimes, in times of stress, she felt more comfortable sleeping in her clothes. Old habits die hard, the cabin was cold, and she didn't have to justify her actions to anyone.

Besides, you never knew when, in a strange place, you might have to run.

Chapter 3

Thwack. Maddie's eyes flew open. Sound waves reverberated up the bed's iron legs, making the bedsprings vibrate.

Thwack.

Throwing off the blankets, she jumped out of bed, squealing when her feet hit the icy linoleum. A dark head passed by the window. Maddie dropped to her knees, scrambled to the window and pulled herself up at the sill.

Jake stood in the driveway, an axe in his hand. Setting a round, stove-length log on a stump, he brought the axe down with tremendous force. Maddie's eyebrows shot up as wood went flying.

He bent to pick up another log and set it on the stump. Then, *Thwack!* Shoulders rippling, he split that piece in two.

Have mercy. She'd never known a man who could swing an axe before—or one who'd even tried. He flipped a log upright with the toe of his boot and split it right there where it stood on the ground with another powerful stroke.

I've got to get a picture of that.

Her eyes glued to the action outside, Maddie patted her chest. Thank goodness she was already dressed. Grabbing the plaid jacket from the chair and her camera from the table, she headed for the door.

* * *

Jake wiped the sweat from his forehead. *Already warming up.*

The new tenant stumbled out onto the porch, pulling on a jacket—*his* jacket. Her eyes were still puffy with sleep and stray wisps of hair caught the sunlight as it curled every-which-way.

He'd always liked that tousled, just-got-out-of-bed kind of

look. A smile tugged the corner of his mouth. "Morning."

"Morning." She squinted, obviously trying to get her mind in gear. "What are you doing?"

"Splitting firewood. It won't burn like this."

Aware of her watching, he set another piece of wood on the stump and brought down the axe, foolishly pleased by how neatly it split.

He turned back to find her aiming a big camera his way. She snapped a quick shot. "Hope you don't mind."

"Guess not," he said, but frowned, not entirely sure.

She watched him for a moment with those sleepy eyes as he set another round of wood on the stump, then she retreated into the cabin.

What *was* he doing here? Good question. Sure, things needed doing around the place, but whatever happened to keeping his distance?

The axe came down hard.

He had rules about women, and a woman from the city living so close to the farm was way outside his safety zone. But the nights were still cold, she was his tenant and, from the look of her, had never split a piece of firewood in her life.

Thwack. More pieces went flying. Slowly the tension in his shoulders eased. He'd always enjoyed the rhythmic sound and motion of splitting wood.

Gotta get more exercise.

* * *

Ten minutes later, Maddie walked out of the cabin feeling more in control, a steaming cup of coffee in each hand.

She watched as Jake leaned the axe against the house and rolled his shoulders loosely, like a cat. Then in one smooth motion he stripped off his grey woolen sweater to reveal a tight black T-shirt underneath that clearly defined the carved contours of his torso. What she'd give to get a picture of *that,* too. But she'd seen the way he looked at the camera and didn't want to press her luck. Not yet.

Jake turned to her and raised one eyebrow.

Her brain stalled for a moment, then she remembered the cups in her hands and thrust one toward him. "Sorry. It's black. I don't have any milk or sugar yet."

"Thanks. This'll be fine." As he reached for the cup, his blue eyes swept over her, the hint of a smile sparking that damn dimple again.

Maddie took a quick scalding gulp of her coffee, watching him over the rim.

He tested the rocky step with one battered work boot. "I'll get to this."

"No rush."

He took a sip of coffee and looked around the yard, seemingly content with the silence that followed.

Maddie was never comfortable with silence. It felt like an itch she had to scratch. She sipped, shifted her weight, her brain screaming, *say something*.

"I'm a photographer."

She hadn't meant to say *that*.

"Really."

She nodded. More silence. Grinding her teeth, she took another sip.

Jake cleared his throat. "Going to take some pictures around here?"

"Yes. I hope to."

I hope to? Where did *that* come from?

"Well, good luck." He glanced at his watch, gulped down his coffee and handed her the empty mug. "Thanks. I've gotta go."

Grabbing his sweater off the woodpile, he hung the axe on a nail on the wall and said, "I'll chop some more when I get a chance." Then he turned and strode up the long leafy drive, sweater slung over his shoulder, his lean frame in motion a joy to watch.

She couldn't suppress a sigh. Then shook her head and grinned. *Stop that right now.* The last thing she needed was a complication like that. With her show coming up and Jenny to see to, she didn't need any complications right now. Anyway, she was better off on her own, making her own decisions and sticking to her own plans.

She bent to pick up an armload of split wood.

Don't wish for something you can't have. Relationships were too risky for people like her. The only thing she knew about 'family' was what she'd learned on TV, and she was pretty sure that wasn't enough to make it work.

She cast one last look down the empty lane. But those blue eyes and that dimple when he smiled? That man was going to be trouble.

And, "good luck." What exactly did he mean by that?

Inside, she dropped the armload of split logs into the wood box and rubbed her hands on her arms. The cabin was as cold as a meat locker. She contemplated the wood stove in the corner.

It wasn't going to light itself. Getting down on her knees, she swung open the iron door. The same log from the night before sat scarcely charred, cold as a dead fish on a small bed of ash. Pressing her mouth in a determined line, she lifted out the log, put in some crumpled paper, the last of the kindling, and topped it off with a piece of freshly split wood.

Half an hour later, the cabin was full of smoke and yet, when she checked, the fire was out. What was she was doing wrong? Coughing and choking, she opened the windows, grabbed her list and headed to town.

At the Fortune Bay sign, she slowed the Beast. On her left, barely hidden by a fringe of trees, an old industrial site looked like a bomb had exploded. Not a tree or building remained, only a listing sign that read, *Fortune Bay Sawmill.* Beyond it, the lake sparkled blue in the sunshine. Her eye immediately began constructing abstract compositions from the rusting coils of wire and broken concrete slabs that littered the lot. The old mill site definitely had picture potential, but right now she was on a mission.

She pulled into the gravel parking lot of the general store

and cut the motor. Bright blue paint on the one-story building was peeling in places from the sun. Bleached-out ads for outdoor gear were plastered to the windows and posters proclaiming community events were taped to the door.

Sitting in the car, she watched battered cars and monster pick-ups come and go for mail and supplies. At least the Beast fit in perfectly here. She'd always thought it looked out of place parked between the Lexus' and Beamers in front of Eileen's uptown gallery.

A small group of people stood chatting in the parking lot, shooting curious glances her way. She recognized the attitude right away—small town, like the towns where she'd grown up. Gritting her teeth, she got out of the car and climbed the steps to the store, sending a cheery smile to the group in the lot.

Another fresh start, like when she moved to Seattle. It was all good.

Inside, three customers stood at the cash. They stopped talking and turned as one to look her over in silence, like the first day at every school she'd ever attended. And there had been many.

A woman behind the counter stopped packing a bag, arms raised, and looked inquiringly at Maddie over wire-framed glasses. The tantalizing aroma of fresh coffee wafted out through the open archway next to the cash.

"Coffee?" Maddie asked.

The woman hitched her head toward the archway. "In the café."

'Café' was a pretty fancy term for the backroom diner. Sunlight poured in through an east-facing window onto small tables, but Maddie chose to sit on a red-topped stool at the lunch counter instead. Two men in baseball caps stopped their discussion to stare and, tired of being the new girl in town, she smiled, raised a hand in greeting, then turned to the woman behind the counter and ordered a coffee.

The woman, whose nametag read 'Louise', was tall and stick thin. Her straight black hair was cut in an asymmetrical bob with one vermillion stripe on the longer side. With her striking hair, tall rangy figure and decidedly retro wardrobe, she could have been an artist, or a runway model.

Louise slapped a heavy white cup and saucer on the counter and poured in the steaming brew. Maddie added some cream, lifted the cup, inhaled the rich dark aroma and drank. Not the non-fat-soy-latté she ordered in the city, but it was good. Very good.

Louise re-filled her cup, then leaned back against the stainless-steel prep-counter and looked Maddie over with undisguised interest. After five long seconds, Louise finally cracked a wide grin. Her eyebrows jacked up in ready humor. "Hard night?"

Maddie smiled and over her second cup told Louise about the two logs that still lay in her stone-cold stove.

Louise nodded as she started Maddie's order of hotcakes and bacon. "That's Stephanie Murphy's cabin. It's been empty a long time. Must be chilled right through. You could check to see if the damper on the stove is open. It's either that or something's nested in the chimney."

Like what? "The damper?" she asked hopefully.

"The metal handle half-way up the stove pipe. You need it open to get the fire going, then shut it down to keep it from burning too hot. Open to start but close it later."

"Open to start, closed later." Committing the mantra to memory, Maddie cut into the stack of steaming hotcakes smothered in syrup that Louise set in front of her.

When she finished, she stocked up on supplies in the general store. They had everything she could possibly need from coffee to duct tape, flash drives to rubber boots.

Back at the cabin, she followed Louise's instructions and started the fire without a hitch, the smoke drifting obediently up the chimney. *Piece o' cake*, she thought as she wiped her sooty hands on her jeans.

Grime coated the windowsills, so she filled a pail with hot soapy water and went to work. Soon the bathroom shone and the fridge sparkled. She felt a palpable shift in the atmosphere and could have sworn the old building heaved a contented sigh.

After washing the pretty mis-matched china, she was wiping down the open kitchen cupboards when she discovered a wooden box on the top shelf. Small enough to sit in the palm of her hand, someone had carved a scene of the lake on the top. She opened the lid and the scent of sweet spices wafted into her nostrils, clearing her head like smelling salts and making her vision strangely focused.

Yellowing recipe cards filled the box, the names written in a spidery hand: *Sunday Dinner Blackberry Cake, October Relish, Children's Delight Cookies.* The names—or was it the smell? —conjured visions of a woman in an apron with flour streaked across her cheek like a character in an old movie.

Maddie didn't have any hand-me-down recipes. Most of hers came from magazines. Her mother Cindy, who never cooked and certainly didn't own an apron, had spent most of Maddie's childhood on the couch, watching her soaps with a beer in her hand.

Inhaling one last breath of the sweet, spicy aroma, Maddie reluctantly closed the lid and placed the box on the windowsill over the sink where she could see it and admire the carving.

Pleased with her morning's work, she took a kitchen chair out to a patch of sunshine on the drive and put her feet up on the chopping block while she ate her lunch. Across the lake, spring green ringed the far shore below a wave of blue-green conifers that surged up the side of the mountain. Hard to believe this view was all hers for the summer.

Her mind drifted back to Jake's morning visit and she squirmed in her seat at the memory of his shoulders working under the tight black T-shirt as he wielded the axe. She'd never had any positive male influences in her life and felt uncomfortable in the presence of so much raw testosterone. That right there, probably explained her failure as a wife.

Her mother, Cindy, was always bringing home some new

weak-kneed schemer, always hoping he was "the one." They drank their way through her booze, spent her money and ate their food, and then, every time, left her mother drunk and besotted. In the end they were all the same. They all just spelled trouble.

She thought about Jake and the thrill she'd felt as she watched him splitting wood in the driveway. Then how he'd walked away without a backward glance.

Nope, she didn't have any instincts where men were concerned so, for his sake as well as her own, she'd leave this one alone.

Chapter 4

The following morning the cabin felt substantially warmer than it had the previous day and, as she got out of bed, a smug smile formed on Maddie's lips at the thought that she'd mastered the wood stove.

A beam of sunlight had worked its way through the tangle of branches outside the window and danced across the bedroom floor. Dressing quickly, she grabbed her camera and set out to explore her own magical piece of forest.

More used to the dry interior of the state and the slick city streets, the stand of firs that protected the cabin seemed like a jungle to her. As she started to work, her mind shifted gears and she began to see patterns in the light shafting through the dense boughs overhead. Unexpected bursts of angled sunshine highlighted strong shadows in the forest, spotlighting individual ferns and glistening foliage.

She began with the big views, using a wide-angle lens to capture the massive height of the trees. Working in black and white, the graphic contrast of tones in her photographs was particularly important. She looked for dark against light, the sun silhouetting trunks of giant firs, a bright fern caught in a shower of morning light, or the way the low side-light accentuated the rough texture of bark.

Following the light through the trees, she worked ever closer to her subjects until, by the time the sun shone high overhead, she was lying on her stomach on the dry ground, the musky scent of forest decay filling her nostrils and her macro lens focused on a tiny white spider working his way across a blushing peach mushroom cap.

The color wouldn't show of course, however by now she could visualize how it would look in black and white, anticipating the shades of grey and feeling the delicacy of the spider contrasted with the smooth, velvety volume of the dome, all set off against the dark shadow behind.

The morning flew by, but eventually her stomach growled, reminding her she hadn't eaten breakfast. She sat back on her heels. Breeze off the lake. Clean forest air. Inspiration. *Perfect.*

Gathering up her equipment, she started back to the house, eager to print the roll of film. She knew exactly what she wanted to capture. Morning in the forest. The damp air and the earthy scent. But first she needed a darkroom.

After a quick lunch, she fingered the roll of film in her pocket as she looked at the pile of darkroom equipment still lying in a heap on the living room floor. In their tiny Seattle apartment, she worked in the bathroom, so that was where she headed.

As she walked through the laundry room, her eyes ranged over the bare bulb in the ceiling and the wringer washer rooted in the far corner. A deep concrete laundry sink sat in the other corner and an old painted dresser stood against the back wall.

She stopped. Water, no window. The perfect darkroom.

Light was always a danger in the darkroom, and swirling dust highlighted the rays of sunlight slanting in through cracks between the wallboards. She'd have to fill the cracks, but luckily there were piles of stuffing behind the porch couch—that, no doubt, thanks to the mice. The wringer washer however, a metal monstrosity that looked like a medieval torture device, had to go.

Feet planted wide, hands on her hips, her shadow fell like Wonder Woman across the laundry room floor. She gave the washer an experimental tug, surprised by how easily it rolled on the tiny casters across the linoleum floor. Maneuvering it into the doorway in front of her, she pushed down on the rim, tipped the washer toward her and gave the quadruped a mighty shove. The front legs dropped neatly across the raised threshold and onto the porch. *Piece o' cake.*

Grasping the rim, she lifted with all her strength but the behemoth may as well have been nailed to the floor. She leaned against the wall, catching her breath. She wasn't getting the same leverage lifting as when she'd pushed down on the rim. She knew she could do it from the other side, but the brute totally blocked the door.

She peered into the tub. Climbing over it would mean climbing into the tub, over the agitator and ringer. Biting her lip, she bent over and peered underneath. Crawling between the four metal legs looked marginally easier.

Heaving a sigh, she got down on her belly, arms waving in front of her like squid tentacles as she wriggled along the dusty floor.

Almost there. A few more inches.

Then the motor, hanging beneath the tub, grabbed her white T-shirt, slicing its talons into her back.

She stopped with a quick intake of breath. Digging her palms into the floor, she tried to back up but couldn't shake the motor loose.

She dropped her forehead to the floor with a thud. This was a big mistake. She should have climbed over. Too late now— she couldn't go forward and couldn't go back.

Shifting to one side, she tried again, but a sharp piece of metal dug into her ribs, tearing her T-shirt and slicing into her skin. Sure blood was oozing from the gash, she tried to snake a hand down her side to check, but only managed to scrape her arm against the rough edge of one metal leg.

Tears sprang to her eyes. One splashed on the floor an inch from her face. She took a deep breath, dust doing a delicate dance in her nostrils. She felt a sneeze building—she tried to fight it, screwing her eyes shut and biting her lip—but the dust won and the sneeze erupted like a small explosion. She smacked her forehead on the floor. Stars circled behind her closed eyes and she collapsed, forehead resting on the dirty boards.

So independent—*so stupid*—renting a cabin in the woods

with no other houses in sight. She would waste away until she was thin enough to slip free. If she still had the strength. It would be weeks before anyone missed her. Probably not until her rent was due.

Above her, a deep voice asked, "Can I help?"

Maddie's eyes flew open. *Thank God.*

She dragged her cheek across the dirty floor in the direction of the voice and came nose to toe with a beat-up work boot.

Oh no. She'd seen that boot before, resting up on the broken step. *Jeeze!* What could she say? Her mind was a blank.

Jake cleared his throat. "Brought you some kindling."

Craning her neck, she tried to look up but could only see as far as the strong forearms cradling a bundle of split pieces of wood.

"Thank you," she mumbled, then closed her eyes and dropped her forehead back onto the floor with a *thunk*. If only she could dissolve right through the floorboards.

The silence blossomed, getting larger and stickier by the second. Was he going to make her beg?

"Looks like you could use some help."

That catch in his voice—he was laughing. She squeezed her eyes shut. The mortification.

Kindling clattered to the floor and one boot fell on either side of her head.

"I'm caught."

"I'll be careful."

The washer rose up and Maddie grabbed her shirt and yanked. She heard a loud *r-r-rip*, but then she was free. Wriggling out between his legs on her elbows and knees, she crawled over to the porch railing where she sat, cautiously resting her stinging back against the spindles.

He lowered the washer and turned around. He wasn't laughing now. A vertical frown-line formed between his dark brows and she dropped her head into her hands. She must look a wreck.

Then he picked something, God only knows what, out of her hair. She pulled away, her back hitting the railing. It stung like road burn, and she gasped at the pain.

"Are you all right?"

"I'm fine."

"Let's see." He came down to her level and gently turned her around. "You have a bad scrape here." His finger, through the hole in her shirt, brushed across her skin like fire. She sucked a sharp breath and pulled away. "There's some grease in it. We should clean it out and put something on it."

She struggled to her feet. No way was she letting him clean her up. "I'm okay. It was a stupid thing to do—"

"Pretty ambitious all by yourself—"

"—it rolled so easily at the start."

"—someone should have gotten rid of it years ago."

He grabbed the rim of the tub and tipped it toward him— *Oh sure. It's easy from this side*—then he pulled and turned and pushed and soon the washer stood in the corner of the porch looking like it had been there forever.

"I'll get rid of it," he said.

"It's okay. It's really not in the way."

"Should have gone to the dump years ago."

They stood for a moment in awkward silence. Being gracious was never her forte, but Maddie took a deep breath and forced a smile. "I'm glad you came by. Thanks for the help. And for the kindling."

"Should make it a lot easier to get the fire going. Maybe I should take a look at your back-"

"No, thank you. I'll take care of it."

"Okay." Jake pushed his long dark hair back off his forehead with one hand as he backed away, tripping over the broken step.

"I'll get to that, soon," he said, and disappeared around the corner of the cabin.

Maddie   shook   her   head,   wincing   more   from

embarrassment than from pain. She must have looked like an idiot, trapped under that machine. Giving the washer a withering look, she staggered into the bathroom.

With the window boarded-up, the room was dark, so she switched on the light, groaning when she saw herself in the mirror. Streaks of dirt ran across her face, stuffing was caught in her curls and her forearms looked like road burn. Grease saturated her T-shirt, but that didn't matter because with two gaping holes, she wouldn't ever be wearing it again. Pulling the shirt off over her head, she threw it in the garbage.

Lips pressed in a tight line, she ran hot water into the tub. She hated being rescued. How could she face him again after making such a fool of herself? The only upside to the whole fiasco was that now she could rationalize a long soak in the big old tub. The humiliation alone rated a dollop of her rationed French bubble powder.

Moaning, she sank into the hot, steamy water until only her face and knees rose above the bubbles. Her shoulder muscles, wound tight from the move, gradually began to relax. There was still a lot of work to do before her darkroom was functional, but surely she deserved to soak for a few minutes in the hot fragrant water. Her eyes drifted shut.

A screech rang out above her like a banshee's cry. Her eyes flew open. Whatever it was, it screeched again and the room became noticeably brighter.

Her mouth formed a hollow O as the boards came off the window.

She shot up until she was sitting in the tub, covered by a patchy slick of translucent foam that was all that was left of the bubbles. The boards fell away, or rather, someone threw them aside, and a man's face—Jake's face—appeared in the window above her. His eyes dropped to her chest and she cupped one breast with each hand.

His eyes bounced up to meet hers, widening to reflect her horror at the situation. She sank back into the water and he twisted away, yanking the ladder away from the wall. He wavered for a moment in mid-air. His jaw dropped and his eyes flew back to hers, the whites growing wider as he slowly fell backwards and disappeared from sight, ladder and all.

Maddie stood up in the water and grabbed a towel. It wasn't large, but large enough to cover the important parts. She leaned over and looked down through the broken window at Jake, who lay sprawled in the lilac bush under the ladder.

"Are you all right?"

He groaned in response.

"Just wait, don't move. I'll put on some clothes and come and help."

She jumped out of the tub and tugged on her jeans, then remembered her t-shirt was in the garbage.

"Don't bother," she faintly heard him say. "I should have known you'd be getting cleaned up." A bush rustled outside the window. "I'm sorry."

She clutched the towel to her chest until the rustling in the bushes ceased, then peeked out the laundry room door. Seeing the coast was clear, she rushed across the porch and into the cabin. She was destined to make a fool of herself with this guy. He must not be hurt, he made a pretty quick getaway, but he obviously didn't want to talk to her—and she felt the absolute same.

Face flaming, she pulled on a fresh T-shirt and returned to the laundry room. Closing both doors, she poured her adrenalin-fueled energy into organizing the darkroom. A while later, she heard a noise at the bathroom window but she didn't open the door.

When she was finished working, she listened at the bathroom door. All was quiet.   Opening the door to take a peek, she saw a new pane of glass in place and, thank God, Jake was gone.

Chapter 5

A few hours later, Maddie emerged from the laundry-room-now-darkroom, tired and dirty but pleased with her progress. As she brushed the dust off her jeans, she considered taking another bath, but decided she'd had enough naked trauma for one day.

On the edge of her peripheral vision, a white blur—some kind of animal—flashed across the driveway and disappeared into the brush on the other side.

She hesitated, watching in case something bigger and meaner was on its trail but when nothing appeared, she followed the flash through the fringe of trees on the far side of the driveway. Peering into the neighbor's yard, the phantom had vanished.

From the safety of the forest shadow, Maddie took in the one-story bungalow surrounded by tidy flowerbeds. In a fenced vegetable garden in the middle of the lawn, a woman knelt planting out seedlings, a large-brimmed hat hiding her face. The woman sat back on her heels and pushed the hat farther back on her head, leaving a streak of dirt across her forehead.

Maddie stepped back, deeper into the shadows, but it was too late. The woman called out a greeting, brushing the dirt off the knees of her pants as she stood.

Maddie's back stiffened. Running her fingers through her hair, she pulled out a rogue piece of stuffing. She didn't do neighbors at the best of times and now she felt gritty and grimy, but there was no place to hide.

The woman walked toward her, a smile crinkling her toffee-brown eyes. She looked about thirty, maybe five years younger than Maddie herself. She was short and round, although the bulky work clothes probably added extra inches, and a heavy brown braid hung down the center of her back.

As she approached, she took off her work gloves and extended her hand, giving Maddie no alternative but to shake it.

"I followed an animal through the trees. Maybe a cat?"

"A white cat? Her name is Spirit. She kind of comes with the cabin."

"I just moved in."

The woman laughed. "That's already old news in town." She waggled her eyebrows conspiratorially. "Anything I can add to the rumor mill will be golden for me. My name is Frankie. Would you like to come in for a cold drink?"

Maddie hesitated. Her immediate instinct was to decline, but it did sound good. She'd been working hard—and something about Frankie's open smile encouraged her to accept. "Thank you. And it's Maddie. But maybe you knew that already."

Frankie laughed as they walked toward the house. "As a matter of fact I did."

The living room windows faced the lake and the mountain that rose across the bay. A marble countertop separated the living room from a kitchen filled with gleaming stainless appliances.

"Louise told me," Frankie explained as she filled two tall glasses with iced tea.

They took their drinks out through a set of patio doors to a lakeside deck scattered with well-padded garden furniture. Maddie sank into the nearest chair, suddenly aware of her aching back. The soft breeze blowing in from the lake was heaven, and she took a long pull on her drink and leaned back. "So, what can I tell you?"

"To begin with, what are you doing in Mrs. Jorgens' cabin?"

"Mrs. Jorgens? I thought it belonged to Mrs. Murphy."

"It does now. Augusta Jorgens was Stephanie Murphy's aunt. Augusta died about fifteen years ago—before my time—

and Steph inherited the cabin. She also inherited the farm across the road from her husband's uncle, old Mr. Murdoch. It's still Jorgens' cabin and the Murdoch farm though." Frankie laughed. "Things don't change that fast in Fortune Bay."

"I rented the cabin from Jake," Maddie said.

Frankie nodded. "Stephanie's son. One of them anyway. He takes care of the cabin."

"He came by to chop some wood." The washer debacle still stung too much, both physically and mentally, to retell, and she didn't even want to *think* about the bathroom window.

"Right."

Frankie smiled her Cheshire cat smile again and for a second Maddie thought she knew the whole embarrassing story. But then Frankie said, "Did you get your stove working?"

"How do you know about that?"

"From Louise. But I'm telling you all of this and you haven't given me anything yet. I won't be able to show my face in town."

"Okay." Maddie's pulse kicked up the way it did whenever she stumbled into the spotlight. "I'm a photographer," she began boldly, but then quickly back tracked. "Trying to be. I have a show coming up, in Seattle in the fall. My daughter is with her dad for the summer so I'm here to work on the photographs."

"When is it?"

"Mid-October." Maddie closed her eyes and shook her head from side to side. "Too soon. I haven't even started. I've been in a slump and I don't have anything to exhibit. Yet."

"What do you usually photograph?"

"For the show I'm working in black and white, developing the traditional way in the dark room. Usually I photograph the people in my Seattle neighborhood. It's a real melting pot. There's a lot of scope. Some of the people are very exotic."

"Sounds fascinating," Frankie murmured.

"First I stuck to candid shots." Maddie laughed. "You gotta love that telephoto lens. It lets me stay well back and get shots of people going about their business. Then I met a young woman who works at the Asian grocery store where I shop and I showed her my pictures. She introduced me to her grandmother who agreed to let me photograph her." Maddie blushed. "It sort of became a thing in the neighborhood to be photographed by me."

"So you have those pictures to show."

"Unfortunately, no. They were in a show last winter at a gift shop near my apartment." Her eyes widened and she lowered her voice, as if saying it aloud would jinx it. "The owner of a *real* gallery saw it and offered me a solo show. She's raising all of my prices and handling the opening." Maddie's voice quavered. "It'll be great."

"I'm sure it will."

"But she wants all new work. This is so much more stressful than the last time." She closed her eyes and shook her head. "That one just sort of happened."

Frankie went into the kitchen and poured three glasses of red wine, bringing two of them out to the deck. "Don't worry, Fortune Bay has lots of characters. And believe me, they're all dying to get to know *you.*"

There was the sound of tires grating on gravel and their gazes met. Quick footsteps clattered on the front stairs and Louise breezed into the living room. She picked up her wineglass on the way through the kitchen and stepped out onto the deck.

Throwing herself into one of the lounges, she downed the wine as if it were water.

"I'm exhausted." She flicked back the asymmetrical fall of shiny black hair that threatened to cover half her face and looked expectantly at the two other women. "What's up?"

"Maddie's been telling me that she's a photographer," Frankie said. "She has a show coming up in Seattle this fall."

"Cool."

Although it all sounded great coming from Frankie, Maddie couldn't restrain the urge to downplay it. She opened her mouth, but before she could get the words out, she caught Frankie's slight shake of the head.

"You have to start living the part," Frankie said softly. "It's hard, but you have to start now, before the show. No one will believe in your work if you don't believe in it yourself."

She was right. Sometimes being a successful artist seemed to be at least half chutzpa. "I know. You have to make them believe."

"It's sort of like a fairy tale," Frankie said. "A lot of the magic is in the telling."

"Same with cooking," Louise added. "Half the impression is in the presentation."

Maddie smiled at them in surprise. "That's exactly right." She turned to Frankie. "But that's enough about me. What about you? Do you live here alone?"

"Yes, I do. I bought this house three years ago. I teach high school English."

Frankie flipped her hand as if to say, *nothing special,* but a single woman Frankie's age buying a house? Pretty impressive.

"She's done so much with the place," Louise exclaimed. "You wouldn't believe the mess it was when she bought it."

Maddie watched as Louise regaled them with stories of the first summer at the new house and Frankie covered her eyes and laughed.

What would it be like to have that kind of friendship? Maddie had always considered friends a luxury she couldn't afford. It took all her energy to keep her life on track without having to fend off intruders and critics. Maybe now, though, when Jenny was gone and she was alone, she should try making some friends. Problem was, she wasn't sure how. She sensed that this was an opportunity though, and decided to take it slow and see how it went.

Louise started describing the dark, fake-wood paneling that had covered the living room and kitchen walls when Frankie moved in.

Frankie laughed. "It was awful. We tried to pull it off but half the drywall underneath came away with it. We had to cover the whole thing with fresh drywall." She turned to Louise. "Remember how we worked covered in plaster dust all that summer?"

Still laughing, Frankie stood to get the bottle of wine and returned to refill their glasses. She looked at Maddie's in surprise. "You haven't touched yours."

"I don't really drink."

"That's okay," Louise said, reaching for the glass. "I'll drink it for you."

"But thank you so much." Maddie rose from her seat. "I'd better go. If I sit here much longer, I'll never get out of this chair. Thanks for listening, and for the tea. It's good to know I have such nice neighbors."

Frankie walked her to the steps. "Come back any time."

"I will," Maddie said and, with faint surprise, realized she meant it.

At the entrance to the dusky path through the trees, Maddie turned and waved good-bye. At the deck rail, Frankie and Louise raised their glasses in a return salute and Maddie felt a tightness bloom in the vicinity of her heart. She'd dreamt of a friendship like that ever since she was a child, but it had never worked out. In recent years she'd been too busy to try, or at least that's what she always told herself.

This time, although she recognized the tang of envy for the friendship they shared, she also felt a whisper of hope. *Maybe,* she thought as she slipped through the darkening trees, *maybe it isn't too late.*

The cabin was cool and dark and empty. She turned on all the lights, opened the fridge and rummaged inside for something to eat.

The electronic disco chimes of her cell phone rang and

her pulse leapt. *Jenny.* She raced to the hooks by the front door, searching frantically in her shoulder bag for her phone. She had called her daughter several times since arriving in Fortune Bay, but it always went to voice mail.

Finding the phone, she stabbed at the *call* switch, afraid she'd be too late. "Hi Honey. It's good to hear your voice." She stood by the door, holding the phone in both hands as if that would keep Jenny from slipping away. "Are you getting settled?"

Her good-mom side hoped her daughter was happy, but she couldn't deny the bad-mom on her other shoulder who wanted to hear that living with her dad wasn't all Jenny had hoped it would be. That she wanted to come home.

"It's great! I have an awesome room on the second floor that looks out at the back yard and the pool. The pool is only tiny, but really cool with a whirlpool and everything."

"That sounds nice, Honey. You'd like it here too. I found a cabin right on the lake."

Jenny rushed on as if she hadn't heard. "Kate took me shopping to these cool little stores. She calls them 'boutiques.' They're not like the stores where we live. She bought me the cutest jacket with ribbon woven through for trim—you'd have to see it—then we walked and walked along the beach—all the way back to the house. Dad had to work most of the weekend, but he says I can learn to play tennis this summer. They belong to a club."

Ah yes, the club. Snobby women in perfect clothes. It probably all seemed exciting and sophisticated to Jenny though. Maddie's throat ached, wanting to warn her daughter of the strings attached, but knowing it could turn Jenny even more against her.

In the end, the call was too short. She suspected it had been Mark's idea and somehow that left her lonelier than before. Was it only four days since she'd left Jenny at Mark's? She should be happy their visit was going so well. It was a great opportunity. A chance, as Jenny had said, to move up in the world. And didn't she want the best for her daughter?

But how could she compete with what Mark had to offer? What if she lost Jenny for good? She just had to believe that their bond was strong enough to bring her daughter home.

But the sharp pain in her heart remained, reminding her of the times when, as a child, she'd reached out to her mother and been slapped aside. Eventually she'd stopped reaching and a callus had formed over the spot in her heart where her mother's love should have been. Now her daughter's defection had torn open the old wound. Maddie had made a point of being a different, better, mother to Jenny. She'd hugged her every day and told her often how much she loved her. But was that enough?

Her appetite had disappeared, so instead of making dinner, she lit a fire in the wood stove. Leaving the stove door open, she sat and stared into the flames, wondering exactly what she was doing here, so far from home.

* * *

Jake stood at his front window staring into the settling dusk. A wisp of smoke rose from the center of the stand of fir trees across the road. A smile quirked the corner of his mouth as he remembered finding Maddie stuck under the washer. She'd done pretty well getting it as far as she did, but what was she thinking trying to move that hulking machine by herself?

Then a vision of her naked in the tub flashed through his mind. He hadn't seen much, but still, that image would haunt him for nights to come.

He rubbed his hand over his face and sighed. She was intriguing, he'd give her that. He had to remember she was only here for the summer. If he could stick to his rules, everything would be fine.

"Daddy!" Sarah called from the kitchen.

Dragging his attention away from the woman across the road, Jake went into the kitchen to help his daughter.

Chapter 6

By the following afternoon, Maddie had the darkroom up and running and had developed the first roll of film. The set-up needed tweaking, but it was twice as big as her bathroom darkroom in the city and, overall, she was thrilled with the results.

Later, when the low afternoon sun cast interesting shadows, she slung her SLR camera loaded with black and white film around her neck, rested her tripod on her shoulder and with a new lightness in her step, walked out to the road.

Seemingly overnight, a carpet of blue and white flowers had opened in the field at the farm across the road. The swath of blooms led the eye seductively up to the log farmhouse, the backdrop of heavy dark logs setting off the fresh fragility of the bluebells. She set up the tripod on the road and snapped the camera on top. A study in contrasts, perfect for black and white, the scene in her viewfinder made her almost giddy.

Who planted these flowers? Probably the first woman to live in the log house. She would have brought a few bulbs from home and over the past century those few had multiplied into thousands of blooms.

Maddie had seen the framed, black and white photographs on the café walls showing how the men cleared these fields one hundred years ago, cutting down giant trees with cross cut saws, then using the logs to build the house.

She zoomed in on the old farmhouse. Back then, of course, the road didn't exist. No road and nowhere to go. No neighbors to visit or to call on for help. What a hard, isolated life it must have been.

So she planted a few bluebells to remind her of home.

Temporary. The blossoms so fragile, they lasted only a few days. But enduring, returning year after year. How wonderful to have that kind of solid family history. So many memories.

Maddie's only memories were of transient rooms and trailer park rentals, of moving on before she ever truly felt at home.

The brooding farmhouse, while fascinating from a distance, was anything but inviting. She wanted to get into the yard though, closer to the flowers. Putting the tripod on her shoulder, she marched down the dirt driveway that ran alongside the field of bluebells and up to the house. Now was as good a time as any to meet her landlady, Mrs. Murphy.

Leaving her gear in a pile on the grass, she approached the gloomy farmhouse. There was no garden to speak of, just a small orchard of twisted fruit trees. A shiver went through her. Forbidding and forgotten, she couldn't help thinking it was the perfect setting for a murder mystery.

Skirting the stack of firewood on the porch, the only real sign of habitation, she made her way up to the heavy front door, scarred by claw marks at the bottom and flanked either side by tall gothic windows of wavy antique glass.

She knocked and, as the seconds ticked by, began to wonder if Mrs. Murphy was old and infirm, possibly unable to make it to the door.

Then footsteps echoed inside the house. Maddie fought the urge to turn and run.

The door swung open. It wasn't Mrs. Murphy; it was Jake. A dishtowel was thrown carelessly over his shoulder and behind him she glimpsed the chaos of toys scattered across the living room floor. Somewhere inside a child squealed.

He arched one dark, impatient eyebrow.

Okay, she'd caught him at a bad time. Maddie's shoulders spread and she rose to look him in the eye. "I'm sorry. I thought Mrs. Murphy lived here."

"No. I live here."

He wasn't nearly as friendly as when he came by the cabin. Although that wasn't saying much. She wasn't here to make friends though, so, taking a deep breath, she plunged on.

"I'd like to photograph the flowers. They're so beautiful, and such an interesting contrast to the house. Which is also so beautiful. So old."

So stupid. Of course it's old.

He didn't respond, just lowered his brows. In thought? In anger? Who knew?

She forced a smile. "Do you mind if I take a few pictures?"

In the silence that followed, his gaze travelled down to her sneakers and back up to her face. Her cheeks burned as sparks shot between them. He definitely looked annoyed, although she didn't for the life of her know why.

Finally, he gave his head a slight shake. "Sure. Go ahead."

"Great. Thanks."

Despite her racing pulse, she turned and walked slowly back to where she'd left her tripod, fighting the urge to keep on walking right down the driveway.

Okay then. I'll take the darned pictures. So he had a family. What did she expect? Nodding sharply to punctuate her thoughts, she set up her equipment.

Annoyed with herself for caring, she tried to unravel the nagging feeling in the pit of her stomach. He was obviously married, so that took care of any fantasies she might have entertained about a summer romance. Just as well too. She didn't need to complicate her life.

Maddie put her eye to the viewfinder and fell instantly under the meadow's spell. As black and white studies formed in her mind's eye, delicate trumpet bells against the charcoal background of the house, she got down to business, Jake and his unfathomable moods forgotten.

* * *

Jake watched through the wavy glass of the living room window.

How long was it since he'd gone out with a woman? Months. Maybe six months. No, he realized, eyes widening, over a year. Far too long. What had happened to him? He was still young—in his prime in fact. Wasn't thirty-five supposed to be your prime? No wonder he'd latched onto the first new woman to move into the area in years.

He jerked the dishcloth off his shoulder and pulled it roughly through his hands.

He loved women. Not just the sex—although, by God, he loved that too—but loved them as a species. His life was full of wonderful women. So full, sometimes he couldn't think, or breathe...

The vision of Maddie wavered through the antique glass as she knelt on the front lawn surrounded by nodding blue and white blossoms. The tripod held her camera a mere foot off the ground and, eye to the viewfinder, totally focused on her next shot, her hips swayed as she leaned forward on her knees, the thin cotton of her pants straining over her rear end...

He groaned. Was he reduced to this? Watching through the window as she crawled away?

"Daddy." The high-pitched squeal yanked him back to reality. His tunnel vision sprang back to wide angle, taking in his wreck of a living room and the dog playing tug of war over his ball mitt with his favorite little woman-in-training.

Six-year-old Sarah. The love of his life. A sigh deflated all deviant body parts back to their normal size. What kind of father was he? He couldn't think about sex and Sarah in the same breath, the same room. He had done a good job of keeping his meager sex life away from her—miles away. Keeping her world safe.

So far his rules had worked just fine. He could see women, but not at the farm. And he'd make damn sure to keep them away from Sarah. He wouldn't let her get attached to some woman only to lose her again. He knew what that felt like, firsthand.

With a weary smile, he retrieved his mitt from the dog and went into the kitchen to fix Sarah a snack. When he returned to the window, Maddie was gone.

Exhaling sharply, Jake closed his eyes and dropped his forehead against the cool rippled glass. This was going to be tough, but he could do it. He just had to stick to the rules.

* * *

Late that night, a velvety darkness hung in the darkroom, so thick and palpable Maddie could almost touch it. As she waited for her eyes to adjust to the inky blackness, she searched for any rogue beams of light creeping in through cracks in the walls, fingers reaching out to destroy the fragile images on the film.

She didn't understand Jake at all. He'd been downright unfriendly when he answered the door. It wasn't a social call. She didn't care if he was married. She didn't need any complications. She had a job to do and no time for distractions.

She chewed on the ragged edge of a fingernail. Still, chopping wood and bringing her kindling had seemed like friendly gestures. Could he be embarrassed about seeing her naked in the tub? Why not? She was certainly embarrassed.

Expelling a frustrated breath, she turned to her work. She couldn't read men at all. Why did she even try?

Although it was dark inside and out, she automatically stuffed the old laundry room mats into the spaces beneath the doors with her foot. You couldn't be too careful at this stage of the process. The exposed film in the camera was still alive, the light-sensitive coating not permanently set, and even moonlight could flash the film and ruin the images forever. Later she would work under the red darkroom light, but for this stage she needed total blackout conditions.

After fumbling for her tools in the dark, she finally switched on the red light to locate the stainless-steel developing tank. Soon she would get used to her new setup and be able to visualize where everything was, even in the dark.

She turned off the red light and, working by touch alone, popped open the metal casing on the roll of film and pulled out the light-sensitive filament. Then she carefully rolled the film back up and placed it in the lightproof developing tank.

Once she'd screwed the lid back onto the tank with the precious roll of images inside, she could breathe easily again. She fumbled for the red light and continued the process, the alchemy of the developing fluids that would permanently set the negative image on the film.

When she poured the last acrid rinse out of the tank, she twisted off the lid and pulled out the film. This part was pure magic and, as always, her heart sped up. As if in a chrysalis, the chemicals in the tank had transformed the film into a roll of negatives. Flipping on the incandescent light overhead, she held up the long dripping strip to review the images burned in microcosm on the film. Then she hung the negatives with a clothespin on the drying line strung across the end of the room, rinsed the tank and set it to dry.

Unlocking the door, she stepped into moonlight streaming onto the porch. The full moon cast the water in an enchanted glow, illuminating the mountain across the bay so clearly that the white blossoms of dogwood trees ringing the shore glowed ghostly in the dark.

Suddenly she was back in the zone, reaching for her camera, not feeling the midnight chill in the air as the heat of the hunt sped through her veins.

Chapter 7

A storm rolled in the following day, rattling the windows and beating branches against the cabin walls. Maddie spent the day in the darkroom, developing the moonlit shots she'd taken the night before. With the rain pattering on the tin roof, she scarcely noticed the wind at all.

In the evening, she spread her new prints on the kitchen table and pulled out her plans for the show. The sound of the wind in the trees was hypnotic and she wasn't aware of how long it took until she tuned in to a repetitive sound coming from the attic.

Creak, creak. A branch rubbing against the siding? No, the noise sounded too measured for that. A regular beat like a rocking chair.

Creak, creak. A chill ran up her arms.

It seemed to come from directly overhead. Her eyes shot up to the painted ceiling boards, a single layer of wood between the kitchen and the attic. As she sat, listening, her muscles ratcheted tighter by the second and her shoulders crept closer and closer to her ears.

Creak. Wide-eyed, she stared at the trap door in the ceiling, nerves taut as a violin string. Her breath came in pants as sweat pooled under her arms. No way she was going up there alone, in the dark, to see what was making that eerie sound.

The wind rose to a frenzy and the creaking increased in counterpoint to the rhythm pounding in her chest.

Then—CRASH! The sound exploded like cymbals. She screamed as panic seized her by the heart. Hand on her chest she held her breath and listened. Nothing, just the wail of the wind.

Grabbing a flashlight, she crept outside. The wind tangled

her hair in her face and rain pelted her back as she scanned the roof and upper window half expecting a ghostly form to appear.

The narrow beam of the flashlight pierced the dark, sweeping across the upper windows to the tin roof of the darkroom where a large broken branch rustled in the wind.

Just the wind. She patted her chest trying to slow her heart.

Hurrying into the cabin, she stood dripping in the middle of the kitchen floor, the hair on her arms standing on end as she strained above the noise of the wind to hear if the rocking had started again.

Nothing.

Giving a half-hearted laugh, she rubbed her hands down her arms. Then, glancing at the ceiling, she walked over and plugged in the kettle for tea.

She wouldn't do any more work tonight.

* * *

By the following morning the storm had blown through Fortune Bay leaving the air soft and still. Low clouds shrouded the mountaintops and all day a mist fell almost soundlessly, tapping faintly on the tin roof of the porch, dripping from the leaves and creating ripples on the mirror-like surface of the lake.

Another day stuck in the house was beginning to rub on Maddie's nerves. By evening the sky was starting to clear and as the sun set, a ragged band of fiery orange burned between the bruised purple clouds and the low mountains at the head of the bay. Quickly she set up her camera on the porch to capture the fleeting effect.

Framing a shot through the lens, she thought, *I'll call this one 'Silence.'*

Her eye on the viewfinder, a rustle in the bush announced a visitor approaching. She glanced up, expecting Spirit, but instead of the cat, Jake came around the corner.

Her breath hitched, but she forced herself back to work. This light wouldn't last long.

He climbed the stairs and stood beside her. "Just wanted to check on the cabin. After the storm."

Maddie kept her eye on her camera. "Give me a minute. This won't last."

She adjusted the levers and screws on the tripod by touch, keeping her eye on the viewfinder. Then she stood back and pressed the shutter button on the remote and, seconds later, she heard the click.

"The timed delay keeps the camera still," she murmured, then reframed the shot in the viewfinder and repeated the process. Then again.

When the last of the orange light left the sky, she turned from the camera and gave him a smile. "Great light."

* * *

It was the light that had drawn Jake to the shore. That, and he wanted to check on the cabin.

Yeah right. The real reason he'd come was he couldn't get her out of his mind.

Suddenly he realized she was watching him, that it must be his turn to talk. He turned toward her.

"So. You weathered the storm all right?" He was staring. Couldn't seem to help it. God, he felt like a teenager. He forced himself to look out at the water again.

He missed the view, which wasn't nearly as good from the farm. But that wasn't all. He also missed sitting on this porch at the end of the day. Those first days of his marriage, when he and his wife were still in love, they had sat here together every evening. Those had been among the best days of his life. Until it all went bad.

He missed it, he realized, and wanted it again. The closeness. The partnership. The peace.

Not with a woman who wouldn't stay for the long haul though. He shook off the longing like a cat would water. No time for dreaming. He had to get back.

Maddie gestured to the roof. "A big limb fell down. I don't think it did any damage. The windows really rattle though, when the wind comes down the lake."

"I know," he said. "I'll come by later and get that branch down. I'm glad you weren't hurt." His eyes sketched out the darkening mountains across the bay. "This has always been my favorite view. In any weather."

She nodded. "I feel lucky to have it. Even just for the summer."

He nodded. *There it is.* She's only here for the summer.

They stood side by side, looking at the lake, and after a moment Maddie started fidgeting with her tripod. She always seemed nervous when he was around, except when she was working.

Just as well, because this would be a big mistake. And besides, Sarah was waiting.

"Gotta go," he said, and taking one last look at the lake, he headed for home.

* * *

Maddie watched Jake walk away, her heart beating an unsettled tattoo in her chest.

Did he feel it too? The tension? Or was it all in her head? Probably just the landlord's job to check for damage after the storm. No point reading too much into it.

Maybe next time, though, he'd stay for a while, instead of always hurrying away.

Chapter 8

Saturday morning, Jake sat across the kitchen table from Sarah, arms crossed firmly on his chest. She too had her arms crossed over her tiny chest in a funhouse version of himself, her scowl almost daring him to blink.

Between them sat the cause of the altercation, a bowl of porridge, grown cold and solid in the standoff.

Jake had to say something or he would snap, and he couldn't do that because then she would have won. Again. And that was not going to happen.

He raised one brow. "I can sit here all day." His bored tone sounded false, even to himself.

Her reply was quick. "Me too."

He studied her in the silence. Stubborn Sarah, only six years old but already a force to be reckoned with. Even her stubby brown pigtails seemed to scream, '*I have a mind of my own*'. The pink and white face scattered with freckles, sometimes so angelic, now had twisted into a demonic scowl.

Where had she gotten that stubborn streak? Not from him. If she'd just eat the damn cereal, he'd show her how reasonable he could be. The clock on the wall ticked off the seconds.

The screen door swung open with a bang and in strode his brother Sean, a fairer, more compact version of himself. Annoyingly cheerful as usual.

"Good day to you both. Isn't today a beautiful day. And don't we deserve it?"

Jake dared not break eye-contact to greet him. "You're early Sean."

Throwing his hat on the hook by the door, Sean swung a chair backwards to straddle at the table. "And what have we here? A small bowl of porridge?" He poked the solidifying mass with a spoon.

"A big bowl," Sarah said, her arms still crossed resolutely over her narrow chest, her eyes never leaving her father's.

"And you are Goldilocks, I presume?"

Her tight lips quirked as she tried not to smile.

"And this must be Father Bear himself."

Jake's focus wavered, and when his brother whisked the bowl off the table and took it to the counter, he lost it completely. "What are you doing?"

"Heating it in the micro. It's like glue. I can't eat it like this."

Sarah squealed as Sean dropped some raisins into the bowl. "It's not yours—it's mine."

His eyes twinkled as he brought the warm bowl and two fresh spoons back to the table. "Won't you share it with your old uncle Sean?"

"You're not old," Sarah said, taking a spoon from him and digging in. "You're the baby brother."

Jake's scowl relaxed, mostly in resignation. He pursed his lips. *He makes it look easy.* Sean made everything look easy, always had. How did he do it? With an exasperated sigh, Jake stood up and said, "Five minutes, both of you, in the truck." Then grabbing his hat, he stalked out the door.

Five minutes later, on the dot, Sean and Sarah walked into the yard, laughing and wrestling, all signs of the argument forgotten as they climbed into the truck.

"Where are we going Dad?" Sarah asked.

"Yeah, Dad," Sean echoed. "Where are we going?"

Sarah laughed in delight. "He's not your father; he's your big brother."

Jake wasn't listening. He was getting that washer, not going to see Maddie. "First we take you to your Gran's. Then Sean and I have a job to do."

"Can I come?" Sarah hopped up to kneel on the seat and peer out the side window.

"Bums on seats. Sean, help her get her seat belt back on.

We're doing a job for a friend and Gran specifically asked for your help this morning. Something about cookies."

Ignoring Sean's questioning look, Jake frowned at the road ahead.

* * *

Stephanie Murphy sat in the sun on her back porch studying a book of Monet's paintings and drinking her morning coffee. She'd put on her gardening clothes first thing—time to move the tomatoes out of the cold frame, but there was no hurry. Warming up though. Almost warm enough to take the storm windows off the screened-in porch.

She looked up when she heard tires crunching on gravel and the old pickup truck her sons shared pulled into the driveway with Jake at the wheel. Sean was with him. That was odd. He'd left a while ago to help Jake with a job. He'd been vague on the details.

Stephanie drifted out the door, mug in hand, and smiled when her granddaughter hopped out of the truck.

"Hi Mom," Jake said. "Is it okay if Sarah stays with you for a while? We have to take Aunt Augusta's old washer to the dump."

"All right." Jake was hiding something. She could always tell.

"Are we making cookies?" Sarah asked, chattering and clapping her hands as they walked back toward the house. "I was a good girl and ate all my porridge this morning."

Stephanie followed her granddaughter into the house. Although Sarah often stayed with her when Jake was at work, and they both ate many meals with her during the week, on weekends, Jake usually wanted Sarah to himself. She gave her sons one last quizzical look, but Sean just returned it with a smile and a shrug.

She'd get the story out of Jake sooner or later. Although with Jake, it would probably be later.

* * *

Jake knew that smirk on his brother's face. Sean was

enjoying this way too much.

"What's your problem?" he demanded, slamming the truck into reverse, shooting up gravel as he roared out the drive.

Sean sat back and crossed his arms casually on his chest. "No problem. Glad to help." Jake had never been able to hide anything from Sean.

Moments later, they drove down the dimly lit lane to the cabin.

"What's her name? Maddie? I haven't met her yet," Sean said. "But I hear she's pretty sweet."

"You keep away from her," Jake growled.

Sean held one hand up, palm out in a placating gesture. "Nice. I mean nice. I heard she's very nice."

"Yeah," Jake said, getting out of the truck and slamming the door. "Real nice."

He walked around to the back of the cabin, lifted a ladder off the hooks on the wall and brought it back around to the front. Maddie stepped onto the porch wearing nothing but a long T-shirt that came to mid-thigh. As she pushed her hair back from her face, he saw a tattoo of a chain around her wrist that faded into—he wasn't sure what. But the contrast between her soft fiery curls and the tough-girl tattoo was sexy as hell. His blood started to simmer. He wanted to grab her hand and pull her in for a closer look, but instead leaned the ladder against the roof.

"Morning," he said. "We've come to take the washer. Thought I'd get that branch off the roof while I was here." He started to climb.

She squinted up at him. "Sure."

He'd told himself he could get the washer out without running into her. Well he'd lied. And now with her standing there in her nightshirt, *damn*, he couldn't think of a thing to say.

And there was no way he was introducing her to Sean. His brother had enough luck with women. He could take care of himself.

Jake threw the branch off the roof into the forest, and climbed down.

Sean stepped up onto the porch and extended his hand, smiling that stupid smile that women loved. "Hi, I'm Sean."

Maddie shook his hand. Her ears turned pink.

"Let's get this out of here," Jake said, walking between Maddie and Sean, forcing them to step apart.

With a grunt, the men hoisted the washer, balanced it against their shoulders and worked their way down the porch stairs and around to the truck. With an echoing boom, the washer landed in the bed of the truck.

Sean turned back to smile and wave to Maddie. She raised a hand in reply.

Jake climbed into the truck and when he dropped his head onto the steering wheel, Sean didn't even try to conceal his smirk. "Smooth, big brother. Very smooth."

"Oh shut up," Jake said, lifting his head, firing up the truck and roaring up the drive. "She's got a damn tattoo."

Chapter 9

A few days later, Maddie hopped out of the car at the Fortune Bay store. You could feel the summer energy building. The parking lot was full of cars and on the weekends, motor homes clogged the roads, more strangers than locals filling the store.

Fiona was at the till and Maddie waved to her as she passed through to the café.

Taking the last available stool at the counter, Maddie said to Louise, "Busy today."

"The summer people are starting to roll in and everyone's excited about the Festival this weekend. There's a parade with floats and a logger sports competition, local guys, real fallers, not professional competitors like some of the big shows."

On her way out, Maddie picked up a few groceries in the store. At the till, Fiona's assistant Phil tugged at his ball cap and told her that his favorite part of the festival—next to the barbeque—was the dance.

"You've got to come. Busted Muffler always plays. Just a bunch of guys from town, but they're really good."

She gave him a non-committal smile. "We'll see."

He winked. "Save me a dance."

Maddie was determined to be in the front row at the daytime events getting the shots she needed, but she wasn't so sure about the dance. Too many painful high school memories with little to counter them since.

Out in the parking lot, the volunteer firemen extended the ladder of the new fire truck out over the road. Sean waved to her from the top of the ladder, then stretched out to finish hanging a banner.

Fortune Bay Festival—Fun for the Entire Family

She just wished that Jenny was here.

* * *

Festival morning arrived sunny and cool. As Maddie loaded her tripod and camera into the Beast, a brisk breeze blew in off the lake fueling her excitement.

In the store, she paused at the arched entrance to the café. Every seat was taken and people stood clustered in the corners. Louise saw her and pointed to a spot at the end of the counter where a cup of coffee and a banana nut muffin were waiting. The layers of voices around her rose like the hum of a cocktail party as people discussed their plans for the day.

"Meet you after the parade."

"They were up until midnight decorating their bikes..."

"The wall of the shed is a mess from Mike practicing..."

"Are you going to the dance?"

She almost choked on her muffin when she recognized the last voice. Her head jerked around and she found herself elbow to elbow at the counter with Jake, his bright blue eyes watching her from beneath the brim of a black cowboy hat.

"Going to the dance?" he asked again, and flashed a crooked smile that made the muffin turn to dust in her mouth.

She didn't know what to say, so she raised her eyebrows and shook her head.

"Tonight at the hall," he said. "The band is playing from seven 'til nine for the family portion, then the DJ takes over."

"Oh." She blushed, embarrassed to have thought for a minute that he was asking her to go with him. "Maybe. Actually, no. I don't think I will."

He leaned into her gently with his shoulder. "Come on, everybody goes." He glanced at the clock, downed the remainder of his coffee and with another quick smile, tipped his hat and made his way through the crowd to the door.

So hot. But so married. Why did she have so much trouble with the concept? Although she had never met his wife, he was clearly in a domestic situation that he was obviously not inclined to talk to her about. Or maybe he thought she knew.

He was probably just being nice because he was her landlord. Anything more was just wishful thinking. A relationship with a married man would be really bad, but he was so helpful, and so hot, and had that cute dimple in one cheek when he smiled—

Louise gave her a nudge and Maddie realized with a start that the café had almost cleared and the parade was starting in ten minutes.

"I'm taking most of the day off," Louise said, giving the counter a quick wipe. "I know you want to take some photographs, but let's meet at the logger sports event."

Maddie nodded as she stuffed the last bite of muffin into her mouth and washed it down with the dregs of her coffee. She ran out to the car, pulled her equipment out of the back, spread the legs of the tripod and snapped her camera on top.

As soon as she put her eye to the viewfinder, she slipped into the zone. The rest of the world receded as the image before her eye captured her full attention, a sensation akin to donning visual headphones. She swiveled the lens left and right, experimentally zooming in and out, finally deciding on wide-angle to catch the atmosphere of being smack in the middle of the crowd as the parade passed by.

But for now, she zoomed in on the people across the road, already ensconced in a row of lawn chairs that lined the route. More townspeople stood behind them, arms folded across their chests, chatting with neighbors in the warm sunshine.

She was amazed at how many people she already knew. Ms. Bowden, the former teacher who Louise had introduced her to at the café, sat in her lawn chair talking to an elderly gentleman who had set his chair next to hers. Then another face she recognized filled the viewfinder, Lindy Smit from down the road. With a little widening of the view, Maddie saw Lindy had the baby on her shoulder and that tired glow that only new mothers had. She snapped the shot.

Another man leaned in to share a laugh with Ms. Bowden

who seemed to be quite the belle at this affair. Maddie's finger pressed the shutter button, catching these two local pioneers, heads together sharing a joke as everything around them receded into soft focus.

At the blast of a horn, everyone clapped and cheered and the parade began with a '54 Ford fire truck leading the way. Over the bulbous front bumpers, the Fire Chief waved out the window. The new fire truck came next, two years old and the pride of the community, with Sean in the driver's seat.

Every Wednesday evening Maddie heard the sirens at the Fire Hall wail, calling volunteer fire fighters to practice. The men gathered at the hall other nights too, ostensibly to check the gear and wash down the trucks, but equally, she suspected, to enjoy a beer around the dartboard with the rest of the crew.

More horns proclaimed the parade floats. Bob's Outboard sported an antique cedar strip motorboat on a flatbed truck with a couple of local guys fishing on the blue plastic waves of the Bay. On the Fortune Furniture float, grinning teenagers, blasting out music and waving to the crowd, relaxed in handmade, wooden patio furniture.

A pole affixed to the forest company's float promoted the logger sports events they were sponsoring after the parade. From ten feet up the pole, a faller waved to the crowd and threw hard candy that scattered on the asphalt, luring squealing children out onto edges of the road.

Maddie's shutter clicked like the flutter of a hummingbird's wings at the arrival of the squadron of kids on bikes, all decorated to the nines with streamers and balloons. Two boys hauled a wagon holding a small building with a half-moon cut into the door that, much to their delight, drew hoots and catcalls from the crowd. Maddie took the camera off its mount and got down on one knee for a shot of a blonde boy leading a goat.

After the last of the kids passed by, the crowd, so well behaved on the sidelines until then, dissolved into a melee of floating faces before the camera's lens. Kids with balloons and ice cream raced by. Adults pushed babies in strollers decorated like the bikes and carried tote bags loaded with supplies: a picnic blanket, bottles of water and maybe something a little stronger for later in the afternoon.

Maddie straightened up and rubbed the kink in her lower back. When the crowd threatened to knock the tripod into the road, she packed up her gear and stowed most of it in the back of the Beast. Then she lifted the camera to her eye and continued her search for new subjects.

A little girl, not much more than six years old, with big fairy wings strapped lopsidedly to her back was attacking a bright red candy-apple. Tilting her head from side to side, she tried to get purchase on the shiny orb with her combination of baby and new half-grown teeth, her pigtails bouncing with every attempt.

Maddie zoomed in until only her face and the apple filled the frame, freckles standing out in relief on her pale snub nose, face-paint adding whiskers and colorful cat's eyes. She clicked a couple of shots—you can't have too many with a young, moving subject—then a smile split the pixie's face.

Snap. A keeper.

The girl thrust the sticky apple up at a man in blue jeans who scooped her up onto one hip. Together their faces filled the viewfinder and Maddie's heart skipped a beat as Jake took a bite of the apple.

The little girl giggled and shrieked and tried to hold the apple out of his reach, and Maddie's heart continued its erratic patter as she took a few more shots. Finally, she dragged in a ragged breath and lowered the camera.

Jake scanned the crowd, his eye stopping on a woman in a bright Indian cotton skirt and tight, scoop-necked T-shirt that highlighted her voluptuous figure. Gold earrings dangled as she bent to talk to a small boy holding another candy-apple.

Jake put the little girl down beside the boy. The family resemblance was unmistakable. Jake slipped his arm easily around the woman's waist and gave her a squeeze, whispering something in her ear.

Go, go, she gestured with a wave of her hand, then he gave her a kiss on the cheek and loped off across the park, quickly disappearing into the crowd.

The woman picked up a toddler, his cheeks sticky pink, and like a mother hen, gathered the two older children beneath her wings and followed Jake across the field.

Maddie dropped the camera to her chest, her arms suddenly too tired to hold it up any longer, her core hollow inside. If that billowing, motherly woman was his type, he certainly wouldn't be interested in her tall skinny self.

A crackling loudspeaker boomed across the park announcing the logger sports events and jolting her out of her thoughts. She'd been staring vacantly as the parking lot emptied, people migrating toward the two tall poles that had sprouted overnight in front of the hall at the far end of the park in the center of town.

Darting back to her car, Maggie grabbed her tripod and a folding chair, and sprinted across the playground looking for Louise in the crowd gathering at the sandy sports pit.

Louise had snagged them front row seats. Maddie sat down in her chair, snapped the camera on top of her tripod and sat back to take stock.

At least twenty guys, all exceptionally fit, most in their late twenties, a few older, stretched and preened—hard to tell which was which—muscles rippling on bronzed shoulders and backs as they waited for their events.

"Holy moly! This is Logger Sports? You were holding out on me."

Louise snickered gleefully. "It's what we come for."

Maddie fired off a few shots, then she caught sight of Jake off to one side, getting his family settled on the grass at the edge of the sandy pit.

The games began and the events unfolded in a whirl of men with bulging biceps and tight T-shirts, many of them stripped off and thrown aside as the sun rose and the temperature soared.

Big burly guys lined up for the axe throwing competition, throwing heavy, deadly, double-headed weapons with astonishing speed at a bull's-eye twenty feet away. Maddie laughed and groaned along with the crowd, her voracious camera eating up the action and the wicked guy-candy. There was definitely a photo essay here that she could probably sell to a magazine, so every so often she switched to her digital camera.

Jake sauntered toward the pack of contestants waiting by one of the tall poles. Her camera was on him like a magnet on steel. These men were generally lighter and more agile than the axe throwers, but in his mid-thirties, Jake definitely tipped the older end of the scale. They were all attaching leather harnesses with razor-sharp cleats to their boots, then they proceeded to climb the smooth pole one by one, like monkeys on speed.

Jake was second from last to climb. When he started up the pole Maddie held her breath, almost forgetting to click the shutter when he rang the bell at the top.

He slid down the pole with the winning time, raising his arms in triumph when his boots hit the ground. A crowd of bare-chested guys swallowed him up, all slapping him on the shoulder, the back and the butt.

Beside her, Louise whooped with the rest of the crowd. "Whoo-who. Get me some of that action."

Even from that distance, Maddie could see the crooked half-grin on his face that never failed to turn her insides to mush.

They quickly moved on to the final event, Jake showing his stuff again by chopping through a downed log with an axe, chips flying as the V deepened. Boy could that man swing an axe.

He came second this time and although she grinned like a fool until her cheeks ached, Maddie managed to get a few excellent shots.

Then suddenly it was over. People stood up and started to mill around and she quickly gathered up her gear.

"See you in a minute," she said to Louise, and started over to congratulate Jake.

When she was just a few feet away, the little girl with fairy wings ran up and took his hands, bouncing on her toes in excitement. Maddie veered off at the last second.

What was she thinking? Butting in when he obviously wanted to be with his family.

Hiding in the shadow of her big-brimmed straw hat, ears burning, she slunk away, hoping he hadn't noticed.

The tantalizing aroma of barbequed salmon lured her across the park lawn to a circus marquee where the local firefighters were serving lunch. Frankie and Louise waved to her from the crowd and she joined them in line.

"Was that great or what?" Louise hooted.

Maddie held out her plate to a burly firefighter who was manning the grill dressed in nothing but shorts, an apron and a fireman's hat.

"Nice outfit Blue," Louise said as she gave the man a friendly pat on his firm buns.

He grinned back good-naturedly. "Happy to please, Louise."

The women grabbed three seats at a long, paper-covered table and once they were settled, Frankie asked, "Going to the dance?"

Maddie winced. Jake was bound to be there with his family. "I don't think so."

"Come on," Frankie coaxed. "It'll be fun. Everyone will be there, young and old. You'll get lots of good pictures."

There was that, and against her best instincts, she agreed. "If we can go together."

"Sure. I'll drive. It starts at seven but we don't have to get there until eight thirty. That's when the kids thin out."

By late afternoon, Maddie's camera-case pockets bulged with rolls of spent film. Hot, dusty and tired of the crowd, she packed up her gear and headed for home.

As she drove out of town, her thoughts returned to the photographs in her bag and the prospects for the evening ahead. She was not sure she was doing the right thing by going to the dance.

She gave her head a shake. *Get over it. It could be fun.*

Chapter 10

Maddie pulled a slithery black dress with a low neckline off the rod suspended in the corner of her bedroom that acted as her "closet." Slipping it on, she turned to study herself in the speckled mirror. Way too seductive. Totally inappropriate for a community dance. Why did she even own this dress? It's not like she ever went on dates.

And why was she even going tonight? She knew exactly what would happen at the dance and it didn't sound at all like fun. Jake would be there, dancing with his wife, surrounded by his family, and that would be hard. She should have stuck to her guns and stayed home.

She pulled off the dress and tried on a black pencil skirt and a white blouse with a pointy collar. Now she looked like she was going to a business meeting.

"What on earth am I supposed to wear?" she asked the empty room.

She had no idea what was appropriate. She hadn't been to a dance since high school.

Maybe going to the dance and actually seeing Jake with his family was the kind of tough love she needed to make her stop mooning over the man who was, after all, just her landlord. She rapped her knuckles on the top of her head trying to make the idea stick. Because lately, she found herself hoping to run into him every time she went to town and if she did, she relived their chance encounters repeatedly in a way that made her heart pound and her cheeks burn like a teenager with her first crush. It was downright embarrassing.

He wasn't part of the plan. Remember *the plan*? Get the photos, make a success of the show, and get Jenny through her last year of high school. No mention there of a man—and definitely not one who was *married*. She didn't need that kind of problem right now. Or ever.

In frustration she looked at the rod in the corner. An outfit hung on one end, a drifting white skirt and a turquoise blouse, complete with a soft pashima shawl in case the night was cool. She didn't remember putting it there, but it did look perfect.

She pulled it down and tried it on. The skirt swished against her legs and she felt—beautiful. Misty and soft and vaguely seductive. Like she might actually want to dance. Like it might be fun.

She shook her head to clear it. Where had *that* idea come from?

She checked herself out in the mirror. She had never worn these clothes together before, but they might be perfect for the dance.

Images from the day flashed through her mind: bright streamers of the kid's parade, the sun flashing off powerful shoulders and broad backs, and the pixie face pulled up beside the strong face of her father. Jake with his arm around his wife, giving her a lusty kiss on the cheek, surrounded by their happy children.

She blew out a heartfelt sigh. It didn't really matter what she wore. Anything would be fine. It wasn't like she was meeting someone special tonight.

Slipping the shawl over her shoulders, she went out on the porch to wait for Frankie.

* * *

The evening sun burnished the hall with gold as Frankie's Mini pulled into the parking lot. Laughing children ran through the shrubbery and music spilled out the open door where people stood, laughing and talking, enjoying the cool evening air.

Inside, the hall was decked out like a high school dance. Colored lights hung from the rafters and sparkling disco balls twirled from the ceiling. Maddie spent the first few minutes greeting people she knew, while the band blasted a country-rock cover in the background.

Finally, she glanced up at the stage, doing a double take when she realized it was Sean on guitar with someone, the salmon-serving-fireman behind him on drums.

Then she saw Jake, prowling the stage, a bass guitar riding low on his hips. She sucked in a breath and from that moment on she could hardly peel her eyes off the stage. Could barely string two coherent words together. Could scarcely remember her own name.

Sean leaned in to the microphone, Jake joining him on the harmonies. Dressed all in black, he channeled the bad boy she'd heard he had been in his younger years, the black cowboy hat that—*oh, yeah*—really suited him on his head.

Their eyes met across the room and her throat tightened. He inclined his head a quarter of an inch and then sunk back into the music. When Fiona's assistant Phil asked her to dance, Maddie tore her eyes away from the stage. Before she could refuse, Fiona stepped up, took the camera out of her hands and said, "Don't worry, I'll watch this."

Phil was looking cool in a lime green shirt and matching ball cap. He took her hand and led her onto the floor and before she knew it she was doing steps she'd never done before with just the touch of his hand.

Maddie was still reeling from the exertion when old Mr. Weatherby moved in next for a slow number. His suit jacket may have seen better days but his white shirt was clean and pressed. He smelled faintly of peppermint, and, holding her at a respectful distance, made small talk through a done-her-wrong song as they moved smoothly around the floor surrounded by dancing parents and children.

He had barely finished his polite thank-you bow when Maddie felt an arm snake around her waist and Tom Findley, Frankie's neighbor-on-the-other-side, whispered in her ear, "I think it's my turn, darlin'."

Maddie stiffened at his touch. She'd only met him briefly once, but Louise had warned her about Tom. That he wouldn't take no for an answer. Now though, aware of the crowd, all she could do was clench her teeth and smile.

"Nice to see you Tom." She attempted to disengage herself from his arm but it was wrapped like Velcro around her waist. Inching toward the refreshment table, she clutched her throat. "You know; I haven't had a chance to try that punch yet."

"Great idea," he said and, taking her arm, led her off the dance floor.

* * *

Trapped up on stage, Jake had no choice other than play through to the end of the set. Ever since Maddie arrived, all he could think about was if he'd get a chance to hold her on the dance floor later on, even just for a few minutes. Meanwhile, he watched her dip and dive with Phil and quirked a corner of his mouth when she curtseyed to Mr. Weatherby's bow. His eyes narrowed under the brim of his hat however, when Tom grabbed her—*what else could you call it?*—took her by the arm and led her away.

Hands off Buddy.

His thoughts skidded to a halt. Not his place to say who she could dance with. The bass lines were coming more by instinct than memory and hearing them growl, he dragged them back to a mellower riff. But his eyes were on Maddie like a hawk.

A few minutes later, when Tom took the drink out of her hand and led her out onto the floor, Jake's insides started to burn.

What was she thinking, dancing with that snake? Jake had heard him talking about women more than once over a beer the Elks Club. That man couldn't be trusted.

The bass growled on.

* * *

Out on the dance floor, Maddie had her hands full. Or rather, Tom's hands were full of her. She tried to head him off at the pass but didn't stand a chance. Finally—*thank God*—the song ended. Tom loosened his grip and Maddie grabbed her opening. Chattering her excuses, she rushed to the sidelines where Frankie and Louise stood together.

Louise had to turn away to hide her laughter. "I think he likes you," she whispered, as they whisked Maddie away.

A few minutes later, when Maddie was sure Tom had moved on to his next conquest, she made her way to the open doorway. The room was hot and crowded and she luxuriated in the cool brush of lake breeze over her body. Inhaling deeply, she caught a hint of the sweet flowering cottonwood trees.

I'm not ready for this, she thought. But if not now, then when?

Sean appeared at her side. He put a paper cup in her hand and leaned against the doorjamb in a way that could have been intimidating in another man. Sean had a way about him though, kind of like a brother, that you couldn't help liking. He wasn't as tall as Jake and Maddie could almost look him in the eye.

"I hope it's not spiked," she said with a smile.

"I would've if I could've, but the bar is still closed." He had a spark of laughter in his voice. Who did he have his eye on tonight? Surely a guy like Sean wouldn't be alone for long.

She took a long grateful drink of the watery soda and before she could comment on the band, something over her shoulder caught his attention. Toasting his paper cup to hers, he moved away down the hall.

Maddie turned to see what had scared him off and saw Jake, up on the stage, set down his electric bass with deliberate care. Her eyes widened when he jumped lightly to the floor and set out on a path across the room straight towards her. Blood rushed to her head and her ears began to ring. Jungle drums pounded in her chest. She took a deep breath and plastered a stiff smile on her face.

What would she do if he wanted to dance? The band might have finished, but the DJ rolled right on playing popular country favorites, old and new.

Maybe he wasn't even coming to *her*, although he was headed directly her way. She tried to look away, but couldn't. From the single-minded determination of his stride, he was definitely after something. But whatever he wanted, she wasn't ready.

A sparkly bundle in a pink tutu ran into his path, but he didn't even break stride, just scooped up the fluffy bundle and continued toward her.

He stopped right in front of Maddie. She was aware of the goofy smile on her face but was helpless to do anything about it. She stared back at him for what seemed like eons.

Finally, Jake broke the silence. "This is my daughter, Sarah. Sarah this is Ms. Tedesco."

Maddie blinked. Same blue eyes. No question, she was his daughter. "Hello Sarah, call me Maddie." Her cheeks froze in a smile. "And where is your mother?"

Behind her, Louise whooped with laughter. Maddie pressed her fingers to her lips. Did she really say that? Her eyes flew to Jake whose gaze was firmly on her, as if waiting for her reaction.

"We don't know," Sarah said, and with a, "nice-to-meet-you," wriggled out of her father's arms.

Maddie took her hand away from her mouth, but she couldn't tear her gaze away from Jake's. In her peripheral vision, she saw Sarah's sparkly skirt as she ran over to an older woman who was heading their way. Sarah took the woman's hand and walked beside her, skipping sideways so she could talk as they continued over to Maddie and Jake.

Jake spoke without breaking eye contact. "Mom, this is Maddie Tedesco. Maddie, my mother. Mrs. Murphy. Your landlady."

"So nice to finally meet you," the woman said. "Call me Stephanie."

Maddie gave her head a slight shake and tore her gaze away from Jake to smile at the striking older woman. A pair of red lacquered chopsticks held her graying hair in a knot on top of her head, showing off her gorgeous cheekbones. "Nice to meet you too."

"I understand Jake is being very helpful taking care of the cabin," Stephanie said.

Maddie's mouth opened but no words came out. Her cheeks flushed as she remembered how he'd caught her more than once in her night shirt, how he'd found her under the washing machine and, worst of all, his shocked face at the bathroom window.

"If there is anything more we can do, please let us know."

Maddie knew she should reply, but all she managed to do was nod.

"Well." Stephanie looked from Maddie to her son. "It's late. I'll take Sarah home. You can pick her up in the morning Jake."

That snapped his focus off Maddie and onto his daughter. He scooped up Sarah and kissed her on the cheek. "I'll pick her up later."

She wrapped her arms around his neck, returning his kiss. "Night Daddy."

As Stephanie carried Sarah away, Jake looked Maddie directly in the eye. "She has no mother."

Maddie blinked, then frowned. "But who was that woman?"

"What woman?"

"In the parking lot."

Jake frowned and shook his head, obviously confused, so she searched the hall until she found the woman in the bright cotton skirt, laughing and dancing with the young boy. Maddie pointed. "Her."

Jake's gaze followed her arm and his face cleared. "That's my sister, Colleen."

Maddie snapped back as if hitting an invisible wall. This changed everything. Maybe she had read his intentions correctly. Maybe he had been coming onto her, albeit somewhat clumsily.

She smiled. There was more to say, but not here, not now. Apparently, he had the same idea. "I'll drive you home."

"Okay, but I have to take some pictures first."

He nodded. "I have to pack up my guitar." Then he turned and headed back to the stage.

Maddie found Fiona sitting on the sidelines, fanning herself with the day's program, keeping an eye on Maddie's camera. As she reclaimed her gear, Maddie was shocked to realize how acclimatized she had become. In Seattle she would never have left her camera on a chair and gone dancing.

In Seattle I never would have danced at all.

She spent the next half hour laughing and taking pictures of her new friends. Most of them, after their initial embarrassment, got into the fun and hammed it up for the camera.

Phil doffed his cap to Marie, who curtsied shyly back.

Mr. Wilson, a short gentleman, two-stepped happily around the room with willowy Louise in her black and white pony vest, lime green cat's eye glasses and fuchsia streaked hair.

Sean had a busty redhead in a cinch, and they dipped and dived out on the floor. She had a friendly smile and hair big enough to handle the country music the new DJ was spinning.

Then Maddie took her camera to the half-darkened entranceway. The angled light spilled out the doorway creating dramatic images of the young crowd lingering there.

That was where Jake found her. He came up from behind and slid her soft shawl over her shoulders, then brushed his hands down her arms, leaving a trail of sparks behind.

"Are you ready?" he asked, his voice low and intimate in her ear. She glanced over her shoulder at him. So close, she could smell his woodsy aftershave and see the fire smoldering in his eyes.

She shivered. After ten years of divorce and a lifetime of disappointment—was she finally ready to try again?

Chapter 11

In the steamy cab of Jake's pickup, sweat trickled between Maddie's breasts as he drove her back to the cabin. The silence stretched between them like warm taffy and out of the corner of her eye she watched Jake's white-knuckled hands on the steering wheel.

He had every right to be furious. She should never have asked Sarah about her mother. She of all people, she who would crawl into a hole filled with spiders rather than talk about her own mother, should have known better.

She snuck a sideways glance at his stony profile. Lust was no excuse. She'd have to apologize.

He pulled into the parking spot beside the cabin, turned off the motor and cleared his throat. She opened her mouth to say the words but he beat her to the punch.

"I'm sorry."

She jerked around to face him, staring in amazement. "*You're* sorry? *I'm* sorry. I never should have asked Sarah about her mother. It's none of my business. Sometimes I surprise myself with the things I say."

"I never should have ambushed you back there." His hands relaxed on the wheel enough for him to peel one off and run it over his face. "I should have told you sooner about Sarah. But really, I thought you knew."

"How could I?"

"I was sure someone would have told you." He gave a hoarse laugh. "They've been gossiping about us in town already. Seems like they've been talking about me ever since I was a kid." She saw a shadow of that boy in his self-conscious glance. Then he stared into the dark forest again. "I'm not really that interesting."

Maddie's hands worked a knot in the fringe of her shawl.

"Where is her mother?"

"She left pretty soon after Sarah was born. Couldn't handle the isolation I guess." Jake stared out the window as he spoke. "After university, when we first came back here, she thought living rugged in the backcountry was an adventure. That didn't last long. She was young, but not that young—mid-twenties. I was younger too."

He glanced at her out of the corner of his eye. "Kids make you grow up fast, don't they?"

"They sure do."

They sat quietly in the dark cab for a few minutes more, watching the moonlight dance on the water. Finally, he said, "It didn't take long before she wanted to go back. Truth was, it was bad almost right from the start. When she found out she was pregnant, she tried to convince me to leave, go back to the city where we met."

His voice took on an urgent note and he turned toward her, clearly determined to make her understand. "I couldn't go. My job was here. And, well, this is my home."

Maddie didn't know how to respond, but was saved the need when he turned his eyes to the lake and started again. "After Sarah was born things just got worse. I don't know, maybe Rena had post-partum depression, but when Sarah was a year old, we finally agreed that Rena would go back to Seattle for a couple of weeks. Alone, for a break. To visit her girlfriends." His voice dropped. "She never came back. Mom offered to help out and has been helping ever since."

The pain in his voice tugged at Maddie's heart.

He pushed out a ragged sigh. "She couldn't stay here and I couldn't leave, and she knew I would fight for Sarah. In the end I didn't have to though."

Sensing he wasn't finished, Maddie let the silence hang between them.

"We phoned back and forth for a few months, tried to work things out. Or I tried. I wanted her back. A little girl needs a mother. But she wanted to untangle herself from our life. My life I guess. She never made any kind of life for herself here.

"We never hear from her anymore."

Maddie barely managed to restrain herself from crying out, *her daughter should have been her life.* Instead, she asked, "How long were you married? How long was she here?"

"Two years, altogether."

With a start, Maddie realized how much of a life she had made for herself here already, in less than a month.

"A little girl needs a mother," Jake repeated quietly, as if talking to himself. "But not a mother like that.

"So." He turned to face her. "That's my deal. My life is complicated."

Maddie blinked. *His* life is complicated? She turned toward him, elbow up on the seatback and let fly.

"I have a daughter too. She's seventeen going on twenty-five. You think your life is complicated now? Wait until Sarah's a teenager. When one day your cute little pixie comes down the stairs in a tube top, with breasts and blue eye shadow and black eyeliner and says she's off to school. Or worse, just off—to who knows where. And so sure of herself that she feels no need to fill you in on her plans. You did such a good job of raising a self-assured young adult that she doesn't need you anymore. Or thinks she doesn't, because one look at her and you know she *really* needs you now. More than ever. But can you talk to her? No-o-o."

She stopped and buried her face in her hands with a laugh. "Don't get me started. You don't know what complicated is until you have a teenager and an ex-husband."

He laughed. It sounded a lot like relief. Then he climbed out of the truck, walked around to her open window and crossed his arms on the window ledge.

She sensed the dreaded after-the-date moment. Even though it hadn't even been a date. She was rooted to the seat, unable—or unwilling—to open the door. Heat rose to her cheeks and she couldn't seem to blink, just stared straight ahead. Slowly she turned to face him. He had a grin on his face and, reaching in, took her face in his hands and kissed her, gently, on the lips. Like sealing a pact.

At first she didn't react, still feeling frozen in her seat. Then the warmth of the kiss spread through her. It had been *way* too long since she'd felt this, this wanting to melt into someone's arms, and she moved eagerly toward him.

That's when he stepped back and removed his lips from hers. She could hardly resist following them out the window, but instead she put her hands on his, holding them to her cheeks, their eyes locked on each other.

He smiled, pulled his hands away and swung open the door. Taking her hand, he helped her out of the truck, talking about the dance and the band as he walked her to the door. He took her key and slid it in the lock, put his hip to the cabin door and nudged it open. A dim light burned on the porch and another on the old electric stove in the kitchen.

She chewed nervously on her lip and her stomach fluttered like the wings of a bird. This time though, she was ready. Ready for the kiss. Bracing herself, she half-closed her eyes and swayed in his direction.

Luckily she could see through her lashes because instead of leaning toward her, he lifted his hand in a wave and jumped down off the porch.

She jerked back. She could have sworn...

Hands in his pockets, he walked back to the truck, whistling one of the band's catchy tunes.

Her chest deflated like a day-old party balloon as she watched him walk away, wondering what the hell had just happened. Wondering if she'd imagined the kiss in the car.

* * *

Jake drove to his mother's house to pick up Sarah with a feeling of danger averted. But later that night, back at the farm, after he'd put Sarah to bed, he stood in his wreck of a kitchen and tried to work his mind around the renovation he'd started months before. Not having a kitchen for months on end hadn't mattered all that much to them. His mother had helped more than usual with meals, and he and Sarah had managed.

Like they managed everything, pretty well, so far.

Cracking open a beer, he leaned against the shell of the old counter. Maddie's words rang in his head. Even now at six years old Sarah was a self-assured young lady, something he already found hard to handle. Like this morning, standing in the poufy princess dress Colleen had given her last Halloween, hands on her hips, demanding to wear it to the festival.

And the glitter—his head ached at the thought of cleaning up the mess she had made in the living room with that. He glanced at it through the doorway and shook his head.

It wasn't much of a living room anyway. More like a kid and dad's playroom with toys on the floor and a big screen TV mounted on the wall. Not a place you'd want to invite anyone into, except maybe Sean to watch the game. Definitely not a woman, and certainly not for dinner. He wandered back into the kitchen, took a hit of his beer and studied the partial demolition.

And what had she said about breasts? The very thought of Sarah with breasts made his shoulders seize. He forced himself to unclench his fists. He would chase away any boys that came sniffing around, but she'd need more defenses than that. At some point he'd have to talk to her about sex.

And what about when she got her period? When did that happen? He was pretty sure he had a few good years yet, but the years flew by, as he well knew, and how was he going to handle that hurdle? Just doing the laundry once a week already overworked his feminine side.

His eyes narrowed. What exactly was a tube top anyway? He took another hit of his beer.

He could count on his Mom and Colleen—they always stepped in when needed—but it wasn't fair to them or to

Sarah, and this was not how he'd envisioned his own family turning out.

He'd told Maddie Sarah needed a mother and that was true. In the dim, after-midnight hours however, he could admit to himself that he needed a mate as well. A warm woman in his bed at night instead of cold sheets and a quick tumble every few months. Someone to sit with on the porch in the evening, talking over their day and watching the sun set. Someone to be a mother for Sarah and to make this shell of a house a home.

Could Maddie be that woman? She was easy to talk to and he bet she'd warm the sheets just fine, but was she a good mother? If she was, why wasn't her own daughter here with her now?

He had a lot of questions, the biggest one being—what would happen when the summer was over?

She'll leave, that's what.

He straightened up and shook his head. He wasn't going through that again. Better to stick to his rules: keep it casual and keep Sarah out of it. No way he was letting Sarah get attached to a woman who would leave in September—leave and break her heart.

He tipped up the bottle and drained it.

No way.

JUNE

Chapter 12

Maddie's pile of photographs grew, eating through her darkroom supplies. When she had no choice but to restock, she and Frankie decided to go to town. Not Fortune Bay, or Majestic at the head of the lake, but all the way to Port Townsend, an hour and a half drive away.

Pulling the money sock out of her dresser drawer, she gritted her teeth as she peeled two fifties off the roll. She had no other choice. She needed supplies.

Before she left, she leafed through the pile of proofs on the darkroom counter. Some were of neighbors: Bob Foster who she often met out on the road where he walked everyday as therapy after his logging accident, Friday the Golden Retriever who greeted her joyously at his fence and Lindy Smit pushing her stroller, trying to lose the new-baby weight.

And then there were the shots of the festival and the farm. A blush rose up her neck and into her cheeks as she stared at the picture of Jake surrounded by six other bare-chested guys after he won the pole-climbing contest. Her mind swirled on to the end of the day when he brought her home after the dance. And then, the kiss.

Now granted, she didn't have a lot of dating experience—not that they were dating—but the kiss didn't strike her as particularly passionate. More like sealing a pact. The single parent, I-don't-really-have-time-for-this pact.

And wasn't that exactly what she wanted? No complications?

Maybe. She didn't know anymore. Sharply, she tapped the

prints into a pile and filed them away. *Whatever.*

In Port Townsend's harbor, the historic architectural beauties had her repeatedly pulling out her digital camera. These would be great on her new website with the best of her digital photographs of Seattle. If she ever got the website started. It was hard with no wifi.

Sticking to her budget, she didn't buy much, just her darkroom supplies. Frankie, however, bought a hat with a big floppy brim and a deck of tarot cards at a shop that smelled of incense and had a bright cosmic eye on the door.

Finally, they crossed a busy street and Frankie led her down a quiet lane to a restaurant with a patio overlooking the water. They ordered pizza and sat in the sun, watching the boats in the harbor.

"Do you read tarot cards?" Maddie asked.

"I used to, in university. It's been years since I've done a reading though. After I've practiced a bit, I'll do one for you. Maybe at our solstice celebration."

"What's that?"

"June twenty-first, the summer solstice. Louise and I celebrate every year. We want you to come this time. I could practice reading on you and Louise."

Maddie smiled. "Sounds like fun."

Nerves fluttered in her chest. *Look at me, planning an evening out with the girls.*

* * *

Jake pounded the last three-inch spike into the new porch step.

Where was she? Not that he'd been waiting.

He wiped the sweat from his forehead with the back of his hand and threw his shirt on the porch, rolling his shoulders to ease the strain. Getting soft. Too much time behind the desk.

A twig cracked on the path through the forest and there she was, like a wildflower in her bright sundress. Soft and clingy, it hugged her curves, exposing a flash of long, bare leg.

When she saw him, she stopped. A jacket hung over her

arm, along with a shopping bag with a photography store logo. The sun had pinked the bridge of her nose and the curve of her bare shoulders.

Crickets sang in the wall of hot air between them.

She stepped forward. "You're fixing the step."

He glanced down. "Right." He couldn't seem to string a complete sentence together when she was around. With her oversized sunglasses on, he couldn't tell if she was glad to see him or not. He reached for his shirt and slung it over his shoulder.

She smiled. "That's great. Thanks."

One side of his mouth quirked in a half smile. "It's my job."

She didn't move. "Thank you."

Silence hummed and a boa constrictor of tension circled his chest. Finally, he cleared his throat and asked, "Did you get some good shots of the farm?"

She blinked and, with a quick intake of breath, came to life. "Yes. Thank you. Do you want to see?"

Not really. He'd seen flowers before. It was just something to say to fill the silence.

But in a flash she was up the steps, across the porch and into the laundry room. Looking at him over her shoulder, she beckoned for him to follow.

He had no choice but to go, and stepped tentatively into the room. Same old laundry room—bare stud walls, homemade shelves, old cement sink in the corner—except the washer was gone and she'd made a counter on each side of the room from boards he'd left in the shed behind the cabin.

She stood with her back to him, shuffling through a pile of papers. Equipment he didn't recognize rested on the counter beside her and plastic trays and glass jugs lined the shelf below.

When she turned to face him in the cramped space, they were almost nose-to-nose. Clutching a stack of papers to her chest, he saw a flash of indecision in her eyes.

He held out his hand. "Okay. Let me see."

Her chin came up and her shoulders straightened—smooth sun-pink shoulders he wanted to touch—and she handed over the eight-by-tens.

Jake laid them in the light on the counter next to the door.

He didn't know what he'd been expecting—but not this. She'd captured the lake in its many moods; brooding, fragile, laughing with sparkling water. The forest glistening after the rain; delicate ferns and rugged tree bark.

Then the farm, dark, almost somber in its lines, and in front of it, a field of flowers. He knew there were a lot, but somehow she had managed to make it look like a million. In the next picture, she'd zoomed in closer—three graceful stems filled the page, each lined with trumpet bells. Grey and white traced the full, sensual lip of each bell, the house a dark, indistinct background. A shiver trickled down his back.

The last shot zoomed in closer still. One stem took up most of the frame, this time silhouetted against a charcoal blur that set off the fragility of the flower perfectly.

He was speechless—completely out of his depth.

She was so close. Tension radiated off her like an energy field. He glanced up. Her eyes were round, waiting, her tongue darted out to wet her lips. She drew in the bottom lip with her teeth. Agonizing to watch, he dragged his thoughts and eyes back to the photographs in his hand.

* * *

Maddie was getting light-headed. She would have to breathe soon or pass out right there at his feet. She inhaled a ragged breath and the intoxicating scent of a man who'd been working in the sun. Despite the warmth of the room, goosebumps rose on her arms.

His broad shoulders seemed to fill the tiny space, and although he'd put his shirt back on, he'd left it hanging open making it impossible for her to think about anything else but the flat of his stomach above his jeans and the fine sheen of dark hair on his chest.

She dragged her gaze back to his face. So silent. What was he thinking?

He looked at her, but his face was blank. Didn't he get it? Maybe he couldn't see what she was trying to capture. He was bound to see everything differently. This was his home.

He carefully put the photographs in a pile on the counter and turned to her. "Very nice."

He didn't like them. In art circles, "nice" was the kiss of death. Almost as bad as "interesting."

She snatched up the pile and held them to her chest. "These are just a few. I'm going to make them bigger." Right, because if they aren't any good now, making them bigger would definitely help.

The sun streamed into the tiny room sending the temperature soaring. He was so close, she had to look up to see his face. To see what he was thinking.

Jake nodded. "Very interesting."

She winced.

He looked around the room and frowned. "You've changed the room."

"I hope it's okay. That's why I needed to get the washer out."

He didn't comment on that debacle, thank goodness. In fact, he didn't say anything for a minute, or two, as the temperature spiraled even higher in the tiny room.

"Well, I guess that's it," he said politely.

"Yes, well, thank you." She wished he'd stay longer but couldn't think of any other jobs for him to do.

He picked up his tool kit from the porch, dropped it into the back of the truck and climbed into the cab. Maddie watched with a sinking heart as the pickup rolled down the drive.

"Thanks for fixing the step," she called.

Jake didn't look back, just raised a hand in salute out the window of the truck.

* * *

He needed a beer and he needed it now. There were none in the fridge at home so he'd just have to drive into Majestic. Maybe stop at the Elks club, spend some time with the guys. Sarah was fine with his Mom and anyway, sometimes a guy just needed some space.

Maddie's pictures were great. Better than great. Probably art, not that he'd know good art if it hit him in the head. Her photographs caught the history though, of the place and the farm and the wilderness he'd loved since he was a boy.

Must be part of being a photographer—being intuitive and insightful. Seeing what other people didn't know they saw, then putting it out there for them to recognize and appreciate. How could she see that when she'd only been here, what? A month? It was something his wife had never seen.

He'd never seen the point of taking pictures, particularly of stuff you see every day. But those pictures of hers...he could see why people wanted to hang them on the wall and stare into the worlds she caught on film. He shook his head. He would have to re-think his first impression of her as a flaky artist-photographer.

But what had he heard? She had a show coming up in the fall. In Seattle.

There was the rub. This was just a diversion for her. The summer would end and she'd go back to the city. He'd been right to keep his distance. No way did he want to go through that again. His wife had been eager to come to Fortune Bay too. At first. But look how long that lasted.

In his experience, city girls go back to the city. Period. End of story.

Problem was, now he wanted to see more. More of the pictures and more of the woman. More of her shoulders and those long, long legs.

With a cloud of confusion circling his head, Jake drove into town after that beer.

* * *

Maddie stalked into the house, threw off her sundress and

pulled on a t-shirt and shorts. The golden glow of early evening drew her like a magnet back onto the porch and down to the shore. Although the sun had dipped below the mountains and the air was cooling off, the giant slab of rock where she settled at the water's edge still radiated warmth against her bare thighs.

Wrapping her arms around her knees, she tried to calm the turmoil in her head as she watched the sky darken to indigo. Her conversations with Jake always left her churned up. She didn't understand him. Friendly one moment, cool the next, he always left abruptly and then, just when she thought she'd seen the last of him, there he was, confusing her all over again.

She'd thought that maybe, after the dance... but no. Apparently, nothing had changed.

Well, it wasn't her problem. She wasn't looking for a relationship. She would just keep her distance.

It had been hard though in the tiny darkroom, with him so big and so...male. That raw masculinity swirled around him like a force field, infusing the air and hitting her like a drug to her system, leaving her confused and overwhelmed, with a head full of thoughts and feelings she didn't understand.

In the past, she'd reacted to that kind of power with fear. Growing up, it had only meant trouble, the kind of trouble that, at sixteen, had forced Maddie to run. A man named McCoy was the last straw. One of Cindy's 'friends', Maddie never knew his first name. He always said, "Just call me McCoy."

One night, when he'd been coming by pretty regularly for a couple of weeks, her mom had passed out in the living room while Maddie was watching TV with the sound low in the bedroom at the back of the trailer.

Suddenly McCoy loomed in the doorway.

He watched her silently, making the skin crawl on her back, but she kept her eyes focused on the screen. She finally glanced up, an involuntary action, but that was all the invitation he needed.

He stepped into the room. She hugged her knees to her ribs trying to disappear, her heart pounding painfully in her breast. Time stopped for a moment as he leered at her, swaying slightly from side to side. Then he lurched toward her and her adrenalin spiked. She jumped off the bed and tried to run, but the room was too small to get around him.

He grabbed her arm and slammed her against the wall, holding her there with his hot sweaty body, breathing alcohol fumes in her face. His whiskers burned a trail across her cheek as he put his mouth to her ear.

"Your Momma teach you any tricks?"

Strangled with fear, her breath coming in pants, Maddie shook her head.

"I got a soft spot for young girls," he slurred in a low drawl. "I could teach you a few things myself."

He was a big man, and she wasn't sure he was drunk enough that she could fight him off herself. Maybe drunk enough to trick, though.

"I'll just go to the bathroom. You know, to get ready." She forced a smile. "Don't you go anywhere."

He loosened his grip on her arm and stepped back, slightly off balance as he hit the bed with the back of his knees. She pushed him hard, on the chest, and he fell back on the bed.

Maddie flew down the hall and out of the trailer, hiding in the first place she saw—under the front stoop. They hadn't lived in the park long enough for her to have any friends, so she spent the night shivering in that smelly hole under the steps.

McCoy left first thing the next morning, her mother a few hours later. Maddie helped herself to the crumpled bills in Cindy's stash jar, which, thank God, McCoy hadn't found yet, and hit the road.

She felt like she'd been running ever since and was sometimes so tired she just wanted to stop. But she didn't dare. Jake seemed like a nice man but she was afraid to let down her walls. It had been a long time, though, since she'd met a man who made her want to try.

Goosebumps rose on her arms as a chill descended with the dusk. The glow on the mountain across the bay faded and clouds gathered on the horizon.

She stood, brushed the fir needles off the seat of her shorts and filled her arms with a load of chopped wood, hoping a fire would fight off the dark memories that lurked in the corners of her mind.

Chapter 13

A storm blew up the following day forcing Maddie to work inside. She kept the fire going, made a pot of soup from a recipe in the carved wooden box, then opened her laptop on the kitchen table and settled in to work. If she wanted to make a go of her photography business, ever hoped to make it pay, she had to get organized. That meant a website, a marketing strategy, the works.

She needed wifi to get her website up and running, but she could start without it, by organizing her thousands of digital photographs of Seattle. Black and white art-photography was her first love and she appreciated having the freedom to work on her show, but she also had photographs of Seattle that she hoped she could sell to magazines. Once she'd built the website and uploaded her samples, she could start sending query letters to editors and local businesses.

She got down to work with one ear cocked to the attic, but this time no unsettling sounds emanated from above.

Late in the afternoon her phone rang. She hoped it was Jenny, but the display showed an unknown local number instead. She answered with some reservation. In her experience, nothing good ever came from phone calls.

"Hey there." It was Frankie. Maddie's shoulders relaxed.

"How're you holding up," Frankie asked. "I thought you might be getting cabin fever."

Maddie laughed. "I'm cocooning. Making soup."

"Sounds good. I'm starved."

Maddie paused. She'd been to Frankie's house a few times for tea and talk on the porch in the evening, but Frankie had never been to the cabin.

"Why don't you come over and try some." When she heard the words come out of her mouth she went cold with panic. *Please say no.* She never had friends over. Ever.

"I'd love to. Be right over." The line went dead.

Maddie stood in the middle of the kitchen, clutching the phone. Her heart beat double time, forcing the blood to rush through her veins, each beat crashing in her ears like a snare drum. She fought for breath, trying to force the air around the lump that was blocking her throat.

Her eyes darted around the cabin. *Empty glass on the coffee table. Sweater over the back of the couch.* She scooped up the sweater and threw it in the bedroom, aiming for the bed and swooshed the curtain closed. She grabbed the glass on her way to the sink, registering the ring it left on the table.

She stopped at the sink and put her hands on the rim. *Relax. It's only Frankie. Isn't this what you've always wanted? Friends dropping by?*

She let her weight drop into her arms and her head hang down, stretching the taut muscles in the back of her neck.

Breathe in, one, two. Out, one, two...

When she got to ten, her knees were still weak but the pressure had eased in her chest. She sucked in a restorative breath and, picking up the dishrag, forced herself to walk slowly over to clean the ring off the coffee table. For good measure, she gave the kitchen table a careful wipe, hung the washrag on the hook she'd screwed into the wall by the sink and turned to inspect the room.

Fine. Not perfect, but fine.

A knock sounded on the door, almost inaudible under the rush of the wind but in her head it sounded like an alarm. She straightened her shoulders and opened the door.

Frankie shook herself like a dog on the porch and then stepped inside. Hanging her dripping raingear on the hook behind the door, she looked curiously around the room. "I've never been in here before. It's been empty since I moved next door."

As she smiled, Maddie felt an artificial stiffness in her cheeks that signaled a glazed expression she'd seen on her face before.

Relax. It's okay. She knew it was okay. *Say something.* "It must have been empty for a long time. There was a lot of dust."

She took a deep breath and looked around, trying to see the cabin as Frankie would see it. Everything was in its place. Her shoulders descended another notch and she lowered her head to one side to stretch out the tension in her neck.

"Cute little figurines." Frankie picked up one of the china figurines off the shelf, checked the bottom and nodded. "Royal Dalton. I thought they were quality."

"They were here when I moved in."

Maddie watched until Frankie put the figurine back on the shelf, then she walked over to stir the soup.

Frankie followed her over to the stove and sniffed the pot. "Smells good. Homemade soup is a treat. I can't cook worth squat."

Maddie looked at her in surprise. "Really?"

Maddie cooked for survival. She didn't consider it a skill. She'd tried the soup—it *was* good. Her shoulders relaxed another notch.

The box of recipe cards that sat on the kitchen table. Funny. She was sure she'd left it on the windowsill. She rarely misplaced things.

She opened the box and the scent of cinnamon and nutmeg drifted out. It was the smell of comfort. As she inhaled, warmth traveled through her body and her tense muscles finally relaxed. She took another quick breath and handed the box to Frankie.

"The recipe for Corn Chowder was in this box of recipes. It was here when I moved in. It's easy. Basically you mix Creme of Mushroom soup and a can of creamed corn."

Frankie laughed. "Sounds like my kind of recipe."

Maddie smiled. "Well, there is a bit more to it than that."

This was going great. She took two pretty, matching china soup bowls with wide flat rims off the shelf and two little plates for bread. Giving Frankie the plate that matched the bowls, she set to slicing the bread.

"What makes it taste smoky?" Frankie asked, taking a taste from the ladle before scooping the soup into the bowls.

"Ham."

"Mmmm."

Maddie got out two glasses, and the milk from the fridge.

"Is this your daughter?" Frankie asked from across the room.

Maddie swung around, her heart pounding, milk sloshing over the rim of the jug. She set it on the kitchen table and hurried over to where Frankie stood in front of the old TV, examining one of the pictures of Jenny she had carefully arranged on top.

Please don't touch. "Yes, my daughter Jenny." At the beach and after the school play in full theater makeup, with lipstick smeared across one cheek.

"She likes acting?"

"She registered months ago for summer acting camp, before she knew she was going to stay with her dad. Luckily, he lives quite close to the university campus where she's taking the classes."

Frankie picked up another photograph, this one of Maddie and Jenny together, their grinning faces filling the frame.

Maddie's fingers twitched to grab the picture, but instead she twisted her hands together.

"She's so pretty. Looks just like you." Frankie put the photo down.

Maddie forced a smile. "Thanks. Let's eat."

Frankie turned back to the table and Maddie pushed the picture frame back half an inch, where it belonged.

As Frankie took her seat, Maddie's eyes scanned the place settings. *Plates, food, glasses. Napkins!* She grabbed some cloth napkins out of the drawer, quickly folded them and set them in place. She checked the table again.

Catching herself, she laughed self-consciously as she took her seat. "I don't have people over often."

Ever.

Frankie dug right in. "This is delicious."

The smell of cinnamon drifted by again. Maddie breathed it in, smiled and picked up her spoon.

"So what happened the other night?" Frankie asked, a sparkle in her eye.

"What do you mean?"

"I looked for you after the dance but you'd already left."

"Yes. Sorry. I got a ride. I had to get out. Must have been the heat."

"Hmm. Louise said you left with Jake."

My God, he was right. People were talking about them.

"Yes. He was kind enough to drive me home." *And kiss me.* She could never tell Frankie that.

"So, your daughter is staying with her father? You must miss her."

Jeeze. Each new topic was worse than the last. Was this what having friends was like?

"I miss her a lot, but I understand why she wants to get to know him better. He *is* her father."

"Get to know him? Doesn't she see him much?"

"Hardly ever. He's very busy." Maddie pressed her lips together and concentrated on her soup.

"I know what that's like. I grew up with just my dad and he was never around either."

Maddie looked at her intensely. "Did you ever want to go and live with your mother?"

The silence lasted a second too long and Maddie guessed the answer before Frankie spoke.

"My mom died when I was very young. I didn't have that out." She smiled. "Probably would have taken it if I had. Most kids that age would."

Maddie nodded eagerly. "That's what I've read. The magazine called it *The Grass is Greener Syndrome.*" Her eyes strayed to the photo of her and Jenny on the old TV. "I just never thought it would happen to us."

"Is she coming back to live with you in the fall?"

Maddie nodded. "That's the plan." She focused her eyes back on her soup hoping to hide her concern.

Frankie leaned over and tapped the laptop on the corner of the table. "Working on something?"

"A new website, for my photographs, but it's almost impossible without internet."

"I couldn't live without wifi anymore," Frankie said.

"I don't care about email, but at some point I'll need wifi to put my website online. I don't know what to do. It hardly seems worth getting cable or a dish just for the summer."

"You can use mine," Frankie said, helping herself to a slice of bread. "It might reach this far, or you can come over anytime."

"That's very kind," Maddie said.

"Let's try it and see. I'll give you the password." Frankie pulled the laptop toward her.

Maddie stood up and reached for it. "I'll do it."

Before Frankie left, they had it working. The signal was weak, but Frankie repeated her offer to come by anytime and Maddie figured she could sit on Frankie's porch if she needed more power.

"It's just wifi," Frankie said.

Later, when she had gone, Maddie hummed as she tidied the kitchen. She'd had a friend over and it had gone well. Very well. Still, the visit left a jittery residue.

She kept a small fire going in the woodstove that evening and, clutching a cup of warm chamomile tea, stared into the flame through the open door, running the evening through her mind, looking for any reason to worry. They'd talked, shared confidences—not about everything perhaps, but they had shared—and Frankie hadn't seemed to notice anything was amiss.

Cautiously, Maddie decided it was all okay.

Chapter 14

Overnight, the storm blew itself out, leaving Maddie eager to get outside. As she walked down the drive past the bedroom window, she noticed a speck of blue paint caught in the weathered grain of the shutters. In a flash of unusually clear insight, she envisioned how they must have looked painted that color and suddenly wanted to see them that way again. It wasn't baby blue or turquoise, but a subtle periwinkle with a hint of lilac; a color she'd seen dripped down the side of one of the paint cans in the lean-to shed attached to the back of the cabin.

Gripping her broom like a weapon, she threw open the shed door. Cobwebs hung from the rafters and swathed a pile of decrepit aluminum garden furniture and a bicycle pump on the floor in the corner.

Swinging the broom left and right, she cleared a path to the shelves across from the door. Half-used tins of paint lined the bottom shelf, hardened drips of color running down their sides. The pale green was from the bedroom, but where on earth had they used the bubble-gum pink? Beside it stood a gallon of exterior white and the rusty tin of periwinkle blue.

Pulling a paint-splattered work shirt off a hook on the wall, she tugged it on over her T-shirt and rolled up the sleeves. Gathering the paint, brush and everything she'd need, she dropped it all in a pile on the ground beneath the bedroom window. A stick of kindling worked to stir the paint and she dipped her brush into the rich swirl of blue. One bold stroke of the brush and, yes, the cabin came to life.

When she finished, she stood back, enjoying the luscious effect of the color and the still-wet sheen. Wiping her hands on a wet rag, she nodded, pleased with the job.

A sigh whispered, "*yesss-s-s,* "the sound slowly fading away on the breeze. Maddie froze, her mouth half open, waiting for more. She searched the forest shadows for the source of the voice, but she was alone.

Slowly she let out the breath she was holding, putting her fingers to her lips as her eyes searched the bush one more time.

Then she smiled and nodded. "It is better this way."

* * *

Jake checked his watch as he walked down the lane to the cabin. Nine a.m. A civilized time to drop by.

This time, though, he had no excuse. No wood to deliver, no window to fix. No problem. He'd think of some reason for dropping by.

As he walked by the cabin, the freshly painted blue shutters jumped out at him, stopping him in his tracks. His thoughts went to the feisty old woman who had painted them that soft blue the first time.

Aunt Augusta. She'd seemed ancient when he was a boy, but from his new vantage point of thirty-five years, he could see she must have only been around sixty, the same age then as his mother was now.

As he came around the corner of the porch, the sight of Maddie backlit by the sun hit him like a punch to the gut. Her hair curled, bright as a flame in the sun, and her long bare legs stuck out from under a paint shirt. *His* shirt. He watched her work while he steadied his breath.

She turned to recharge her brush and when she bent over to dip the brush in the paint the shirt hitched up at the back revealing the shortest shorts...and he lost his train of thought again.

She pushed the hair back from her eyes leaving a broad swath of blue across her cheek.

He should help. He smiled at the thought, turned on his heel and headed to the back shed.

* * *

Out of the corner of her eye, Maddie saw Jake disappear

around the corner of the cabin.

Leaping up, she dropped her paintbrush into the can and followed him at a sprint. She probably should have asked before starting to paint.

They met at the far corner of the cabin. He had a paintbrush in his hand.

"Whoa." He stopped her with a light grip on each arm to prevent her from crashing into him. "Where are you going?"

Her heart beat a rapid tattoo. "After you. I wanted to explain."

"Explain what?"

She glanced at the shutters. "Why I did it."

He surveyed the shutters. "Looks good. Why did you?" He walked back to the front of the building and checked out the half-finished blue door.

"Last evening, I saw blue in the cracks and the paint in the shed so I started on the shutters. They looked great when I finished, but then..." Her voice trailed off. She wanted to tell him about the voice in the wind but in the cool light of morning it seemed too fantastic.

"Then what?"

She bit her lip, and took the plunge. "I thought I heard a voice say—it was good."

"Whose voice?"

"I don't know. It might have been the wind, but it sounded like '*yesss-s-s-s*'." She let the word linger and fade, then pressed her lips together, waiting for Jake to laugh.

He didn't, just ran the dry bristles of his brush through his fingers. "That would be just like Aunt Augusta to want the last word. She always did."

Maddie blinked, not making the connection. "Your aunt?"

"She painted it this color the first time." He dipped his brush in the can of paint and worked it around the turned posts below the railing. "I guess I should have kept it up after she died."

Maddie wasn't sure what she'd just heard. "Are you saying...that your Aunt Augusta...?"

Jake nodded, his eyes on the job. "Yup, a ghost. Well I don't really like to call her a ghost—sounds so hokey—but I don't think her spirit has moved on, as they say."

Maddie shook her head slightly from side to side, eyes squinting in concentration. Jake seemed like a serious guy, not flakey at all, and he seemed to believe it. "Really? And you didn't think to tell me that when I rented?"

He grinned. "She's harmless. And I mean that in the best possible way. When I lived here I always felt she was nudging me in the direction she thought I should go. I couldn't really put my finger on it. Little hints she'd leave around."

Maddie's frown deepened as she thought of the almost tranquilizing aroma of spice that floated through the cabin during times of stress. And the outfit that appeared on the rack when she was stuck for something to wear to the dance.

She smiled. "Really?"

Jake was up on the porch, working on the spindles, so when Maddie finished the door, she went down and stood carefully in the flowerbed. Stealing glances at his dark brows and ridiculously long lashes, she worked opposite him in silence as they worked on the spindles along the front of the porch.

Soon the sun climbed above the firs, warming her back. Jake whipped off his T-shirt and she couldn't help watching the muscles of his shoulder ripple as he wielded the brush.

He glanced up and caught her staring. He grinned, making the dimple pop in his cheek. "Get to work Slim."

Picking up her brush, Maddie scrubbed the color into the wood. "It would help if you'd keep your shirt on."

"I would, but you're always wearing my work clothes."

"Oh!" She looked down at the paint shirt now covered in blue smears.

He didn't really seem to mind though, was already back at work.

She searched for something to say. "What was she like? Your Aunt Augusta."

"Great-aunt," Jake said. "Fearsome and fearless." He paused to reload his brush. "She came out here in the thirties. Things must have been pretty rough back then. There were a lot of Swedes here working as loggers. She married Uncle Sven and for years they lived on a float house up the lake at Boston Camp." The hypnotic tone of his voice matched the regular sweep of his brush.

"Float house?"

"Houses that float." He grinned at her through the railing. "Where the bush was too thick for them to build on land, they built on rafts on the water. That whole camp was float houses, houses and gardens and places for kids to play. Augusta never had any children though."

He plied a few more strokes. "I never knew my uncle. He died before I was born. Logging accident. But Augusta was tough. She stayed on in the cabin for the rest of her life."

"It couldn't have been easy living there alone."

"She was stubborn. Didn't want to live anywhere else."

"When did she move here?"

"When Uncle Sven died, Augusta had the house towed here and pulled up on land. This is it."

"The float home?" Maddie stopped painting and stepped back to reassess the cabin. No longer quite the same abandoned building she'd discovered that first day, it seemed to sparkle, pleased with the paint and attention.

She went up to join him on the porch. "So you've taken care of the place for a while then?" She dipped her brush back into the paint and plied it to the wood.

"Since she died almost fifteen years ago. I was working in the bush and wanted a place of my own, so I moved in here. I helped her out all through high school too though." Jake stopped and looked out at the lake. "I miss this place—especially the view."

"I can see why." Maddie stopped to admire the sun on the

water surrounded by bright spring green. "It's beautiful. I feel lucky to be here."

Turning smoothly back to the paint can, her brush sliced across Jake's bare back leaving a bold streak of blue.

She giggled. "Oh no." Grabbing a rag, she dabbed at the paint on the golden expanse of skin, doing more to smear it than to clean it off.

The giggle dried in her throat. She wanted to rub her hand over the muscles of his back. She bit the inside of her lips, pressing them together into a line.

He craned his neck trying to see the damage she'd done. "Are you getting it off or not?"

"I'll have to get this wet." She started for the kitchen.

"Don't bother."

He put down his paintbrush and headed for the lake. She followed, almost running, down to the shore. "Are you crazy? The water's still ice cold."

"Naw, it's the middle of June. When we were kids we were always in by now." He kicked off his shoes and waded out until he was knee deep in the water. Then he held out his hand. "Care to join me?"

She was tempted, *really* tempted, but when she tested the water with her toe, she jerked her foot back. "It's freezing."

"Your choice." He walked out to waist deep, then dove under in a rush. Seconds later he shot up, sputtering and shaking his head, his hair releasing an arc of glistening drops. Just like a shampoo commercial. An inane grin tugged at her cheeks.

"Perfect," he exclaimed, but he churned up the water in his rush to get to shore where he presented her with his dripping back. "Gone?"

She licked her lips with the tip of her tongue and, just once, rubbed her hand across his slick, wet back. A shiver shot through her that wasn't from the cold.

"Gone," she said. Her voice sounded hoarse. She cleared her throat and tried again. "Gone."

He turned around and his eyes, so blue, met hers. His slow smile told her he knew exactly what she was thinking.

"I've gotta go too," he said. He sounded disappointed. Or was that stupid wishful thinking on her part again?

He picked up his shirt from the porch and as he pulled it on, he glanced at the darkroom door, seeming to hesitate. Then he said, "You want to see more flowers?"

"Sure."

"Okay. Tomorrow morning. Nine o'clock."

She nodded. He started down the drive and when he got to the shutters, he turned to face her, walking backwards, his open shirt exposing abs that were as good as the muscles on his back.

He gave her a grin and a thumbs-up.

She closed her eyes and shook her head. She was toast.

Chapter 15

The following morning Maddie's eyes sprang open, her mind running in overdrive.

He said nine o'clock. What would she wear?

It wasn't a date. Just a morning shoot.

The sun was up, but it was only twenty to six. *Groan.* She never got up this early. Resolutely, she closed her eyes.

Sleep, however, was a distant memory and it wasn't long before she gave up and got out of bed.

The mornings were still cool, but not cold enough to light a fire. Once the sun came up over the trees it would burn the chill off the linoleum floor. Now she only lit the stove occasionally, in the evenings, mostly for company.

Grabbing the plaid jacket from behind the door she headed out to the bathroom. When she opened the front door, she froze in her tracks. Hardly...daring...to breathe.

A bear cub sat in the sun by the water not thirty feet away, round ears sticking up like a cartoon character on the top of its head. And the short brown snout? Adorable.

Although unbroken forest ran from her doorstep all the way to the Pacific coast, she rarely thought about wildlife. But now her blood was pumping hot. Her camera and tripod stood ready just inside the door, and silently propping the screen door open, she ever so slowly moved the tripod into position in the doorway.

The cub heard her, looked up and squawked. His fur looked thick and black through the telephoto lens. Maddie took two quick shots.

Then he cried out, louder this time, and in reply a nasal moan echoed from down the shore. Maddie froze, a prickle of excitement running down her spine. Her eyes searched the shore and, sure enough, Mama Bear was lumbering towards the cabin, her enormous bulk swaying as she called to her cub. She stopped and raised her snout—not nearly as cute as the cub's teddy-bear face—and sniffed the air.

Her big furry head swiveled straight toward the cabin.

Maddie suddenly remembered what Louise had said— *never get between a mother bear and her cub.* She had read the public notice taped to the door at the store: *IF YOU MEET A BLACK BEAR—maintain eye contact, let them know you're a human, speak in a calm voice, back away slowly.*

And the last one, that always sounded stupid to her—*try to appear large.*

The bear stood up on her back legs, suddenly doubling in size. Maddie gasped, gripping the camera. The mother took a few quick steps toward the cabin and raised her nose to sniff.

Maddie's heart pounded and she didn't dare breathe as the predator peered short-sightedly in her direction.

Although her knees were shaking, Maddie pulled herself up to her full height. "Get your baby and go," she said loudly, hoping, praying, she sounded calm. The bear stood still, her nose twitching.

Somehow Maddie's heart had become lodged in her throat. She swallowed hard and tried to maintain eye contact as she slowly moved the tripod back into the cabin. Keeping her body still, she reached out and with a shaking hand, closed the flimsy screen door between them.

The cub cried again and his mother dropped to four legs and sprinted to her babe. She licked the young one's head roughly and whacked it gently with her paw, clearly not amused.

Maddie quietly closed the inside door and rushed to the window. Camera pressed to the glass, she took a few more shots, zooming in to tight focus on their faces before the pair waddled away toward the bush.

The mother turned and shot one last warning look at the cabin. Through her long telephoto lens, Maddie stared right into the mother bear's eyes, black and inscrutable. The threat was clear. *Click*—she pressed the shutter one last time before the forest swallowed them up.

Blowing out a ragged breath, Maddie sunk bonelessly onto a chair.

A smile crinkled the corners of her eyes and spread right across her face. *Gotcha.*

Those photographs would be the centerpiece of the show. She jumped up and looked out the window. No bears. She opened the screen door and checked again. All clear. She dashed across the porch to the bathroom.

After she'd showered and thrown on some clothes—what to wear no longer seemed to be an issue—she packed her gear for wherever it was she was going with Jake and still had two hours to kill.

Tapping impatiently on the counter, she looked to the windowsill for the recipe box—but of course it wasn't there. It was back on the top kitchen shelf, where it had been the day she moved in. Obviously where Augusta wanted it kept.

She reached up and brought the box down, opened it and smiled as the aroma of cinnamon and cloves drifted up. Walking her fingers through the dog-eared recipe cards inside, she decided Children's Delight Cookies sounded perfect. Soon the rich smell of spice drifted out the kitchen door.

At five minutes to nine, Jake poked his head through the door, raised his nose and sniffed the air like the mama bear.

"Children's Delight. My favorite." He stole a cookie from the rack cooling on the counter and stuffed the whole thing in his mouth at once. His cheek twitched, mouth pulled up on one side, flashing a grin.

"I grew up on these." He took another. "Where did you get the recipe?"

Her hands grew cold; she handed him the wooden box. Maybe she shouldn't have touched the recipes. They were private. Family memories.

She stood very still, as he turned the box over in his hands, studying the carving on the sides. "This was Aunt Augusta's. I think her husband made it." He opened the lid and rifled through the cards. "Have you tried any of them?"

"I've tried a few."

"That's good. Feel free to use them. Augusta was a great cook." He put the box back on the counter and took another cookie.

She watched him for a moment, then she said, "It moves."

"What moves?"

"The box."

He grinned and popped the cookie in his mouth.

Then Maddie remembered her news.

She grabbed his arm, halting yet another cookie on its trajectory to his mouth. "You won't believe what happened. When I got up this morning and came out onto the porch, there were two bears on the shore—a mother and a cub."

"Are you sure?" He pulled his hand away and took a bite.

She grabbed the film canister off the counter and shook it in his face. "I have pictures to prove it."

He took the plastic container and his brows contracted. Now she had his attention.

"You're sure?"

"Yes I'm sure. They hung around for a couple of minutes, down by the water. I saw the cub first, then the mother came down the shore. She stared right at me."

"She saw you?"

"Yeah. I was on the porch, trying to get a picture." She described the encounter. "Then they headed down the shore." She sucked a quick breath. "We should tell Frankie."

Jake thought for a moment, then popped the remains of the cookie into his mouth, reached into his back pocket for his cell phone and punched in one of the speed dial numbers.

"We'll do that," he said, his eyes on hers.

A moment later she heard a voice on the other end of the line. Jake turned to the window and greeted someone. She watched, hardly hearing his words as he went through the obligatory small talk. He leaned against the kitchen counter in torn blue jeans, his soft, thin, faded blue shirt begging to be touched. His hair curled over the collar and a dark layer of stubble highlighted the strong planes of his jaw line.

He looked back at her and his eyes, the color of the lake at twilight, were a whirlpool, pulling her in. She felt herself going under and grabbed a cookie as if it were a life raft.

"We had a couple of bears here this morning," he said to whoever was on the other end of the line. "Down by the cabin."

"What time?" he asked Maddie.

"About six."

He relayed what he knew and then nodded. "Thanks. I worry, you know, about the kids."

He flipped the phone closed. "Jesse, the conservation officer for the lake district will look around and see if anything turns up. Said he'd contact the neighbors."

"Great." She couldn't think of anything else to say, being dangerously close to slipping into the whirlpool again.

"You ready?" he asked.

She blinked once, twice, to clear her head, then remembered why he was there. The shoot.

She gathered up her gear. "He won't do anything to the bears, will he? She wasn't aggressive or anything."

"You're lucky." Jake took her tripod case from her hand and slung it over his shoulder, then ushered her out and shut the cabin door behind them. "When it's a mother and cub you've got to be careful. They're unpredictable at the best of times. We like to steer them away from populated areas."

"I was careful. I didn't leave the porch. In fact, I didn't even go *on* the porch. I stood in the doorway with the door propped open."

"And took their picture." Jake shook his head, but he seemed amused.

"I talked to them, like the posters say, and tried to look tall." She grinned and he treated her to a rare smile in return.

A rare *killer* smile that made her stomach do a back flip and her knees turn to jelly, making it hard to keep up with his long stride as they walked up the drive.

At the road they turned toward the farm. "Where are we going?" she asked.

Jake veered into his driveway. "It's a piece of land near the creek where protected wildflowers grow. It's not far, but I didn't bring my car. I didn't realize you'd be schlepping all this gear. We could have driven."

"Only the backpack. It's not very heavy." She stopped to hoist it higher onto her back, then had to jog to catch up. They continued at a brisk clip right past the log house and down the gravel utility road that wound between a cluster of old outbuildings. Some were little more than sheds with light showing through the weather-beaten siding, but one large barn of sun-bleached boards was filled with bales of straw.

"It's so old," Maddie said. Like many of the smaller buildings, the faded boards on the barn no longer lay square. She itched to pull out her camera and take a shot but they strode right by and off across the back field. She looked over her shoulder at the old barn. She'd be back.

"The farm is a hundred and twenty years old," he said. "That's old in lake terms, real old for anywhere on the peninsula. Majestic was just a logging camp back then. My great-granddad Murdoch walked twenty miles up the river along forest trails to get here, from the port at the mouth of the river to the head of the lake, then rowed the rest of the way to claim this land."

"It must be great to live in an area with so much family history."

He thought for a moment, then said, "I wouldn't live anywhere else."

A toppled, split-log fence separated the field from the dirt road that wound around the lake. Jake hopped the fence and held out a hand to help her over. She took it when the weight of her backpack threatened to topple her over, enjoying the solid warmth of his hand.

They crossed the road and Jake led her up a narrow track into a glade of giant maples. "I know every path in these woods. As kids, we spent summers racing stick-boats down the creek and making forts in the giant logs."

Sun streamed through the vaulted canopy of translucent maple leaves as large as the span of two hands, coloring the air around them. It dappled the ankle high pockets of wildflowers, tiny yellow violets splashed across the green canvas.

"It's magic," she said.

Creamy white trilliums towered over the more delicate lilies, all rising above a blanket of young fern and salal. Rangy maples twisted up to grab the light between the stumps of the giant firs that once ruled the valley. Moss-covered logs, some four feet in diameter, lay on the forest floor, nurturing fern, lichen, and even young trees that grew straight out of their decomposing remains.

They walked into an open glade and she drew a deep breath. "What are these?" She quickly set up her camera and tripod.

"Pink Fawn Lilies," he said. "This is what I wanted to show you. They're common in white, but this pink form is rare. They only grow around Majestic Lake."

* * *

Jake was glad they'd come. Maddie photographed the glade from every angle, not taking her eye off her camera.

And Jake couldn't take his eyes off Maddie. He followed her through the paths along the creek, fascinated by the physicality of her process. She squatted and sat, dropped her tripod to mere inches from the ground, then lay on her stomach to zoom in for the closest shots of the tiny yellow dog-toothed violets. 'Liquid sunshine' she called them.

Just when he thought she'd forgotten he was there, she sent him a grin. Then she took the camera off the tripod and lay on her back, shooting straight up at the luminous canopy of leaves and the licorice fern hanging from the gnarly maple trunks.

What did she see? Wasn't she shooting in black and white? Standing in the midst of all this green, he couldn't imagine how the final prints would look. Or how Maddie would feel stretched out beneath him. Or what she was doing for dinner tonight.

He snapped back to reality with a speed that left his head spinning. Things were moving too fast, and he wasn't slowing them down at all by inviting her into the forest, alone. He should be keeping his distance, not getting in over his head.

A field trip to see the flowers was one thing—she'd never have found them on her own—but dinner was out of the question, and anything else was self-destructive lunacy. Because really, nothing had changed. The clock was still ticking on her return to the city.

* * *

Eventually Maddie ran out of steam. Almost like waking from a dream, she came back to reality, lying on her back on the forest floor, the rich, heady smell of damp wood and composting leaves filling her head.

And there was Jake, a few feet away, watching her work. What must he think? She'd ignored him for—how long? Most men would be bitching and moaning by now. She was glad he was there though, watching out for the bears.

She smiled. "This is great. Just a couple more shots."

She set her sights on the creek that flowed through the canyon of maples, an ethereal place, cool and green in the mid-day sun. Then she blew out a breath and straightened up. Her stomach growled.

"I wish we'd brought a picnic," she said. "Or at least some cookies."

Like a magician, Jake produced two crumbling specimens from his shirt pocket. She grinned and snatched one out of his hand.

"You're amazing," she said as she hoisted her backpack

onto her shoulders.

It was almost noon when they arrived back at the cabin. Maddie carried her equipment into the kitchen, then peeked out at Jake through the big front window. He stood, one foot up on the step, arm resting on the railing, chewing absently on a stalk of grass, staring off over the water. So gorgeous, but so distant. She wondered what he was thinking. Taking a deep, shaky breath, she grabbed her camera and stepped out onto the porch.

Raising the camera to her eye, she framed him vertically in the viewfinder and quickly took the shot. His eyes were dark and wary, as if she had caught him at—what? She had no idea.

"Can I make you a sandwich?" She owed him something for taking the time to show her the wildflowers.

Jake glanced at his watch, distracted. "No thanks, I have to get back. But before I go..." He walked over and thrashed through the underbrush between the cabin and Frankie's yard, returning with a branch, four feet long, possibly the branch that had fallen on the roof in the storm. He stripped the broken twigs from its length, ending up with a serious staff that he swung experimentally a couple of times before handing it to her.

She blinked at it uncomprehendingly.

"'Walk softly and carry a big stick,'" he said. "Keep it on the porch, by the door. If you're going out early in the morning I don't want you to be caught unarmed. In a pinch you could use this to scare off a bear."

Maddie looked at the club, eyes wide. His voice softened and he smiled. Her heart did a backwards dive into her stomach. "I don't mean to scare you, but it's better to be prepared. I'm pretty sure you won't see those two again though."

She took the stick out of his hand.

"Thanks for the cookies," he said, then he headed up the drive.

She stood on the porch with the staff in her hand, watching him go but wishing he would stay.

Chapter 16

Mother bear's piercing black eyes stared back at Maddie from the print she'd developed that morning and the tingle she'd felt when they'd met face to face danced across her skin. The bear's gaze sent a powerful visceral message that chilled her to the core. Tiny hairs on her arms prickled and her heart raced as she read the warning in its eyes. *Beware.*

She gave herself a shake that brought her back to the now. That photograph would be one of the stars of the show.

Yesterday's shoot at the wildflower meadow had been wonderful. With Jake by her side she'd felt safe, even after having seen the bears. Safe, yet comfortable enough to get the work done. That was a new feeling for her. She always worked alone.

But afterward, as always, he'd left in a hurry. She wasn't sure why, but sometimes she thought it was because of her. As if he was afraid of getting too close.

Her phone rang and she dug it out of her purse. Jenny was the only one who ever called her, except for that one time when it was Frankie.

Unknown caller showed in the display and Maddie's stomach tightened into a knot. She took a deep breath. "Hello?"

"Hi, Mad."

The peace of the morning shattered around her. Her free hand reached up to rub her forehead. "Hi Mom."

"Now darlin', I told you not to call me 'Mom'."

"Okay. Cindy. How are you doing?"

"Oh, not too good. You know. I've been sick."

Sick was one way to put it. *On a bender* was probably more like it. "That's too bad M—Cindy."

"I'm in trouble Mad. I can't make my rent at the end of

the month. I don't know what happened to my check"—
welfare check— "but the landlord's going to kick me out this
time for sure." Cindy's voice took on a pathetic waver and
despite the fact Maddie knew her mother was scamming her,
she still felt a catch in her chest.

"Look, Mom, I don't know if I can help you, I'm not in
town right now."

"Where are you?"

Big mistake. "Just visiting a friend. Listen, I'll come by
before the end of the month. I can't give you much—"

"A couple hunert should do."

Maddie closed her eyes. "Okay Mom." What else could
she do?

"Thanks Mad. You're a life saver."

How many times had she stepped in and saved her
mother's life? She could kick herself for offering to go by
Cindy's apartment. When Maddie had left home she'd vowed
never to go back and although Cindy would be in yet another
new place—she never stayed in one place for very long—it was
always too familiar, brought back too many memories.

"Okay Mom, I'll call you next week."

Cindy hung up. Message delivered. No, *how are you dear?*
Just, *when can you bring the money?*

Cindy had never been able to take care of herself and ever
since Maddie was a child, she had tried to take care of her
mother. But Cindy didn't want any help. Not really. All she
ever wanted was money. Maddie could handle the
responsibility; what she couldn't handle was the way Cindy
spoiled everything she touched, like a spreading mold.

She tapped herself gently on the forehead. *Stop that. She's
your mother.*

But her lips formed a firm line when she remembered the
day Cindy met Mark.

He was a clean-cut middle-class guy, the kind of guy who'd
never paid any attention to her before, and Maddie was
thrilled when he asked her out.

She'd thought he was the one. How wrong she'd been.

Soon after they married it became clear they had little in common, other than in bed. He expected her to live by his rules; not take any jobs, keep the house spotlessly clean, and entertain his boring corporate friends. Because of Jenny, she stuck it out for seven years, until the day her mother arrived and things got unbearably worse.

Cindy turned up, drunk on their doorstep, looking for a place to crash. Until that point, Maddie had managed to keep her mother a secret from Mark—but once he met Cindy, their marriage didn't last long. He showed his contempt in every look, in every word and soon after that, Maddie took the then six-year-old Jenny and ran.

She took a deep shuddering breath as she envisioned what would happen if Cindy showed up here, in Fortune Bay.

Leafing listlessly through the stack of proofs, she stopped at the picture of Jake leaning against the porch, chewing a long piece of grass. What would he think if he met Cindy? It would probably be the last she ever saw of him.

No, her mother couldn't find out where she was staying.

It was probably just as well that Jake kept leaving when he did, putting the brakes on their friendship. Someone had to, because Maddie was having a terrible time keeping her own thoughts and feelings in check. The kiss in the car after the dance had started a fire inside her.

Get a grip. It would be easy to slide into a relationship with him, but she sensed it would be something she couldn't control. Something she would later regret.

Nope. Not getting involved. Not part of the plan. She had this opportunity, this show. It could change her life. She couldn't blow it.

Control was the key, and that meant staying independent. No men. Ever. She'd learned that much from watching her mother, from seeing the havoc relationships could play— although she wasn't sure "relationships" was the right word for Cindy's liaisons. Her mother's discarded flames littered

Maddie's childhood like a trail of dead soldiers after a weeklong binge.

Putting Jake's picture on the bottom of the pile, she sighed and shook her head.

She could handle it. She always did.

Chapter 17

Hands on her hips, one eye half closed, Maddie stared at the recipe box on the top kitchen shelf. "Okay, Augusta, what game are you playing?"

She *knew* she'd left the box on the windowsill after making the cookies, but there it was on the top shelf again, the same place she'd found it the day she'd moved in. And every day since. She smiled and shook her head. "You win."

She lifted it down and took it to the table where she thumbed through the battered recipe cards, searching for one in particular, *Family Reunion Chicken Wings.* Perfect for Frankie's solstice dinner tonight.

Maddie's cheeks glowed at the thought of the friendships she was forming, slow but steady. She had never had close friends before—the disasters of her childhood had taught her the wisdom of that—but she was surprised to find she was able to relax around Frankie and Louise. With them she could be herself and, in return, they seemed to accept her as she was. They were her first real adult friends and she didn't want to blow it.

Dinner with Frankie the night of the storm had gone very well, but even so, Maddie still always watched for *the look.* The look she'd received hundreds of times growing up. The look that passed between the others, saying more clearly than words that she didn't belong.

As a child she rarely stayed at one school long enough to make friends, and when other kids did invite her home, she invariably felt their parents' eyes burning holes through her ragged clothes and already fragile veneer of self-confidence.

Like Jessica. They met in third grade. Maddie was new in school—as usual—but Jessica smiled at her right away and said, "Sit with me."

Jessica could do things the other girls couldn't, or wouldn't, like sneaking into the orchard and climbing the trees to pick apples. When she invited Maddie to go along, she was giddy with joy. Jessica never seemed to notice what Maddie was wearing and shared her lunch without batting an eye. But then she invited Maddie home.

Maddie walked into Jessica's house with her defenses down. And paid the price.

Jessica's mother asked, "Who is this?" in that brittle voice Maddie had heard countless times before, and that's when she knew she'd made a big mistake.

Jessica's mother's smile was stiff as she marched Maddie into the bathroom, stripped off her clothes and put her in the tub. After scrubbing her down, she dressed Maddie in some of Jessica's cast-off clothes and made a show of putting Maddie's own clothes in the trash.

After that, Maddie learned to wash her own clothes, sometimes standing in the shower with them on or washing them in the bathroom sink. As she grew, she learned to take care of herself and to not become trapped in those situations.

Later, the looks came less often, however she was still always on the alert, waiting for people to realize she wasn't what she seemed.

When she struck out on her own with Jenny, Maddie decided that making their home a place where Jenny could bring friends was more important than having friends herself. She didn't really mind. The fewer people in her life, the easier it was to maintain control.

So far here in Fortune Bay, no one had given her *the look,* and she planned to keep it that way. She had promised herself that while she was here she would try new things, so she would go tonight and she would have fun. After all, it was just dinner at Frankie's.

She'd seen party recipes in women's magazines so she knew *Family Reunion Chicken Wings* was the perfect thing to bring. Once the wings were roasting in the oven, she went into the bedroom and looked for something to wear, probably something a bit nicer than the jeans and sneakers she'd been wearing every day this summer.

Half an hour later, after trying on everything she owned, she finally settled on a gauzy black top, white capris and silver sandals. She felt positively glamorous.

Too glamorous to visit a friend?

Her knees went soft and she sank onto the edge of the bed. How could she possibly know? They would see through her right away and know that she didn't belong. She might as well have "loser" tattooed on her forehead.

She took a deep breath. *One.* Blow. *Two...*blow. *Just dinner at Frankie's.*

Someone tapped on the door. Maddie jumped to her feet, then laughed at herself when Louise called through the screen door, "You ready?" Help had arrived. Louise would know if this outfit was appropriate. Maddie stepped into the living room.

"You look great," Louise said.

The hitch in Maddie's shoulders relaxed and a smile spread across her face when she saw what Louise was wearing; a short, pleated striped skort—skirt and shorts combined—the likes of which Maddie hadn't seen since her childhood, and a Grateful Dead tee. Obviously anything goes at Frankie's party.

"I'm ready," she said, and grabbed the casserole of wings.

When they walked into Frankie's kitchen, Frankie sniffed the air. "That smells delicious. I love it when people bring food. I made veggies and dip."

Frankie took the tray of wings and Louise's brownies, and put a glass of sparkling water in Maddie's hand.

Maddie sat back and listed to Frankie and Louise banter back and forth. She barely recognized herself, a woman with silver hoops in her ears and a cluster of bracelets on her wrist that tinkled like wind chimes when she moved. A woman taking charge of her life—because that was what they had decided the evening would honor, in the spirit of wise women's solstice gatherings stretching back for thousands of years. Nothing too weird, they'd all agreed, just something to encourage their own awareness of their personal power. They would each ask for, or choose, a direction to follow for the next fertile quarter of the year.

And for Maddie it had to be fertile indeed. The next equinox fell before the opening of her show, the harvest, so to speak, of her summer's bounty.

Frankie was playing high priestess tonight. Over her loose linen pants, she wore one of Stephanie's robes, sapphire silk with a border of white Celtic symbols down the long front lapels. In honor of the evening, she had abandoned her customary single braid and wore her hair loose on her shoulders, adorned with a garland of lavender.

She spoke in a quiet voice as she shuffled the Tarot deck. "Traditionally, the summer solstice was a time of renewal. A time to release all sadness, pain and fear. A time to prepare to reap the abundance. A time to find a husband."

"Bring it on," Louise intoned.

Frankie closed her eyes, a smile on her lips, and continued to shuffle the deck. Maddie concentrated on Frankie's hands, letting the soothing motion settle her nerves.

Placing the brightly patterned deck on the table in front of Maddie, Frankie said, "Think of a question, then cut the cards. Be careful though. The tarot knows the question in your heart."

Maddie smiled and a shiver ran through her as she tried to look deep inside. There was really only one question on her mind. *Will my show be a success?*

Frankie took the deck from Maddie's hands. "This is a basic, five-card spread. Simple, but very powerful.

"The central card represents the present." Frankie flipped over the first card, a knight on a spirited horse, and placed it on the table. "The Knight of Wands."

She squinted at Maddie. "Are you sure your question is about your work? The Knight of Wands *can* be an idea or an approach to life, but most often it's about a man."

"Like Jake," Louise said.

Busted.

Frankie continued. "The Knight of Wands is usually a confident generous person who makes a warm friend or lover. He's fun loving but tends to be unpredictable." She paused, considering the card. "Here he's covered in armor from head to foot, trying hard to protect himself."

"You can say that again," Maddie murmured. Jake rarely let her see his fun-loving side. It was as if he was trying to protect himself. From her? But why?

"The second card represents past influences that still affect you." Frankie turned over another card. "The Eight of Swords."

She laid the card to the left of the knight. On it, eight swords were driven into the ground creating a loose fence around a blindfolded woman. "This woman could free herself from her prison if she dared. What binds her is not the swords but more likely her own fear of the past.

"The next card represents your immediate future. The Five of Cups." A dismal figure in a black cloak looked down at three cups, their contents spilled on the ground.

Maddie's eyes widened. "That looks bad."

Frankie shook her head. "It's not as bleak as it looks. The choice is yours. She still has two full cups, and then there's the castle in the distance."

"From whence my knight shall come?" Maddie asked with a faint smile.

Frankie shook her head. "I don't think so. This reading seems to be all about your choices. More like, 'to which you could go with the two full cups.'"

Maddie frowned. "I'm not sure what the castle represents or what's in the cups."

"Don't worry, you'll probably figure it out eventually. The fourth card is the impediment, that which prevents you from achieving your goal. For you," she said as she turned the card, "it's The Moon. That could also be about facing your fears. They keep surfacing, crawling out of the murky waters of your past like this crab on the card, crawling out of the water. You can push the fear back, but it will keep crawling back out."

Maddie winced. She knew exactly what the crab represented.

Frankie placed a card on the table. "And the last card is the potential, the possible result. Here, the Ace of Wands."

A chill went down Maddie's spine. The picture on the card depicted a hand at the end of a strong disembodied arm holding a staff. It looked just like Jake's hand when he'd handed her the four-foot long stick to beat off the bears that lurked in the forest.

That was when the idea of the cards as mere entertainment flew right out the window. The reading was about Jake all right. And those crabs crawling out of her past? She could definitely put a name to them too: *Cindy.*

"The staff, or club, is for you to use." Frankie paused to consider the entire spread. "Taking it together with the other cards, I'd say it means you can use it to beat off the fears that keep you imprisoned in the past. If you so choose."

"Heavy," Louise said, startling them both into laughter.

"But optimistic," Frankie added.

Maddie stared at the cards as if she could read their meaning in the pictures on each one. "So overall, it says I have a choice? The power to make changes in my life?"

Frankie nodded. "You always have the power."

* * *

The next day, Maddie stood in the patch of sunlight that poured through the darkroom door and onto the counter where she had laid out her photographs. She was fascinated and horrified but not really surprised by how many were of Jake.

Frankie's tarot reading hit surprisingly close to home concerning both her past and her present. The knight had to be Jake: generous and confident and a warm friend or lover.

Her words, not mine.

Although things had changed after the dance, she wasn't exactly sure where they stood. She thought about him often, but hadn't seen him now for almost a week, not since he'd shown her the wildflower meadow. She could go to the farm but somehow she didn't feel he wanted her there.

No, if he wanted to see her, he knew where she lived. If his life wasn't too *complicated* to include her. She certainly wouldn't throw herself at him—in fact, why was she even thinking about him at all? He wasn't part of the plan.

Frankie had stressed in the reading that Maddie controlled the direction her life took by the choices she made, but she cringed to think how much time she'd spent bouncing like a pinball from one obstacle to another, always with someone else working the paddles. Always reacting, never acting. From her mother's trailer to her husband's career to her current life in Seattle where she felt trapped in her job at the gallery, not unlike the blindfolded woman trapped inside the fence of swords.

She thought about that for a moment. She'd read a magazine article about the baggage children of alcoholic parents often carried into adulthood, but she hadn't thought it applied to her. She was doing okay. She wasn't repeating her mother's mistakes. She was a good mother, giving Jenny a good home. Safe, secure.

And she had learned from her mother's mistakes. Learned that a man in your life didn't necessarily equal safety and security, despite what she'd seen on TV.

She wasn't trapped, didn't have a blindfold over her eyes. She was just getting on with getting on.

And hadn't she taken control of the paddles by leaving the city and coming to Fortune Bay? She wanted to believe that from now on she had the power to stand up and take what she wanted from life. To say yes or no.

Her eye fell on a tiny contact image of Jake, stripped to the waist after winning the pole-climbing event. She pressed a soft fist to the smile on her lips. Was it bad to want a little more? Was it wrong to think there could be love in her future?

The roar of a vehicle on the driveway snapped her back to reality. She looked up from the picture as Jake stepped onto the porch. Maddie slapped another photo over the picture of him, but he was front and center in that one too. Mortified, her gaze flew to his face.

He didn't glance at the photos, obviously had something else on his mind and without preamble asked, "Would you like to go out for dinner, Tuesday night?"

Her nerves sprang to attention but she pushed them aside and took a step forward, obscuring the pile of photographs. "Yes."

"Great." His face softened and he smiled. "About six thirty? Wear jeans and boots and, ah, something pretty."

Then he was gone, the roar of the engine taking off down the drive the only proof that he'd been there at all.

Maddie crossed her arms tightly on her chest.

What on earth had she just done?

Chapter 18

Jeans and boots and something pretty. It wasn't much to go on.

Well, she had on the jeans and the boots stood by the door, but the 'something pretty' wasn't as easy. Maddie pulled another blouse off a hanger on the broom handle 'closet' and tried it on.

Such a strange guy, she thought, checking out the plain, white cotton top in the mirror. The date was his idea, yet he hadn't seemed very excited. Just asked and left.

Well, *she* was excited. She hadn't been on a date since that fiasco with the artist when Jenny was ten years old. He actually just wanted her to pose—naked. After that she had stopped dating entirely.

So what has changed? Why am I thinking about dating again?

She studied herself in the pitted mirror. This wasn't the same as last time. Jake was a different kind of a guy. She was different too. Different in ways she couldn't always name.

One thing she was sure of though, she wanted this evening to be perfect. "Help me out here Augusta," she murmured. "What should I wear?"

A sleeveless pink blouse with a wide row of soft ruffles around the neck slipped off its hanger and fell to the floor.

"Really? This?" She picked it up and put it on, then turned from side to side as she studied her reflection in the mirror. It didn't really go with the jeans at all, but it certainly was pretty.

As she added a pair of dangly earrings, she saw in the mirror a black blur streak across the window behind her, accompanied by a floor-rattling growl. Rushing to the window, she gasped as Jake pulled up beside the porch in a cloud of dust, straddling a motorcycle.

He kicked down the stand and swung one long leg over the seat, then pulled off his helmet and shook out his hair. He had on jeans and boots and a black leather jacket that had *wild one* written all over it.

Maddie ran out to the porch and he shot her a grin, moving his hand to the bike in a gentlemanly gesture.

"We're going on that?" She'd never been that girl, the girl-on-the-motorcycle-with-a-guy before, but she was ready to be one tonight.

Jake handed her a helmet and offered her a jacket but, instead, she darted inside the cabin and retrieved her own well-worn leather jacket. She quickly glanced at her reflection in the mirror and hardly recognized the woman who grinned back at her.

"A motorcycle," she whispered, and she pulled out her tube of Crimson Red and applied a cupid's bow to her lips. Then she smacked a kiss at herself in the mirror and headed for the door.

When she walked back out onto the porch, Jake still stood in the driveway, but a shyer, more self-conscious smile had replaced the cocky grin.

"You look great," he said. "Really great."

"Thanks." The shyness seemed to be contagious and all at once she felt like a teenager on a first date.

He pulled on his helmet and settled onto the seat, then looked at her over his shoulder. "Climb on."

Like a child playing dress-up, she put on her helmet, tucking in her curls and fastening the strap under her chin. Tentatively, she lifted her leg over the seat and climbed on behind him. "Where are we going?"

"Potters Cove."

Maddie held lightly to the sides of his jacket as they started slowly down the bumpy driveway. When they reached the road he stopped momentarily, took her hands, wrapped her arms around him, pulling her tight against his back.

"Hold on."

Her eyes widened as the bike sprang forward with a growl, leaving a fishtail of gravel in its wake.

They flew onto the pavement, Maddie clutching his waist, then barely slowed to make the corner to town. Minutes later they flashed by the *Welcome to Fortune Bay* sign and Jake slowed down considerably as they drove through town, waving at neighbors who watched them with interest and raised their hands in reply.

This would be all over town in minutes, how she rode off into the sunset with Jake. But Maddie scarcely had time to form the thought, never mind wonder what people would think, before they reached the far end of town and took off again.

On the sinuous road to Majestic they swayed from side to side as one on the curves. The forest flew by in a green blur pierced by occasional flashes of blue where the late afternoon sun glanced off the lake. They slowed again as they drove through Majestic, but then were jet propelled over the ridge. Time and the blur of the forest melted into the vibration of the bike between her legs and the solid heat of the man in her arms.

The road crossed the highway that circled the peninsula and continued through the farmland of the river valley. As they wound their way toward the sea, she caught glimpses of blue in the distance until finally, after one last bend in the road, they rode into the hamlet of Potters Cove.

Jake cut the engine and she sat for a minute re-adjusting to the abrupt stillness. A couple of houses on a rocky hillside faced a pristine cove surrounded by deep green conifers. An eagle circled above them on air currents looking for its next meal. A natural harbor, it sheltered the wharfs that made up most of the town from the wind and waves.

Maddie stepped gingerly off the bike. Her knees buckled and she gripped Jake's arm for support as she staggered, finding her land legs, a grin plastered across her face.

Jake stepped down and took off his helmet. "How did you like it?"

Maddie tapped him happily on the chest. "I loved it, and we get to do it again going home."

He laughed, helped her out of her helmet and slung his arm across her shoulders as they walked down onto the dock. Still exhilarated from the ride, she wrapped her arm around his waist.

Boats lined the wharfs, runabouts and trawlers, dinghies and yachts. Funky float houses were moored at the outermost wharf, many handmade with whimsically mismatched windows and doors.

A shingled building housed the Dockside Pub. Jake had made a reservation and a waiter led them to a patio table overlooking the tranquil bay. Maddie didn't know what to say when he helped her remove her jacket, but was glad she had taken the time to find the perfect pink blouse. *Thank you Augusta.* He hung their coats on the backs of their chairs and held her seat for her as she sat before sitting down across the table.

The sun skirted the low mountains that ringed the bay, reflecting off the water in an early evening glow that highlighted Jake's prominent cheekbones and strong jaw. The midnight blue shirt, casually open at the neck, showed off his broad shoulders and accentuated his sapphire eyes. *Her date.* A strange and unusual thought.

Her chest tightened as he ran his hands through his hair, leaving it waving gently away from his face like a romantic hero. Her fingers twitched to run through it too. The bike ride had taken a big chunk out of their wall of reserve, but she wasn't quite ready for that. She didn't even know what he did for a living.

She leaned forward, resting her arms on the table. "Where do you work?"

"I work in the bush."

"Are you a faller?" she asked, thinking back to his prowess

in the logger sports events.

"Used to be. I started working in the bush straight out of high school. A lot of the guys here do. I enjoyed it for a while, the pay was good and I was pretty good at it, but eventually it seemed to me that the guys walking around with the clipboards were the ones making all the decisions, not always the right ones, and I was the one taking all of the risks."

He stopped, concentrating on the tiny bowl of flowers in the center of the table, absently playing with a piece of fern. "My uncle, Augusta's husband, died in a logging accident before I was born. My Dad died the same way a few years ago. They were both good experienced fallers, but when the boss says cut you have to cut, even on steep slopes and in dangerous conditions. The high pay doesn't compensate for the risks. I knew how dangerous it could be, so I decided to make a change.

"So at twenty-five I went back to school. Took forestry engineering. Now, I'm the guy with the clipboard. I'm still in the bush most of the time, which I love, but now I'm the one making the decisions on how to cut a section of land in a way that will keep the other guys safe." He shrugged. "I like it."

The waiter came for their drink orders.

"Wine?" Jake asked.

Maddie shook her head. "I'll have a Virgin Bloody Mary."

He gave her a quizzical look. "Don't drink?"

"Never have," she said brightly, hoping he wouldn't pursue the matter, happy when he ordered an imported beer for himself and let it drop.

They studied the menu until the waiter returned with their drinks and to take their order. Then silence descended over the table. The whole restaurant seemed to be holding its breath. Maddie's breathing became tight.

Jake cleared his throat. "You've met most of my family. What about yours?"

"Oh-h-h." Maddie drew out the word, glancing away. She rubbed her hands up and down her arms. What could she say? She chose her words carefully.

"I grew up in a small town in the interior of the state. Chelan. Ever been there?" She glanced at Jake. He shook his head, no. She nodded and looked away again, concentrating on the view of boats tied to the wharf, anchored safely while she was still at sea.

"It's about as different from here as you can get. All bone dry hills, with sagebrush and sandy bluffs. Those were the early days of the wine industry and fruit trees still grew everywhere. Apples, cherries, plums, you name it.

"We lived all over the valley—mostly in trailer parks." She checked his face for a reaction, but his gaze remained steady.

She took a deep breath and forged ahead. "My father was never in the picture, it was just my mother and me. My mom had trouble holding a job, so we never had much money." She shrugged one shoulder. "We got by."

She moved on quickly, skipping the bad times, the nights when her mother lost another job and started drinking heavily again. "After high school I moved to Seattle, got a job and went to art school part time. I was waitressing in a fancy place downtown when I met my husband, Mark. He was a junior account executive and, at the time, I liked his drive. He wanted to do something, be someone, and he wanted me. Or thought he did anyway."

Stop talking! She couldn't seem to stop. Couldn't seem to blink. She shook her head.

"He was never home and after Jenny was born, I had an excuse not to join him for drinks and dinner with the people he worked with."

Shut up. "Not that I drink, anyway."

She felt a blush creep up her neck and silently cursed the nerves that pushed her away from the topic of her mother into the equally dangerous topic of Mark.

Finally she got control of the reins and the babbling stopped. "You're a good listener," she said.

He didn't say anything, just smiled that killer, one-dimple

smile.

"Anyway, eventually we split up and it's been Jenny and me ever since."

"Where is she now?" Jake asked, his eyes never leaving her face.

"Her dad invited her to stay with him for the summer. Out of the blue." Her voice dropped. "And she went." The pain of her daughter's desertion hadn't lessened with the passing weeks.

"You didn't want her to go?"

"He's never shown any interest in her before." The words burst out. She struggled to regain control. "But it is important that she knows her dad. I just hope she's not disappointed."

Thankfully, the waiter returned at that moment with their food. The mood changed and they spent the rest of the meal on the small talk that fills first dates: music and friends, gossip and flirting.

Dusk descended and the moon rose. All too soon they had finished their coffee and it was time to go. She climbed back on the bike and as she wrapped her arms around him, pulled in tight and leaned her head against his broad back, warmth spread through her making her tingle.

Like a dark dream, they flew over the ridge and through the moonlit forest. As they slowed on the driveway into the cabin, her stomach started to churn. She pulled away slightly and sat up straighter.

Where was this leading? *Am I ready to go?* She hadn't had sex in years, didn't even know what was expected after a date. Surely not that. Not on the first date. Should she ask him in? Who knows?

When they pulled up to the cabin, Jake hung her helmet on the handlebars and walked her up onto the porch. Her core throbbed, pulsing down her legs, and not entirely from the vibration of the bike.

The moon was beginning to wane. It sparkled on the water, casting a blue glow on the beach and the branches at the edge of the forest. She couldn't ask for a more romantic setting, and looked up at him shyly through her lashes. "I had a great time."

"Me too."

Then why did he sound so serious? "I loved the bike."

"I'm glad. We'll have to do it again sometime," he answered stiffly.

Who is this dark, moody guy, and where is my easy, funny dinner date?

Jake looked at her seriously, considering—what? She had no idea and her own thoughts were beginning to fray. Something better happen soon or she would lose her nerve.

Something did. He leaned forward and kissed her gently on the lips. Just as she was softening into the kiss, he pulled away, said a quiet "good night," and was gone.

Maddie fisted one hand on her hip. They didn't have to leap into bed, but was a decent kiss too much to ask? With a bit of physical contact thrown in?

She took out her frustration by rattling the handle on the sticky front door, but it refused to budge. "Come on Augusta," she muttered under her breath. "I'm in no mood for games."

Jake suddenly materialized beside her again on the porch. "What are you doing for the Fourth of July?"

Her mind went blank. She blinked. "No plans."

"Good. Come to dinner with my family."

The family? Panic must have flashed across her face because he took both her hands in his as if afraid she would flee.

The thought had crossed her mind.

"My Mom has a picnic every year for the holiday. It's fun. Really. Very informal, outside on the grass, lots of kids and dogs. Mostly family. You've met most of them already; Sarah, Sean, my sister Colleen."

Maddie shook her head. No way.

"No? Colleen was the woman at the Festival. And you met my Mom, well only for a minute, but it's at her place." He ground to a halt. "Please say you'll come."

He still had her hands in his strong grasp and she sensed he wouldn't take no for an answer. She took a deep breath. "Yes."

With the word, the knot in her stomach loosened and it suddenly sounded like a picnic might actually be fun.

He did that guy thing where he nodded his head as if closing a deal. "Okay. Good." Then he kissed her again, quick and hard on the lips, and disappeared into the night.

She smiled, playing her fingers lightly over her lips. The cabin door swung open, but she hardly noticed.

It was easy. Just say yes.

* * *

Jake felt antsy, not ready to go home just yet. In the old days he would have considered ten o'clock too early for a date to end. If she'd been one of the out-of-town women he sometimes dated, he wouldn't have left her at the door at ten. He'd have got himself invited in for a nightcap and then he could take it from there.

Back on his bike, he cruised into Majestic, thinking about a beer at the Elks.

So, why hadn't he stayed? The thought had crossed his mind, standing on the porch, her hazel eyes warm and inviting, the imprint of her body still burned onto his back, soft and tempting under her leather jacket.

Just following the rules. Not getting involved with someone nearby.

Right.

He was breaking those rules, right left and center. Right up front, the date itself was a big mistake. Already he knew one date wouldn't be enough. The more he got to know her—*mistake number two*—the more fascinating she became. It must have been hard growing up with a single mother and then raising a kid alone. It was rough enough when you had family ready to jump in to give you a hand when you couldn't make it work alone.

She had guts, more than he'd figured first time they met. Sounded like she hadn't had much fun in her life. He remembered how her eyes lit up after the motorcycle ride, her cheeks aglow from the wind. She'd never been on a bike before and she'd loved it.

He grinned. *Happy to oblige.* He'd be happy to show her lots of good times.

When he got to the club, the prospect of a noisy pub full of half-drunk people, even if they were his old buddies, didn't sound good to him anymore, so he looped around the parking lot and headed back to Fortune Bay.

Won't be obliging tonight though. No, he'd take it slow with this woman.

But hadn't he already made plans—*mistake number three*—and invited her to the party on the Fourth? Pretty well as his date, right in front of his family. He hadn't thought that part through yet, but still he was smiling, looking forward to the prospect.

He revved his bike on the empty moonlit road, ready to take the risk, ready to break all the rules.

Chapter 19

Jenny phoned the following evening, right on schedule. Although Maddie was expecting her every-second-night-call, her heart sank at the emotional distance that had grown between them.

After a few questions, to which Maddie received one word answers, they lapsed into an awkward silence. She wracked her brain for something, some bit of news from her new life that would break down her daughter's walls. Then she had it.

"I went on a date."

Jenny squealed. "No way."

"Yes way."

"With who?"

How to explain it? "With my landlord."

"Euuuww. like Mr. Gaspo?" Jenny asked, referring to their greasy, sleazy landlord in the city.

"No!" Maddie exclaimed and they both laughed. "This guy is hot." She blushed as she said it, but was having too much fun to care.

"Be careful Mom."

"Jenny!"

"NO, Mom, I don't mean *that.* I don't mean safe sex," Jenny said quickly. "Well, that too I guess, but I just mean be careful. How well do you know this guy? Don't let him break your heart."

So-o-o sweet—advice on my love life from my sixteen-year-old daughter. But what did it say about her love life if her sixteen-year-old daughter thought she needed advice?

"It's okay," Maddie answered solemnly. "I am being careful. Taking it slow. It was just a date. But he picked me up," she paused strictly for dramatic effect, "on a motorcycle!" Her voice rose at the end and Jenny squealed on the other end of the line. They both shrieked and laughed like teenagers, Maddie clutching the phone with two hands.

When they stopped laughing, Jenny said, "I miss you, Mom."

"I miss you too, Honey." Maddie swiped at her tears. "So, you're finished school for the summer. That must make you happy."

"Yeah, I guess."

Was that a less than enthusiastic response? "And your acting classes start next week?"

"Yeah, that'll be fun."

A bit better, but maybe something more than residual anger at Maddie was the reason Jenny had been so uncommunicative for the past two months.

Suddenly, she had to see her daughter. "Do you have plans for this weekend?"

"No. Dad says he has to work—again."

How well Maddie remembered that. "I'm coming to the city. Maybe tomorrow."

It was a spur of the moment decision, but Tori *had* been after her to bring her new photographs by the gallery. And she *had* been wishing she had her framing supplies at the cabin so she could get a jump on all the frames for the show.

There was also her promise to her mother, although she preferred not to think about that.

Mostly, though, she suddenly had to see Jenny.

"I could pick you up at your dad's after my meeting at the gallery tomorrow afternoon and we could spend a couple of nights at the apartment, hang out on Saturday. Then I'll take you back to your Dad's on Sunday morning and head back here." *In time to go to the picnic with Jake.*

"That'd be totally cool."

The excitement in Jenny's voice made Maddie's hopes soar. She might get her daughter back after all.

* * *

The next day Maddie watched through the ferry window

as the city rose up in the distance, the city she had lived in for so many years and which held so many memories. She was eager to shop at her favorite stores for the Italian coffee and good rye bread she couldn't get in Majestic, excited to visit *her* new gallery and was looking forward to spending the night with Jenny at their apartment.

But still, her stomach churned like the choppy waves outside the ferry window and every few minutes she patted the prints in her tote bag to make sure they were still there.

Tori had sounded excited over the phone. Maddie hoped she hadn't made a big mistake switching from urban portraits to so many landscapes. Would Tori like them or would she think they were weak and derivative? It was hard to take an old theme and make it fresh and new.

She pulled the prints out of the bag. On top was a moody shot of the lake with low clouds. Ignoring how it shook in her hand, she moved determinedly on to the next: sparkling raindrops on maidenhair fern after the storm. It was good. Very good. The fern clear and crisp, the background artistically blurred. With a firmer hand she picked up the next print, the deep woods silhouetted against the early morning glow.

She loved them all. Hopefully Tori would too.

As she drove off the ferry, nerves set in again, her stomach unsteady as she drove through the city, the downtown towers seeming to mock the backwoods theme of her new work.

By the time she got to Pioneer Square her stomach was in knots. What if she was completely on the wrong track? Maybe she should have stayed in town for the summer and continued to take gritty city shots. People liked them before—maybe such a big change was playing with fire.

Maybe Tori would change her mind about the show when she saw the proofs.

At the top of the gallery stairs, Maddie wiped her sweaty palms on the sides of her dress and pulled her stiff cheeks into what she hoped would pass for a smile.

Tori was not in the main gallery. Maddie barely registered the colorful paintings that lined the walls. She was early. Too early? She had driven straight from the ferry, unable to think about anything else. Maybe she should have gone to lunch first. Maybe Tori was busy and couldn't see her now.

Her mouth was so dry she wondered if she could speak at all. She'd forgotten her water bottle in the car and coughed hoarsely to clear her throat.

The door in the back wall swung open and Tori burst out. Her broad smile and double-hand clasp immediately dropped Maddie's anxiety level by several notches.

"Come in, you made good time." Tori towed her by the hand into her office. She moved the stacks of paintings off a pair of love seats in the corner, settled Maddie onto one and sat down across from her on the other.

Tori looked at her intently. "How have you been?"

Even over the phone, Maddie had sensed her concern about how the work for the show was coming and wanted to put her mind at ease. "I've been well, working hard."

"Good. I can't wait to see them." Tori tapped a clear spot on the coffee table.

With her heart in her throat, Maddie opened her tote bag and pulled out the manila envelope protecting her prints. She laid the selection out on the table, one by one, facing Tori.

The minutes slipped by, the clock on the wall ticking unnaturally loud. Tori touched first one print, then another.

Maddie's head started to spin. She reminded herself to breath.

Then Tori looked up and gave her a big smile. "Exciting— and unexpected," she said, then went back to studying the photographs.

The vice constricting Maddie's chest eased off. She took a deep breath and blew it all out, allowing her shoulders to drop, pressing her lips together to contain her excitement. Maybe the show would happen after all.

"You've landed on your feet," Tori said, then pointed to

a shot of Jake surrounded by guys at the logger sports event. "Who's this?"

"My landlord," Maddie said, feeling a blush creep onto her cheeks.

"Good for you. He's gorgeous."

"We've only been on one date. It's a little complicated."

Tori picked up the photograph of Jake and Sarah and the candy apple. "The best ones always are."

Maddie opened her mouth to respond, but didn't know what to say. Luckily, Tori moved on.

"Is this where you're staying?" She held a shot of the farm, dark and hulking behind the delicate spring blossoms, and Maddie found herself telling her about the cabin, the town and her new friends.

An hour later, she gathered up her prints, preparing to leave.

"So. We need thirty framed pieces for the show," Tori said. "Sixteen by twenty?"

"Yes. I want to be sure of my choices before I start enlarging them."

"Of course. That's expensive. We have a few 'for-sures' here already, I love that axe throwing shot, the face of the bear cub and the one of, who is it? Jack?"

"Jake."

"Jake and his daughter. They all definitely make the cut. I'd like to see more later. I know what my customers buy and that's the name of the game."

Maddie agreed. The roll of cash in her sock drawer was dangerously slim—this trip alone was taking quite a slice—and the specter of returning to work for Eileen at the end of the summer loomed large in her mind.

They talked for another hour, agreeing on limited editions of thirty prints, three matted and shrink wrapped plus one of each framed on the wall, one hundred and twenty prints in all. Thank goodness Tori liked the simple black frames that Maddie had made for last winter's show. Making her own cut down tremendously on her expenses. But making thirty frames took a big chunk of time with her limited skills and resources.

Too bad Jenny wasn't in Fortune Bay. Maddie could use her help. They had made quite a team before her last show, working spread out all over their small apartment, a veritable assembly line, each with their own jobs: cutting, painting and assembling the frames. She'd paid her daughter five dollars for each frame they finished, a pittance compared to what it would have cost to have the photographs professionally framed, but Jenny was thrilled.

And Tori loved the shots, loved her new direction, loved the pictures, and Maddie left the gallery with her brain on spin dry and a spring in her step.

Until she remembered she had one more stop.

Chapter 20

One more stop. No problem. Swing by her mother's apartment and drop off some cash.

Maddie's hands were slippery on the wheel as she drove through familiar streets lined with seedy apartments, pawnshops and hotels with rooms-by-the-hour.

Her mother had moved, probably had a new man, and Maddie hadn't been to this place before. She found the concrete apartment block—no better but, she was relieved to see, no worse than where her mom had lived before.

Two men slouched against the outside of the building, watching as she locked the car. A chill ran down her spine. For once she was sorry the Beast was a station wagon. Her overnight bag and portfolio were totally obvious in the back, even though she'd covered them with a blanket. Should she leave her camera there or take it with her? They'd see if she took it out of the car and might follow her inside and try to grab it. In the end she left it where it was, hidden in the back of the Beast.

Why was she even here at all? It wouldn't make any difference in the long run. Cindy would be in the same situation again in a week. But it *was* the end of the month. Maybe the landlord would actually get the money before Cindy drank it away. And what else could she do? Cindy was her mother, the only family she had other than Jenny, and Maddie couldn't bear to think of her out on the street. If indeed that were even true.

She usually avoided visiting Cindy at home. It dredged up too many painful memories. Usually they met at a café where Maddie would try to get her mother to put some food in her stomach, but sometimes there was no choice.

She'd tried to call to set up a date, but Cindy must have

called from someone else's phone because the last contact number she had was disconnected. Her mother rarely had a phone of her own and Maddie had given up buying her cell phones. There was always some reason it didn't work. Sometimes she thought Cindy just plain didn't want her to call.

The elevator was out of order so Maddie trudged up the center of the steps in the concrete stairwell, trying not to touch the railing. Thank God Cindy only lived on the second floor.

Maddie walked down the corridor, gagging on the odors of urine and God-only-knew-what. Hand to her nose, she checked the numbers on the doors. The light was burned out and half the numbers were missing making it hard to figure out which apartment came next. Obviously Cindy wasn't the only tenant who wanted to disappear. Finally, she found number fifteen, the five on a rakish angle, held to the door by only one screw.

Stomach churning, breath tight, she listened at the door. The TV was on but there was no other sound. No shouting or other sounds.

She tightened her hand into a fist and knocked, conscious of the money in an envelope in her purse. Should she get it out so she could make a quick getaway, or was it crazy to stand in this hallway with a handful of bills?

No one came to the door. She clenched her teeth and knocked again. Waited... Nothing.

Then, in the stairwell at the end of the hall, running footsteps and laughing voices echoed. The muscles in her neck tightened until she could only look straight ahead.

The voices got louder, then the runners continued up the stairs, right past her floor.

She couldn't wait any longer. Cindy could have gone out and left the TV on, a habit of hers that drove Maddie crazy.

Checking both ways to be sure she was alone, she took the envelope out of her purse and slid it under the door. What else could she do? She was not coming back.

She ran down the stairs, grabbing the railing when her shoe caught a tread. The smells brought back memories of too many places she'd lived as a child. Her stomach churned, she gagged. She had to get outside before she threw up.

Bursting out through the front door, she took a deep breath of the city air. She was shaking, but the car was still there, thank God, and it looked untouched. She glanced up and down the street, afraid she'd see Cindy heading her way on the arm of her latest flame, but the coast was clear.

Maddie hurried toward the car, unlocking the door with the key fob when she was still ten feet away. Wrenching open the door, she jumped in and locked all the doors. She stabbed the key at the ignition, once, twice, until it finally slid home. Turning the key, she gunned the motor and tore away.

The visit had woken an all too familiar fire-breathing dragon in her stomach. After a few blocks she dug around in her purse for anti-acid pills, finding a linty old pack she hadn't used since she'd moved to Fortune Bay. She took two with a cold coffee chaser.

As she drove back across town to Mark's house, she stretched her neck, forcing her shoulders to relax.

Where did she fit in? Certainly not with Cindy, but not in Mark's world either. She wondered if Jenny fit in there. Their last phone call had been warmer but she still wasn't sure if the high life Mark had to offer had seduced her daughter. She chewed on another anti-acid.

When she pulled up in front of the house, Jenny ran out the door and down the stone steps, shouting over her shoulder, "I'm going, Dad."

Mark appeared on the front porch and raised his hand in greeting. Maddie rolled down her window as Jenny slung her bag in the back. "I'll bring her back Sunday morning."

"Fine," he said. "I'll be working most of the weekend anyway."

"Right," Maddie said in a low voice, forcing a smile as she raised her hand in good-bye. Jenny climbed into the car, threatening to strangle her with her hug.

"I am *so* glad to see you," Jenny exclaimed. "*So* glad to get out of the house."

As Jenny did up her seatbelt, the dragon in Maddie's stomach began to uncoil.

"Dad can be so over-protective. He hardly lets me leave the house." Jenny listed his restrictions on her fingers. "Not after dark, not with friends he doesn`t know, not after dinner on a school night. I can't wait for the acting course to begin."

Maddie kept her eyes on the road, but she smiled. So, not paradise after all. Maybe this was the perfect summer to hand the parenting over to Mark. Jenny seemed to be pushing all the same boundaries Maddie herself had set last winter, which had been the source of most of their disagreements.

"What do you want to do?" Maddie asked, happy to be the 'good parent' for a change. "Where shall we eat?" They might be spending the night at their old apartment, but dinner would be somewhere special.

They sat on the outdoor patio of a small restaurant not far from the beach and ordered a variety of tapas; olive tapenade, sausage with roasted tomatoes, toasted almonds. Maddie photographed all of the dishes for a "dining out" article she had in mind, causing Jenny to roll her eyes faking chagrin, but she dug right in.

After they'd eaten, they wandered down to the beach and sat on the warm sand, their backs against a log, and watched the sun set over the water. Although Maddie had a hundred photographs of the scene already, she couldn't resist pulling her camera out and taking a few more as the sunset stained the houses rising up the hillside bright peach.

They talked cautiously, feeling each other out, but Maddie sensed that Jenny might be ready to start over too.

Later, as they tried to sneak quietly up the two narrow flights of steps to their apartment, their overnight cases banged against the walls and their giggles spiraled out of control.

Maddie circled the apartment straightening ornaments

and wiping dust off surfaces. It felt...small. Always her safe place, the place she and Jenny had moved when she first left Mark, now she felt like a guest, and she couldn't help comparing the claustrophobic sloping ceilings to the airy comfort of the cabin where the breeze off the lake swept through the open front door.

They slept in their old beds, and on Saturday morning went out for coffee and pastries at their favorite café around the corner, agreeing that it was the best in the city.

"Dad took me to visit his parents," Jenny said. She had only met Mark's parents a couple of times before.

"How did that go?"

Jenny winced. "Pretty formal. Like, I had to wear a skirt and tuck in my top."

"Did your Dad tell you that?"

"Dad told me to wear the skirt, but Grandma made me tuck it in. We sat in the living room and drank tea. From little cups and saucers. It was kind of creepy."

Maddie stirred the coffee in her chunky stoneware mug. "I never enjoyed visiting them either." *Understatement of the century.*

As Maddie lifted her mug to her lips, out of the blue, Jenny asked the question. The question Maddie had been dreading for years. "Why do we never see your mom?"

Maddie's hand froze in mid-air, coffee sloshing onto the table. Jenny knew vaguely about Cindy, and that Maddie had no father, but she had never asked about either subject. Thank goodness, because Maddie didn't know how to explain illegitimacy and the pain it could cause to a child in the small-town social climate of thirty years ago.

But Jenny wasn't a child any longer and Maddie knew she shouldn't be surprised that Jenny had questions about her unknown family.

"Dad said he met her. Once."

Maddie blanched. God only knows what else he said. She chose her words with care. "You know why we don't see her.

She's a serious alcoholic and doesn't really want our help—or interference."

A shrillness she couldn't seem to stop crept into her voice. "I have tried to keep her away from you. I just wanted to be a good mother—that's all—not like her." She drank down the last of her coffee as if it was a shot of something stronger, and set the cup back on the table with a smack.

Jenny chewed on her upper lip, her eyes serious under lowered brows. She reached out and patted Maddie's shaking hand. "That's sort of what Dad said. Too bad. I would like to have one nice grandmother. I guess I'm just out of luck."

Maddie's eyes filled with tears and she held onto her daughter's hand. "I'm sorry Honey."

Jenny smiled and shrugged. "Hey, not your fault. No biggy."

It was a biggy. Jenny had no idea how big. And Maddie would still keep Jenny away from Cindy, but she felt better as a result of sharing. She had carried the burden for too long. Eventually Jenny would have to meet her grandmother again and maybe if they talked about it now the meeting wouldn't shake her daughter's world.

After breakfast they strolled along the trail at Elliot Bay, enjoying the gorgeous weather of the glorious summer long weekend along with all the other locals. Then before she knew it, Maddie was back in front of Mark's house saying goodbye to her daughter.

"I do want you to visit," she assured Jenny, who was clinging to her in a tearful hug. "As soon as your acting course is over you can come for the weekend."

Then she kissed her daughter goodbye and drove away, already questioning her decision to leave her there with Mark.

They'd enjoyed each other's company this weekend more than any time in the whole last year. That, at least, was something to cling to.

* * *

Four hours later, Maddie put her hip to the cabin door.

The roses wreathing the front porch had opened while she was away, trailing a swath of tiny pink blooms over the railing, their delicate fragrance permeating the air. Too beautiful to resist, she pulled out her camera and took a few shots.

For the moment, the framing supplies could stay in the Beast. She didn't know where she would store them, let alone where she would work on the frames. For now, though, she was happy to open the cabin windows and let the sweet summer breeze sweep through. To put away her weekend gear, check the noisy old fridge for groceries and settle her spirit back into the place.

Seattle had been fun. Jenny seemed genuinely glad to spend time with her and it was nice, in an oddly nostalgic way, to see their old apartment again. She was surprised at how glad she was to leave the city behind though, to fly like a homing pigeon back to Fortune Bay.

Taking a glass of cold lemonade out onto the porch, she watched as the late afternoon sun painted the mountain across the bay deep orange. Whether hidden in low cloud or reflecting the setting sun, this vista had become as familiar as an old glove. She would miss it terribly when the summer ended.

It was only the beginning of July, but this weekend signaled the halfway point in her summer sojourn and, like a cloud over the lake, her return to Seattle had cast a melancholy shadow over the rest of the summer.

She wanted to stay. She had friends here. She peered through the trees to check if Frankie's car was there.

And then there was Jake. She ran her tongue over her lips as she remembered their last kiss.

Yes, she wanted it all: Jake, her new friends, the community she was growing to love, and the work she found so satisfying.

Could she just say *yes*, and make it hers? There was still the matter of Cindy, but what her mother did or who she was didn't seem to matter as much anymore. At least that's how

Maddie felt when she was in Fortune Bay. She was an adult, with a life of her own. She could make her own plans and change them when needed.

Maddie walked down the steps to the stony ground sprinkled with grass and moss, and knelt at the little garden in front of the porch and began to pull out the weeds that had sprung up. Showers had fallen on and off all through June, but now the air had a different finish; it was drier, crystal clear. A typical west coast summer, it could be weeks, possibly months, before it rained again.

She didn't look up until a shadow fell over the garden where she knelt.

* * *

"Hi," Jake said. "Where have you been?"

The second the words left his lips, he knew it was the wrong thing to say. But his relief at seeing Maddie back at the cabin, weeding her roses, knocked the right words out of his head. He closed his eyes, cleared his mind, and then tried again.

"You've been away?"

"Yes." She stood up and brushed the dirt off her bare knees. "I went to Seattle. I had business with the gallery and I wanted to see my daughter."

He exhaled the breath he felt he'd been holding for days. He'd been by, more than once, while she was away, wondering where she was, what she was doing and who she was doing it with. Wondered if she'd make it back for the picnic.

Idiot. He'd never considered her daughter.

He convinced himself the picnic was the reason he came by all those times, but that was a lie. He was afraid she wouldn't return at all.

"Are we still on for tomorrow?" he asked, moving closer, inhaling that smell of lemons and roses that was Maddie.

She smiled. "I'm looking forward to it. What time?"

"I'll pick you up around two." He brushed a curl, soft as

dandelion fluff, back from her cheek.

Her eyes flared. She whispered. "What can I bring?"

He took another step closer, felt the tension, pheromones leaping from her skin to his, almost visible, like thousands of fireflies bouncing back and forth between them. He took one more small step. "Nothing. I'm sure they have it covered. I'm just glad you're back."

He hadn't noticed she was moving too, but now she was standing right in the flowerbed, backed up to the railing. He paused to give her a chance to put a hand on his chest—any indication she wanted him to stop.

Awareness brightened her eyes in a way that could have been a smile. She put her hand on his chest all right, but instead of pushing him away she clutched the front of his shirt. He didn't know if she pulled him or if he moved closer himself, but when he found her, her lips were warm and responsive. He put a hand on either side of her head on the railing and leaned in, tilting his head, taking the kiss a fraction deeper, then slowly pulled away.

Her eyes closed, she shuddered a breath that told him what he wanted to know. This still might not be a good idea, whatever it was they were doing together, but he didn't think the knowing was enough to make him stop.

She opened her eyes and released her hand on his shirt.

"See you tomorrow," he said, running the back of his hand down the curve of her cheek as he regretfully stepped away.

He never had been good at following rules.

JULY

Chapter 21

A pile of discarded outfits lay strewn across Maddie's bed. She grabbed her hair with both hands. In the city, she had never had trouble deciding what to wear—she had the uniform down pat. But what on earth do you wear to a picnic? Her family didn't do picnics. Take out, yes, on a good night, but not picnics. And this was not just any picnic, this was *meeting the family.*

She collapsed on the edge of the bed. *Family.* Such a loaded word. She'd always wanted one, more than anything, but although she'd tried, she'd never been able to make it work. The relationship with her mother was flawed, right from the start, and her experience with Mark's family had always been stiff and uncomfortable. So even though she knew Jake's mother and Sean, and had even met his daughter Sarah, she couldn't stop the ache in the pit of her stomach at the thought of meeting them again today.

Was it too late to call the whole thing off? Where were those anti-acids?

Get a grip. He said informal. Kids and dogs. She stood up and looked at herself in the mirror again. Denim shorts and a red blouse. She nodded to the mirror. Pretty but not fancy. Perfect for a picnic. Tying her hair with a red kerchief into a high ponytail, some curls escaping around the hairline, she was ready to go.

Five minutes later, she stood in the kitchen wringing her cold, sweaty hands. Despite what Jake had said, she wanted to take something but couldn't decide what. In desperation she went out onto the porch.

Flowers. Grabbing a pair of scissors, she started to cut: a couple of peonies with swirling pink heads, blooms so heavy they'd already fallen to the ground. Mauve and white stalks of wild foxglove for a vertical element, and orange and yellow columbine for a punch of color. The columbines seemed wild too, growing in and out of the garden boundaries without compunction.

She'd looked up all of their names in an old gardening book that she'd found in the cabin. It had appeared on the kitchen table just as she began to wonder what the flowers sprouting in the garden were called. She assumed it was a gift from Augusta.

Finally adding some green ferns to fill out the arrangement, she was satisfied with the way it looked and took it inside to wrap it in paper.

A knock sounded on the door and she looked out the big front window. Jake stood on the porch, staring out at the lake. He looked like a celebrity slumming, gut-wrenchingly handsome in a cream-colored shirt and well-worn jeans that rode low on his lean hips. Warmth flooded through her like the heat and vibration she'd felt from his lips the day before. To his silent request for permission to kiss her, she'd answered *yes,* and even though she knew there'd be the devil to pay, she'd say yes again in a heartbeat.

He turned and knocked again. He'd brushed his long hair back from his face, showing off his high forehead. Dark brows dipped low giving him such a serious look, but that only made his rare smiles that much more spectacular. Like fireworks on the Fourth of July.

He caught sight of her through the window and the dimple sparked in his cheek. Maddie's knees turned to jelly. She slapped herself lightly on the cheek and laughed—*pull yourself together.* Taking a moment to add a layer of Candy Apple Red to her lips for strength, she picked up the flowers and stepped onto the porch.

His eyes ranging over her left a trail of heat that made her want to arch her back like a cat under an attentive hand. He smiled, reached up and gave her ponytail a playful tug. Taking the flowers in one hand and her hand with the other, he led her off the porch.

He turned the bouquet over in his hand. "My mom has some flowers like this. Probably got them from Aunt Augusta."

Maddie puffed out a sharp breath. "Then she won't want these."

"Sure she will. They're beautiful. It's like you're part of the family."

Maddie smiled, but it was short-lived when she saw the family-style car he was driving. Oh well. She couldn't have ridden on his motorcycle in shorts anyway.

Minutes later, they cruised down Jake's mother's long driveway. Voluptuous maples in full summer leaf hid the house from the road, offering relief from the blazing afternoon sun. In back, facing the lake, long tables were laid out under more trees.

The yard was alive with people. Maddie stopped, the blood draining from her cheeks. She thought this was only going to be family, but at least twenty adults sat in lawn chairs, chatting with cold drinks in their hands. A swarm of children chased three barking dogs in circles around the trees. Down at the lake, teenagers sun bathed on a dock that bristled with boats.

She hung back, clutching the flowers to her chest like a shield. Jake, apparently unaware of her distress, plowed ahead, towing her behind him, her hand held firmly in his.

They skirted the crowd and went up the back steps to a quiet, screened-in porch overflowing with summering houseplants. Maddie looked longingly at the comfortable wicker furniture. Maybe she could just stay here...

But Jake whisked her through. At the farm-style kitchen door, they paused and watched as four women, laughing and talking, ladled food into banquet-sized serving dishes.

Jake cleared his throat. "We're back."

The women swarmed around them, showering Maddie with greetings. She thrust the bouquet at Stephanie.

"Thank you darling," Stephanie said, giving her a kiss on the cheek.

Maddie's hand went up, her fingers finding the warm spot where Stephanie's lips had touched. She glanced away, then looked back, but Stephanie had already turned away to find a vase for the flowers.

Jake tugged her on to meet his sister Colleen. She was dressed much as she had been at the Festival in a bright peasant skirt and cowboy boots, a tight T-shirt showing off her womanly curves. She shook Maddie's hand briefly, and looked her up and down. "We'll get together later for a chat."

Chat wasn't the word that immediately came to Maddie's mind. Something closer to *grilling* was probably more like it.

Stephanie whisked them out the door with the back of her hand. "Take her outside Jake. Introduce her around. We'll talk later, dear."

Outside, however, lay Maddie's worst nightmare. "Can't I help you in here?" she asked brightly.

"No, go out and enjoy the day," Stephanie insisted, sacrificing her to the horde of strangers in the yard.

No sooner had they stepped outside than they were waist deep in a maelstrom of children. Jake reached into the mob and plucked out a particularly colorful girl with pigtails, fairy wings and a yellow polka-dot bathing suit. She giggled and squirmed and kissed him on the cheek before he dropped her carefully back onto the ground where the unruly gang immediately swallowed her up.

"My daughter," he said wryly. "I see she's in no mood for formalities. I'll introduce you again later."

Jake stopped to grab soft drinks from a cooler on the grass and Maddie leaned against the trunk of a tall maple, arms tight across her chest. Sean slid his arm around her waist, gave her a light kiss on the cheek. She blew out a breath, deflating slightly but, at a glance from Jake, he quickly melted back into the crowd.

Jake gave her a mildly embarrassed smile. "We might as well get this over with." Then taking her hand, he sauntered nonchalantly around the yard greeting first one group then another.

Inquisitive stares pricked Maddie's back, but Jake was clearly in his element. Cousins, neighbors, uncles and aunts, he stopped to shake hands with the men and plant kisses on the cheeks of some of the women. Her mind was reeling at the introductions, but at the same time she was fascinated by this new, affable side of the man.

A group of middle-aged women with big straw hats sat fanning themselves on lawn chairs in the shade while their husbands, off across the yard, huddled around the yawning hood of a vintage Mustang.

One ample-bosomed aunt took Maddie's hand, patting it and not letting go. "Well, Jake, it's about time you brought someone by to meet the family. Must be almost five years since the little one's mother left—not that we've been counting." A twitter of laughter ran through the group.

"It's downright un-natural to see a man like you all alone," another woman put in. "If I was a few years younger, I'd'a gone after you myself." Jake laughed as he pulled Maddie away.

Her eyes glazed over as her brain overflowed with milling names and faces. Then a familiar pair of oversized sunglasses came into view on the blanket below.

"Frankie!" She dropped to her knees and reached out to touch her friend's arm, the first stable lifebuoy in this sea of strangers.

Frankie pulled her sunglasses down on her nose, her eyes laughing over them. "Feel like you've run the gauntlet?"

"It is good to see a familiar face."

Above them, Jake laughed. "Come on, it's not that bad."

Maddie took a deep breath and rolled her eyes dramatically, but smiled up at Jake. She turned to Frankie. "I didn't know you two were related."

"We're not. It's not all family. Some of us are neighbors from along the shore."

That explained the boats tied up at the dock. Shielding her eyes, Maddie looked down to the water where a couple of teenagers were strapping on life vests and climbing into a small aluminum boat with a motor on the back. A boy, who couldn't have been more than ten, was already seated in the stern. He took the throttle and shot off with a roar across the bay.

"I'll leave you with Frankie for a while," Jake said. "I have a few things to do."

After he left, Frankie frowned at Maddie. "Are you okay? You look kind of pale."

Maddie pressed her hands to her cheeks. "I don't do well in crowds."

Frankie patted her arm. "Stay with me. I'll protect you."

Although said lightly, Maddie believed she would, and relaxed back on her elbows on the blanket.

A teenage girl dropped down beside them. She wore a T-shirt over her bathing suit and black-rimmed glasses under a thick fringe of straight, blonde bangs. A handful of freckles were tossed across her otherwise pale nose and cheeks.

"Hi Brandy," Frankie said. "Have you met Maddie?"

"No," Brandy said looking at Maddie with open curiosity. "But Louise told me about you. I'm her sister."

"Brandy and Louise live next door," Frankie explained.

Brandy smiled, exposing transparent braces.

"How old are you, Brandy?"

"Sixteen," she answered, a trifle too boldly.

Maddie lifted her eyebrows. "Really?"

Brandy retreated with a grin. "Okay, sixteen next January."

"I have a daughter about your age," Maddie told her, and Brandy smiled again. "But I guess you know that, too."

Brandy nodded. "Lou told me. Is your daughter coming

to visit?"

Maddie shrugged, lips tight. "I hope so."

Brandy turned to Frankie. "Lou said to tell you she's sorry she couldn't be here. She went to Seattle for the weekend."

"Too bad."

Brandy jumped up. "See ya later," she said, then she was gone, bounding down to join the kids on the dock.

Nice to have teenagers around, Maddie thought with a twinge.

A few minutes later, Jake made his way onto the dock in the middle of a buzzing swarm of children, bullhorn in one hand, a watermelon in the other. Sean followed him, a lethal looking knife held high over his head. Both men had changed into swim trunks, a sight that wasn't lost on the women on the blanket. Maddie pulled out her camera and focused in on the brothers as they organized the children's swimming races. Above the shrieks of the kids and shouts of encouragement from the crowd on the shore, she could hear Jake's calm even voice through the bullhorn.

Using the camera as a shield between her and the crowd, she moved from the children's races to photographing the chatting group of women under the trees, to the beer-bellied men standing around the cars in the field.

She slipped into the kitchen to snap a few shots of the women shrouded by steam rising from pots on the stove. One old woman was shelling peas, aided by a small girl she introduced to Maddie as her great-granddaughter.

How wonderful to grow up with a family like this, where you knew you belonged. You would never be alone. It wouldn't always be perfect of course, but she sensed strength in their numbers.

Stephanie separated herself from the women in the kitchen and took Maddie into the sunporch. "I'm glad to see you again. I hope I haven't been a negligent landlady. I do own the cabin, but Jake has always taken care of it for me. I hope he's taking care of you."

Maddie felt hot spots of color bloom on her cheek. "He's great. I mean great as a landlord. He fixed some things for me. Things that needed doing."

Stop talking.

"Like the step." She couldn't stop, and grabbed the idea like a lifeline. "It was broken. And painting. Last week he helped me paint the porch."

Stephanie's eyebrows rose. "Jake Murphy painting? Interesting." She smiled. "I understand you're a photographer."

"Yes I am." Maddie had noticed large abstract paintings on the kitchen walls. Unusual for a kitchen. "Are you an artist?" Anything to get off the subject of Jake.

"Yes. I paint. Abstracts mostly. But it's just a hobby."

"Really?" Maddie stuck her head back through the doorway and looked at them again. "They're wonderful. So full of life."

"Thank you." Stephanie put a hand on her arm at the door. "I should get back," she said, with a smile. "Come for tea someday. I'd love to hear about your work." Then she went back into the kitchen.

Wow. The woman was amazing. She *looked* like an artist with her long salt-and-pepper hair pulled up in a messy bun on top of her head and the loose silk jacket that Frankie had said she had made herself. A large abstract pattern of black and white swirled across the robe and although obviously one of a kind, she wore it with a casual grace and assurance as if she'd just shrugged it on.

Maddie stood for a moment trying to work out her feelings before stepping outside. Stephanie had been friendly, not judgmental. Certainly not like other mothers she had met before.

When she got back to the blanket, Sean had awarded the last swimming ribbons and Jake was standing waist deep in the water, cutting the watermelon on the edge of the dock into happy-face slices for the children.

Maddie sighed. "He's good with kids."

"Something wrong?" Frankie asked

"No, nothing. It's just...I wish I'd discovered this place sooner. That Jenny could have grown up like this."

"You sound like you might be thinking about staying."

"Oh no," Maddie said with a laugh. "It's too late for that now. My life is in the city. I have to go back. This summer is only a detour."

"Does it have to be?"

For a moment, warm fuzzy thoughts clouded her brain.

"It would be nice...but I have to go back. It's Jenny's last year of high school; I couldn't move her now. I have the show coming up—it's a big opportunity for me—and my job at the gallery to go back to. I hope I don't have to work there forever, but I'm going to need the money in the fall." She shook her head. "No, I have to go back."

After that, she was silent, focused on the man sitting on the dock with the little girl tucked between his legs, watching them spit watermelon seeds into the water.

Chapter 22

When the crowd on the dock began to disperse, Sarah ran over to Maddie and Frankie with a plate of watermelon slices, followed by a large wet dog.

"We get special treatment?" Frankie asked, taking a piece.

Sarah held out the plate to Maddie, watching her intently. "Daddy said to bring you some. I know who you are 'cause I met you before."

"Yes. Hello again. My name is Maddie."

"My name is Sarah. This is Rex. Lie down Rex," she ordered, and with a *harrumph*, the dog flopped down on the corner of the blanket.

"You have a pretty ponytail," Sarah observed, reaching out to pat it with one sticky hand. "And pretty earrings," she added, head to one side.

Maddie felt ridiculously uncomfortable under her scrutiny. "Thank you. You have very nice braids yourself."

"Daddy says they're good 'cause they keep my hair out of my face, but sometimes I'd like a curly ponytail too," she said wistfully, although Maddie doubted Sarah had a curly hair on her head.

Suddenly Jake was heading for the blanket and Maddie barely noticed Frankie slip away. He had changed back into jeans but his white shirt hung open, showing off a sculpted torso that she was sure was the result of manual labor, not trips to the gym. A line of dark hair ran down his taught belly and as he came up beside them she had to stop herself from reaching out and grabbing him by the belt.

Instead, she wrenched her eyes away and brought them back up to his face.

He dropped down beside her, two cold drinks in his hand. He held one out to Maddie and the other to Sarah.

"How are my two favorite girls?" he asked, lying on his side and leaning on one elbow, raking his gleaming wet hair off his face with his free hand. Sarah lowered her brows and Maddie almost laughed aloud. The girl was the spitting image of her father.

"I thought I was your favorite girl," she said, lips pouting.

"You are, but Maddie's my next favorite girl." He spoke easily but Maddie saw he was watching Sarah closely.

She scrunched her freckled nose in thought, then smiled at Maddie in saccharine commiseration, leaned back against her father in an unmistakably territorial way. "Second best is pretty good."

He wrapped an arm around her and kissed the top of her wet head. "You better go, Sport, and get out of that wet bathing suit if you're going to play ball."

Sarah scrambled up. "Baseball? Can I be on your team?"

"You bet. I want all the best players on my team. And don't leave that wet suit on Grandma's floor," he called as she bolted for the house with Rex at her heels.

"She's great," Maddie said, her eyes following the ball of energy as it zigzagged confidently through the crowd. "She's lucky to grow up here."

"I think so."

They were silent for a moment until, without warning, fifty pounds of wet smelly dog bounded up and poised beside them to shake.

Maddie shrieked as the first cold drops hit her. Jake hurled himself between her and the dog, landing on top of her in time for most of the wet, sandy spray to splat on the back of his white shirt.

Rather than pushing him away, Maddie gripped the open lapels of his shirt, hotly aware of the hard length of his body pressing down on her.

The crowd stilled around them. Her eyes locked with his as he held himself above her for a few long seconds. A satisfied smile spread across his face. He had to feel her racing pulse, and she certainly felt the growing effect she had on him.

Then he put his hands on the ground on either side of her and pushed himself up. With a grin, he took both of her hands and pulled her to her feet. They stood hand in hand, toe to toe in the middle of the yard as conversation and laughter resumed.

"Baseball, City Girl?" Jake challenged.

She looked up at him through her lashes as she brushed the grass off her shorts. "I don't know if I'm good enough to be on your team."

"We're pretty accommodating," he said, putting his arm around her shoulders and leading her to an open field ringed by spikes of magenta fireweed at the side of the house.

Jake and Sean were the unspoken team captains and the guests chose up sides, the resulting teams composed of motley mixtures of ages and abilities. The game began and progressed with a cacophony of cheering and heckling, the rules changing to suit the age and skill of the players.

When it was Maddie's turn at bat, Jake's cousin pitched her an easy slow ball, right over the plate. Although it was twenty years since she'd held a bat in her hand, she was pleased to find she hadn't lost her touch.

The bat connected with the pitch with a resounding *Crack!* She took off to first base like an arrow from a bow while the outfielders scrambled for the ball.

Sarah raced around from second to home. Her older cousin Matt, who had been on first, passed her as he rounded third base. Maddie herself got to third before the ball made it back to the infield. Hooting and hollering filled the air and she blushed with pleasure as Jake and Sarah gave her big smiles and thumbs-up from home plate.

Jake hit her in with a home run and soon joined her on the sidelines. He grinned and shook his head. "Well, Slugger, who'da guessed? Welcome to the team."

Maddie didn't even try to hide the smugness in her laugh.

After the game, everyone gathered for the evening meal at

long tables set under the maples. Barbequed chickens and pasta salad with capers and tomatoes, and roasted vegetables fresh from Stephanie's bountiful garden. By the time the sun sank low in the sky, the laughter and ribbing settled into quiet, after dinner talk. Maddie carried a load of dishes into the kitchen, separating garbage and paper plates from cutlery and glasses, dumping the latter into the sink and filling it with hot soapy water.

A moment later, Jake's sister Colleen followed her into the kitchen loaded down with dinner debris.

"You don't have to do that," she said.

"I'm happy to do a load," Maddie replied over her shoulder, up to her elbows in soapsuds. As she put the clean glasses into the drainer, Colleen picked up a towel and started to dry.

"So when did you move here?" Colleen asked casually.

Maddie kept busy in the sink. Where was this going? It was the family cabin, surely she knew. "I moved into the cabin at the beginning of May."

"When did you start going out with my brother?"

Now we get down to it. Maddie rinsed another cup and put it in the draining rack. "We aren't really 'going out'. We only went out once, for dinner, that's all."

"He never mentioned you were seeing each other."

"Because we're not. Not really."

"He's never brought a woman to meet the family before. Not since Rena. His wife."

"I don't know if he brought me 'to meet the family,' or if he brought me to be neighborly. Because, you know, we're not dating."

"Looks more than neighborly to me. How long are you staying?"

"Today? Well, Sarah looks tired and Jake said something about leaving right after the fireworks—"

Colleen turned directly to face her. "No. I mean in Fortune Bay."

There it was again, the question of her leaving. "I'm going back to Seattle in the fall."

"His wife left him too, you know. He's a lot more vulnerable than he makes out."

"Don't worry. We aren't moving very fast."

"Well, that's good since you're *leaving*. He needs a woman who can give him the family he deserves. One who'll be here for the long haul."

Maddie didn't have a response for that, so she kept her eyes focused on the fading bubbles in the dishpan as Colleen hung up the towel and swung out of the room.

Maddie leaned heavily on the edge of the sink, the old burner firing up in her stomach. Maybe Colleen was right. Maybe she shouldn't be spending time with Jake just for her own pleasure. Because although she wished they could have more, that she could be part of the family she'd seen here today, for her it was just a fantasy. She might as well dream of eating cake on the moon.

By the time Jake came in with a heavy sleeping heap of Sarah in his arms, the sink was empty and Maddie was drying her hands on a tea towel. Looking at them, her arms ached for the weight of a warm sleeping child nestled onto her shoulder.

"Time to go," he said softly. "Maybe we'll catch the fireworks from your place."

"Okay," she whispered.

They met his mother in the darkening sun-porch on their way out.

Stephanie took both of Maddie's hands. "Let's get together soon," she whispered. "I want to hear about your work."

"I'd love to," Maddie said, surprised that she meant it. She sensed Stephanie had a quiet strength, was the kind of person you could trust.

At the car, Maddie opened the door to the backseat and Jake carefully lowered the sleeping Sarah into her booster seat, doing up her seatbelt and gently propping her head to one side. Their headlights cut broad swaths in the undergrowth as they swung onto the dusky driveway.

They didn't say much during the short drive to the cabin. He pulled the car up in the driveway so they could see out across the bay. He cut the motor and they sat in the dark for a moment, both aware of the sleeping child in the back seat.

Jake took her hand and asked apologetically, "Trial by fire?"

She laughed. "No, it was fun."

A loud *BOOM* reverberated across the water and a chrysanthemum of brightly colored stars exploded in the dark sky.

"It's magic," she said.

"It could be."

She didn't know what to say to that, so she leaned her head back against the seat and just watched as red and blue spirals shot into the night. Remembering the feel of his body on hers in that moment when the wet dog shook, and the heat in his eyes, she wished he could come in and they could recreate that moment. But she knew that he couldn't. Not with Sarah in the car.

"My mother likes you," he said. She sensed how important that was to him.

"I like her." His sister's words echoed in her head. "I have to go back in the fall, you know."

For a while he didn't say anything, just rubbed the back of her hand with a calloused thumb as the fireworks lit up the sky. "I know," he said. "We'll worry about that later."

Then he leaned over and kissed her. A deep, full-on kiss.

Cracks and booms echoed in her ears and Maddie felt like the sparks were falling right inside the car.

Limp from a day spent out-of-doors, she sank into the kiss. In the darkness of the moment, she wrapped an arm around his neck and pulled him close, letting her feelings lead the way.

When a final shattering boom announced the end of the fireworks, Jake slowly pulled away. His eyes were hooded, hot with promise, as the last dazzling sparks fell from the sky.

Sarah whimpered in the backseat.

"Time to go," Maddie said and opened the car door. "Thank you. I haven't had many days like this."

"I could show you more."

She just bet he could. He had shown her a whole new world today, the family, the friends, exactly what she'd always wanted.

"Thank you," she whispered, and slipped out of the car.

After the car slowly pulled away, tail lights disappearing down the dark lane, Maddie didn't go into the cabin straight away. The night was so lovely, the soft breeze scented with honeysuckle and the shushing waves breaking on the shore, so instead, she sat on the porch and stared at the stars, crazy bright in the dark lake night.

She had breezed—well, maybe not breezed, but not stumbled either—through the day and at times it had actually been fun. Everyone had made her feel, if not quite part of the family, then pretty darn close. What she wouldn't give to have grown up in a family like that. And to have given Jenny that experience too.

And Jake's mother, Stephanie. At first Maddie felt she had bumbled their meeting, but Stephanie had been so nice, not cold and judgmental like Mark's mother. In fact, by the end, she had almost forgotten Stephanie *was* Jake's mother.

Things were changing, *she* was changing, and she was trying to sit back and let it happen because so far, touch wood, it was all good. She didn't mind living alone, her work routine was hitting a rhythm, she actually enjoyed meeting new people and—she smiled, a warm feeling rising up from her belly—she was making some friends. The only thing that would make it better was if Jenny was here. And that was why she had to go back.

No, it was best to focus on her show and making sure

Jenny came back to her in the fall, as planned. But did that necessarily preclude a summer fling with Jake? She was thirty-five, surely she could have a fling if she wanted. They both knew the score; knew she was leaving in the fall.

But she couldn't get Colleen's words out of her head. *He's been left before. He's more vulnerable than he looks.* The last thing she wanted was for him to be hurt again.

Sometimes she almost forgot she was only in Fortune Bay for the summer, forgot that this wasn't really her life. Her brows met in a frown. She had better be careful, not let down her guard. Sure, everyone seemed nice, seemed to accept her, but no one knew where she came from. No one knew about her family. She blew out a breath. Hopefully they never would.

Maddie rested her head on the back of the couch and stared at the stars in the lake night sky. Jenny wouldn't be with her forever and, at the thought of spending the rest of her life alone, always coming home to an empty house, a cold ache grew in her chest.

She thought about Jake and their easy, joking camaraderie as they painted the porch. Who decreed she always had to be alone? Maybe there was someone out there, someone caring and handsome with sparkling blue eyes, who wanted to sit on this couch in the evening with her.

Hey, if you're going to dream, why not dream big?

Chapter 23

The day after the picnic, Jake took Sarah to Colleen's for the afternoon so he could work on the kitchen. He wanted to cut a new window but was afraid to start. His concentration was scattered, all he could think about was Maddie and the tongue-twisting kiss they'd shared the evening before. When he realized he was staring at the blank kitchen wall, he decided enough was enough. He took off his tool belt, hung it on the back of a kitchen chair and headed out the door.

When he reached the cabin, he paused on the porch. The darkroom door was wide open; the room was empty. He stood in the doorway, hands behind his back and looked inside. A row of eight by tens was lined up on the counter. Maddie had never offered to show him how she developed the black and whites, but now he wanted to know. He wanted to know everything about her.

Maddie stepped out of the cabin, onto the porch. Her eyes widened when she saw him standing in the darkroom doorway.

Silence hung in the muggy air between them. "Show me," he said.

Her eyes darted left and right as if looking for a place to hide. She rubbed her palms on her shorts and smiled at him thinly. "Look at any you want."

"No. Show me how you do it."

"Oh, that." She bit her lip. "If you really want to see."

He tried not to look at her lips. "I do."

Nerves shimmered off her in waves. She didn't move, so he took a step back into the closet-sized room to give her room to pass.

She squared her shoulders, stretched her neck to one side as if it had suddenly developed a kink, and crossed the porch to the darkroom door. Flipping over the 'BUSY' sign that hung on the door, she closed the door firmly and turned the lock.

She frowned at him over her shoulder. He could tell he was making her nervous. He shoved his hands in his pockets to make sure he wouldn't reach for her. Not yet.

She took a deep breath and stepped into the narrow room, closing the bathroom door and kicking scatter rugs into the cracks beneath both doors with her feet. Then she went to work.

"This is the wet side of the room," she said. Her voice came out in a hoarse squawk. She cleared her throat. Lining up three plastic trays on the counter, she filled them from three plastic jugs stored on the shelf underneath, then ran water into another tray in the old cement laundry sink in the corner.

She turned to the opposite wall, pulled a binder down from a high shelf and set it on the counter. "This is the dry side."

He looked over her shoulder as she leafed through the pages of the book. On the left were plastic sleeves of negatives, on the right, rows of tiny black and white photographs.

"What are those?"

"Contact sheets." She cleared her throat again. "I develop the negatives in this small size first, to see which ones are good enough to enlarge."

She flipped back and forth in the book, murmured, "I don't know," pushed her hair behind her ear. Finally, she found a tiny picture that seemed to satisfy her and pulled a negative strip from a sleeve on the opposite page. She held it up to the light, then turned abruptly and walked straight into his chest.

"Sorry," he said. He tried to step back to give her more room, but only gained a few inches before running into the laundry sink.

"It's okay," she answered, not looking at him.

"This is the enlarger," she continued quickly, lifting the cover off a piece of equipment that looked like a giant microscope. Instead of looking in through the top though, she fed the negative strip into a high bracket, then switched on a small, red light bulb in a socket plugged into an outlet on the wall.

Look at me, he thought, as if by telepathy he could turn her around and into his arms. He wanted to turn her by the shoulders, but instead, forced himself to follow her movements. She was letting him into her world. He would wait, and see.

Finally, she did turn. His fists clenched in his pockets. She looked him straight in the eye, reached over her head and pulled a string hanging from the ceiling. The room went dark.

The safelight created a halo of red in the center of the room with darkness crowding in on them from the edges. Squished like sardines in a closet, the thick warmth of the small space pressed in on him.

"Could be quite claustrophobic in here," he murmured.

"You get used to it." She brushed past him to reach up to a high shelf on the dry side for a flat box of paper. His fingers twitched, burning to run down her long sides as she stretched up inches in front of him. He tried to keep his mind on her actions but heat and the sweet scent of sunshine radiated off her neck, perfuming the intimate space.

"The paper is extremely light sensitive," she said. "The slightest crack of outside light can ruin it for good, but the frequency of the red light is safe."

She stood at the enlarger with her back to him and he moved in, longing to blow on the soft hairs on nape of her neck where her ponytail was falling down.

Her voice brought him back with a start. "This timer is connected to the enlarger. It only takes a few seconds to imprint the image on the paper." At the flick of a switch, the enlarger glowed, showing a reversed, negative image of a child's face that entirely filled the page below.

He stood behind her, trying to focus on the image. His turn to talk. He cleared his throat. "I see why they call it an enlarger."

Jeeze. Could he sound any more stupid?

Energy pulsed off her body, arching to his across the sliver of space between them. The musk of her skin filled the warm dark. He closed his eyes and breathed her in.

The enlarger light clicked off and Maddie scooped up the paper, turned quickly and walked straight into his chest again.

"Sorry," they said in awkward unison. His arms went out to steady her but he forced himself to drop them and step away to give her room.

She crossed to the wet side, barely two feet away, and swung the arm on the timer around, dropping the still blank sheet of paper into the first pan of liquid.

"Now watch this," she said, her voice soft and diffused.

As she tipped the pan repeatedly, the liquid sloshed gently back and forth. He moved in close, hovering over her, echoing the curve of her body. He didn't feel claustrophobic anymore and his throbbing blood had nothing to do with the confines of the space.

Still, he forced himself to concentrate on the process and, as he watched over her shoulder, the liquid rolled from one end of the tray to the other until patches of grey began to form on the paper. His interest piqued as the image slowly darkened under the clear elixir. Like magic, Sarah appeared on the page, a candy apple in her hand, a look of pure joy on her face.

His own face broke into an answering smile and his hands moved up to rest on Maddie's shoulders. "Wow."

"I know," she said in complete understanding. "It does it to me every time.

"Quick now—move," she ordered, and he jumped out of the way. She lifted the paper from the liquid with tongs, dropped it into the next tray of liquid and reset the timer. "This will stop the image from darkening any further."

All business now, she tilted the second pan of liquid as she had the first, repeating the process in the last tray, then holding the picture under running water in the sink. When she turned around, her eyes wide and happy, she held a dripping picture of Sarah.

"Finished?" he asked, his voice a low rumble.

Her eyes flared, inches away, hot in the red glow.

"Yes," she whispered, but she made no move to turn on the light.

He reached for her then, his lips closing on hers. To hell with September. He wanted her now.

The print dropped from her hand to the counter and she melted into the kiss. Like an addict, relief flooded his system as she wrapped her arms around his neck. This was what he needed, her body pressed against him, her curves molding to his chest.

He swung her around, against the door, bringing her hands up beside her head and pinning them to the wood. He deepened the kiss, mouths moving, tongues searching, exchanging heat for heat until she turned to wax beneath him.

A loud knock sounded through the door behind her. Jake sprang back, but kept her pinned to the door. She didn't struggle. They were both breathing hard.

Frankie's muffled voice called, "Maddie?"

He held her eyes in silence. Maddie's lips pressed together, holding back a laugh.

"Working in here," she called. "Be out in a minute."

"Won't she suspect something?" Jake whispered.

"You can't stop in the middle."

"Tell me about it." He moaned quietly, leaning back in and gently grinding his hips on hers. A giggle escaped her as he gently bit her lower lip. He wasn't nearly done, but he gave her another kiss and pushed himself away.

Maddie sagged against the door as if his weight had been all that was holding her up. Then, with her eyes on his, she reached up and turned on the light.

A slow smile lit her face. He leaned in and kissed her again. A quick kiss. He'd made up his mind. They'd waited long enough.

Sliding an arm around her waist, he unlatched the door and swung it open.

Frankie was standing right outside. She stepped back and smirked. "Oh. Sorry."

Maddie's cheeks burned red as if still lit by the safe light.

"It's okay," Jake said. "She was showing me how it all works in here. I have to go, though. Get back to work. That kitchen won't reno itself."

He took his arm from around Maddie's waist and ran the back of his hand down her cheek. "See you."

She nodded.

"You too Frankie," he added as he jumped to the ground and rounded the corner of the cabin, his heart light and a smile on his lips.

Chapter 24

Maddie dried one of Augusta's china dishes and put it on the kitchen shelf. She couldn't stop thinking about Jake and the kiss in the darkroom two days before. And the picnic. He'd showed her a whole new world; one she'd always dreamed of. She tried to see herself fitting into the picture, but the image was blurred. She didn't know how a family worked. Didn't know what was expected. Didn't know what to do.

A determined *tap tap tap* sounded nearby. *Woodpecker?* Lately they'd been drilling outside her bedroom window.

Tap tap tap. No, not a bird, but she couldn't see anyone on the porch when she looked through the big front window, so she dried her hands and went to look through the haze of the screen door.

A little pixie in a pink T-shirt and shorts, with purple flip-flops on her feet and her arm slung around the neck of her dog, waited on the porch.

When she knocked again, Maddie swung open the screen door. "Hello Sarah."

"Hello. You have a nice house." Maddie recognized the overly-mature tone of an only child who was used to talking to adults. As a child, Jenny had spoken the same way.

"Thank you. Would you like to come in?"

"Yes, please."

Her reply was a little too polite, putting Maddie's maternal radar on instant alert. At first she was afraid Rex would follow Sarah in, but the shaggy old dog waited outside the door as his young owner marched into the living room. He didn't seem to pose a threat, not like the snarling collarless dogs that ranged through the rundown trailer parks of her youth, but still, Maddie wasn't getting too close.

The little girl sat primly on the couch in a way that signaled a formal visit.

"Would you like a cookie?" Maddie asked, her mind racing as she put some cookies on a small fancy plate and poured a glass of milk. Jake would be crazy with worry, if he even knew she was gone.

Of course he knew.

Sarah carefully chose a cookie and said, "Mmm, Children's Delight."

Trying to keep it casual, Maddie asked, "Do you know your phone number?" Sarah rattled it off, far more interested in the cookies than what Maddie was doing as she punched the numbers into her cell.

It only rang once before Jake answered, his voice rasping. "Yes."

"She's here."

A sharp exhalation of breath—she could imagine him running his hand through his already rumpled hair.

"I'll be right there." The line went dead.

She flipped the phone shut and sat down beside Sarah, who had slowed on the cookies and was regarding her intently. Sarah got right to the point. "I have no mother, you know."

"I know." Maddie wasn't sure where to go from there. "But you have your grandmother."

Sarah face twisted in a plaintive smile. "It's not the same." She cast her eyes down, then quickly flashed them up to catch Maddie's reaction.

Maddie crossed her arms on her chest. She knew when she was being played.

Luckily, she didn't have to answer because Jake burst through the door and snatched the little girl up in his arms.

"Where did you go? I looked everywhere. How did you get here?" He held her eye to eye. Anger quickly replaced panic and his brows lowered ominously.

Sarah, however, seemed unafraid. "Across the field. Rex

wanted to come so I had to follow him. He wouldn't listen."

Jake regarded her, one eye squinting, almost closed. "Next time, you let him go and come and get me."

"Yes, Daddy," she said, wrapping her arms around his neck.

Maddie tried to restrain a smile. Sarah had Jake wrapped tight as a twist tie around her little finger. He was going to be toast when his daughter hit her teens, and boy did she wish she could be here to see it.

She held out the platter. "Children's Delight?"

Jake took a cookie and looked at Maddie for the first time. He puffed out a breath. "Thanks."

Maddie smiled, unreasonably happy to have him in the cabin again. "No problem."

"But we've got to go."

Her heart deflated to normal size.

"Can Maddie come for dinner, Dad?" Sarah pleaded.

Jake's eyes widened in panic. "I'm tearing out a wall in the kitchen."

Tearing out a wall? Maddie wondered. *How does he cook?*

"The kitchen is all torn up," he said.

"That's okay," she said, almost simultaneously. "We could eat here. And go for a swim at Frankie's dock first."

"Yeah," Sarah shouted, the same moment Jake said, "We couldn't impose."

"Frankie's away for the week," Maddie said. "She said it would be all right."

In the pause that followed she could see him considering the idea. "I'll bring steak," he said.

"Good," she replied. "I'll make a salad."

For a moment they eyed each other like people jockeying in a doorway. What could possibly happen with Sarah in the mix?

* * *

Maddie lounged in her bathing suit in the hot sun on

Frankie's dock. Summer had blossomed—each day progressing from clear mornings to hot, languid afternoons, and on to golden evenings. She just wished Jenny could be there to share it.

This was an afternoon to remember, as were most of the days she spent with Jake. He and Sarah tried to lure her into the water but she knew if she actually went in, her hair would turn into a ball of curls.

So Jake played in the water with Sarah, teaching her to swim, tossing her squealing up into the air, throwing sticks for Rex who would swim out and fetch. Then they all hauled up onto the dock, Maddie shrieking with laughter when the dog shook freezing droplets of water onto her sun-warmed back.

She volunteered to go back to the cabin for cold drinks and, when she returned, Jake and Sarah were standing at the end of the dock, straining to see something that appeared to be swimming underneath.

"I saw it," Sarah insisted. "It went right under there." She pointed, peering intently under the dock.

"What did?" Maddie set the drinks down and walked out to join them.

"I don't think so." Jake looked underneath, then glanced skeptically back at his daughter. Maddie craned her neck to see what had caught their attention.

Then Sarah shrieked, four wet hands grabbed her, and Maddie was airborne. She had just enough time to take quick gulp of air before—*smack!* She hit the water.

So cold! An ear-piercing scream burst from her lips as she surfaced, sputtering with laughter. By then, though, the water already felt warmer. Lovely, in fact. She paddled around as Sarah wrestled Jake off the end of the dock, his long arm taking her with him at the last minute.

He was trouble in the water, Maddie could see that right away. She could imagine him as a thirteen-year-old boy, terrorizing his brother and sister. He hadn't changed much in the intervening years. Grabbing her leg, he pulled her under, then shot up, wrapped a strong arm around her waist and pulled her to the surface.

No point in sulking; he was clearly unrepentant. Apparently those were the laws of the dock—anyone who doesn't go in on their own is fair game.

Sarah and the dog paddled back to shore. Jake laughed and kissed Maddie on the lips. A hot snake of lust hissed in her belly. She wanted to rub her wet body against him, but instead, he pulled her over to the dock. *Rats.*

They climbed out of the water and lolled in the sun, watching Sarah and Rex play on an air mattress in the shallows.

Jake reached over and stroked the tattoo on her wrist, a chain that wrapped around it, morphing into birds that flew up her inner arm. "When did you get that?"

Maddie laughed, rolled over onto her back and put her arm over her eyes, hiding the birds. "I was seventeen. Young and foolish."

It wasn't that she was ashamed of the tattoo, in fact, part of her was proud of what it represented. Freedom. But Mark had hated it, and her boss Eileen did too. She insisted Maddie keep it covered at work and now, Maddie herself sometimes thought it might be better if she didn't have a tattoo at all.

"I like it," he said.

She rolled back on to her stomach and turned her face toward him.

"What do you do with Sarah all summer?" she said, deliberately changing the subject.

"The woods closed a few days ago because of the dryness," Jake said, squinting at the sun. "It's not safe to work if the forest's this dry. I'll probably be laid off for six weeks and after that my holidays kick in. That pretty well does it."

They rolled onto their stomachs and watched Sarah battle the bucking air mattress in the water, losing more often than she won.

"I guess I'll work on the house," he said. "Kitchen's torn

apart. I'm building some cupboards, replacing the counter. Have to get all new appliances, too."

"Sounds like fun," Maddie said dreamily. "Like building a house." She had never thought about building a house before, had never considered the possibility, but now that she had, it did sound like fun. Permanent. Settled.

"I've always wanted to build a house in the field next to the cabin," he said. "It's got the same great view as the cabin and with very little work could have a nice beach and a dock. Then I'd get a boat."

"We'd be neighbors," she said. But even as she said it she remembered—she wouldn't be here. The playful mood abruptly went south. In an attempt to recoup, she sat up briskly and said, "I think I'll go back and start dinner. Don't hurry. Come over when you're ready." She stood up and waved to Sarah as she hurried off the dock.

Back at the cabin, she changed out of her wet bathing suit and into the shorts and tank top that had become her summer uniform, adding earrings and a splash of lipstick in a nod to dressing up. Unfortunately, there wasn't much she could do about her hair, which had dried into a mass of red curls.

She checked the refrigerator. The jellied salad had firmed up nicely. She didn't actually have to work on dinner. It wasn't the real reason she had rushed off the dock. She had just needed some distance.

The pull of this man was strong in her belly, but she couldn't trust the feeling. Growing up, she'd watched her mother go through it, again and again: the exhilarating early days with a new man, always *the one*, followed by the frightening descent into depression and self-abuse when he inevitably left.

Although, in this case, she'd be the one who was leaving.

She huffed a half laugh. Maybe the stick in her tarot reading was really for her to use to ward off her feelings for Jake.

When he and Sarah arrived, Maddie met them at the

door. They had been home and changed into dry clothes, their wet slicked-down hair intensifying the strong similarity between father and daughter. Jake held tightly to Sarah's hand as she danced on the spot in excitement. Rex waved his big tail and sported a red bandana around his neck. He nosed his way in and gave Maddie's hand big slurp with his tongue. Startled, she gave him a cautious pat on the head.

Sarah looked cute and huggable in turquoise overalls and she immediately told Maddie they were, "brand new from the store." Jake looked gorgeous and huggable too, his drying hair curling irresistibly at the collar, the soft blue shirt, open at the neck.

He fired up the barbeque, a rusting hulk that Maddie never dared to use, a remnant of his residence at the cabin, he said. In the kitchen, she wrapped potatoes in tin foil and brought them out with the steaks to where Jake was watching the flame. Then she made up a plate of cheese and crackers and joined them on the porch.

When the meat was ready, Maddie put the jellied salad on the table on the porch. Sarah clapped and giggled as it jiggled and shimmered, orange carrot shreds folded in lime green light.

They ate on the porch, lined up on the couch with Sarah in the middle. Jake's eyes sought Maddie's over Sarah's head.

How long can we keep doing this? she wondered. *Keep putting Sarah in the middle like this?*

"I love this jelly," Sarah said. "It's like the one Grandma makes."

"Maybe it is," Maddie agreed. "It's from that box of family recipes in the kitchen where I found the Children's Delight."

"Mmmm, Children's Delight," Sarah moaned, making Maddie laugh.

"You might think I'm crazy," Maddie said to Jake, a blush spreading from her throat to her cheeks. "But I could swear I put the recipe box on the window sill every time and yet it's always on the top kitchen shelf when I look for it."

"You think it's Aunt Augusta." It was a statement, not a question, and since he kept right on eating, she couldn't judge his reaction.

"Sometimes I do," she admitted, laughing.

He looked up and smiled, but she was relieved to see he wasn't outright laughing at her.

"There were things I wondered about when I lived here, too," he said. "For one, I never felt she approved of my standards of tidiness. Augusta liked things done just so. I always thought she was picking up after me. I'd find my jacket hung up when I knew I'd left it on the couch, and beer caps on the counter were a definite 'no'."

"Are you talking about a ghost?" Sarah asked, wide-eyed.

"Yes, but a friendly ghost," Jake answered. "An aunty ghost who likes to clean."

Sarah giggled.

The telephone rang and Maddie walk over and rummaged through her purse. She frowned when Mark's name came up on the display.

"Is she there?" he asked before she could speak. The panic in his voice turned Maddie's insides to ice.

"What do you mean?"

"Jenny's run away."

Chapter 25

"Her dad doesn't know how long she's been gone. He doesn't seem to know anything."

Maddie stood in the doorway, phone clutched to her chest. From her voice, Jake could hear she was teetering on the cliff edge of panic. He put his hands on her shoulders and held her gaze with his eyes, willing her back from the edge. He knew exactly how she felt. He'd been teetering there himself only hours ago.

Focus on the facts.

"Take a deep breath," he said firmly. "How long has she been gone?"

"Mark doesn't know. Five, maybe six hours. It must be something or he wouldn't have called. He said they'd had a fight. She's turned off her phone."

Maddie clutched her chest, obviously having difficulty breathing. Jake steered her to a kitchen chair.

"He doesn't like the kids she met at the acting course. She wants to stay out late; he wants her home. He asked if I knew where she would have gone.

"How would I know?" Her voice rose dangerously again. "*I* haven't been there. *I* haven't met her new friends. By the sound of it, neither has he."

"Okay, it's okay." Jake stroked her hair while he thought. "It's only been a few hours. It's still daylight. She's a big girl, in her own territory. She'll be okay."

He was running out of comforting things to say. "Let's make some coffee and wait for her to phone." It wasn't much, but it was all he could think of.

"Who's Jenny?" Sarah asked. He'd forgotten she was there, sitting quiet and wide-eyed on the porch couch. Maddie sent him a look and went and sat down beside her. Jake went inside to make coffee, but watched them through the window.

Maddie put her arm around the little girl's shoulders, Jake suspected as much for her own comfort as Sarah's.

"She's my daughter."

"A little girl like me?" Sarah's voice was pinched.

"Oh no, a big girl, like Brandy."

Sarah nodded. "Brandy's almost a grownup. She'll be okay." Mimicking her father, she patted Maddie's hand.

Jake brought out the coffee and together they tried to figure out where Jenny could have gone, but eventually they fell silent. The minutes ticked by. Twilight settled and Sarah fell asleep between them.

Jake lay his arm across the back of the couch and massaged Maddie's rigid shoulder.

"I knew Jenny and Mark were having problems," she whispered. "But I never dreamed anything like this would happen. She has never run away before. I should never have left her with him. I knew what he's like—totally inflexible. She told me she was unhappy and I made her stay."

"It is not your fault. Kids that age are loose cannons; you never know what will set them off."

She turned to face him, her face twisted with worry. "You don't understand. I ran away when I was exactly her age. Ran and never went back. I can't lose her. She's all I have." Tears spilled over and ran down her cheeks.

Christ. Not tears. He had to think of something to say.

"We were wild at that age," he said. "Kid's stuff mostly, but we frightened our parents more than once."

That got her attention, so he wracked his brain for a story to distract her. "One time, just after I got my driver's license, I took Mom's old beater and drove Sean and Blue to Bremerton on a Friday night, just for the hell of it.

"We were supposed to be at a dance in Majestic. Of course, it took a couple of hours longer than we figured to get there and back. We were almost home when we had a flat and had to change the tire. That took hours too. We didn't have a clue. Eventually, our neighbor Bob Foster drove by and stopped to give us a hand. I don't think he ever told our folks. I guess he figured we'd get in enough trouble just for being so late.

"Our curfew was ten o'clock and it was after midnight when we got home. We were scared shitless by that time. Mom hit the roof. Dad wanted to take us out back and teach us some respect, but Mom convinced him to stop. We were grounded for a month though—no car for two. But we'd been okay the whole time. Just witless." He was rambling, but it seemed to ease her mind, gave her something to think about besides her daughter.

He got up and went into the cabin and filled their cups. He set both cups on the table and lifted Sarah's sleeping head onto his lap so he could sit beside Maddie.

He put his arm around her shoulders and they sat together watching the darkness fall over the lake, her mood spiraling from hand wringing down to a blank-eyed stare.

Occasionally she'd say something— "Where would she go? There is nowhere for her to go." —then she'd fall silent again.

Jake remembered the hollow dread he'd felt when Sarah was missing—and that had only been for a few minutes. He didn't think he could have handled any more.

"She'll be okay. She's a smart girl." He hoped so. He didn't know what else to say. The tension crawled along his skin. All this caffeine couldn't be helping so he decided to make some herbal tea. And look for some cookies. He had to do something.

The phone rang. Maddie stared at it for a moment, then looked at Jake as it rang again.

"Answer it," he said. "Maybe she's home."

Jake focused his attention on Maddie's face as she put her cell phone to her ear, willing it to be good news. His heart sank when she closed her eyes and a tear leaked out.

Then she said, "Where are you?"

The fear and tension drained from her face and her body went limp as she listened to her daughter on the phone. He exhaled a breath of relief.

"What time do you get in? Okay. I'll be there. Wait for me. Don't—go—anywhere." She snapped the phone shut, took the hot drink from his hand and, closing her eyes, sank back into the couch.

"That was Jenny. She's on the ferry. She did run away, but thank goodness she's running to me."

* * *

Jenny found an empty row of seats on the ferry and slid all the way across, tight to the window, hoping no one would come and sit beside her. Her knee hopped as she thought, her heel drumming on the thin carpet. The chocolate bar and coffee she'd bought at the terminal hadn't done much to calm her down.

She couldn't tell if her mom was mad. She'd sounded sort of relieved at first on the phone, but then? She didn't know. Her heel, tap, tap, tapping on the floor, was driving her crazy, so she brought her feet up under her on the chair, glancing over her shoulder, hoping no one would tell her to put her feet down. She'd never been on the ferry before. Outside the window the lights of Seattle receded in the darkness.

It was really dark; her dad would be having a fit. No news there. She couldn't seem to do anything lately without him freaking out. Yeah, okay, this was over the line, but she'd had to do something to get his attention. And her mom's.

Since her mom's visit, she'd been sinking further and further into a dark lonely hole. During the day at acting camp with the other kids she was fine, but every evening, she dreaded going back to her dad's house. It was just fighting and yelling and "Go to your room!"

Sure she fought with her Mom, but through it all she knew that her mom loved her. Her dad? She wasn't so sure. She felt lonely most of the time. At first it was cool, so grown up being there without her mom. Her dad didn't really know her and at first he gave her some room.

But then he changed. Now he seemed pissed all the time, working late every evening. And so was Kate. So she started staying out later too, hanging with some of the kids she'd met, but then he threw a fit if she wasn't home, in her room, when he got home. Why the hell should she be?

After the fight they'd had last night, she'd felt sick to her stomach all day at the thought of spending another lonely month in that big empty house. She was too far away from her school friends to see very much of them and the kids in the new acting group lived all over the city. Once the camp was over next week they'd go back to their old friends and she'd be alone.

Her mom didn't seem to want her anymore either. A tear spilled over onto her cheek. She'd just left her there, in the city, alone. Probably glad to get rid of her. Jenny felt a twinge of conscience remembering some of the fights they'd had last winter, some of the things she'd said, but she never thought her mom would *leave*. Even when her dad called and invited her for the summer, she thought her mom would be there, at the apartment, and she could at least see her every little while. She never thought she'd leave the city *completely*.

She had to talk her mom into letting her stay. She just had to.

* * *

Jake had turned into a mother hen when Maddie left to drive to the ferry. Of course she could drive herself. If Sarah hadn't been there, she'd bet he would have insisted on coming along. Still, it was kind of nice to have someone who shared your concern.

When Jenny walked out of the terminal building, she looked more like a college student coming home for the holidays than a little girl running away. Maddie hugged her, then scolded, then hugged her again, but as soon as they got in the car, Jenny started to rant.

"You *have* to let me come and live with you for the rest of the summer."

This was exactly what Maddie wanted to hear, but although her heart cried 'yes', she forced herself to retain a stern demeanor. At least for the moment.

"He's horrible," Jenny moaned.

Knowing her daughter's penchant for drama, Maddie took her words with a grain of salt. But she also knew her ex, so she could understand her daughter's anger. She managed to restrain the "I told you so" that hovered on her lips.

"Well, dear, you agreed to the arrangement." *Jumped at it is more like it.* "Now you have to make it work."

"I can't," Jenny wailed, sounding barely any older than Sarah.

"You have to. We'll talk about it in the morning. I spoke to your father after you called, but now I want you to call and tell him you're all right. He was worried sick."

Serves the bastard right. But Maddie was determined to take the high road on this. Take the high road, and still win in the end.

To her surprise Jenny didn't argue. She meekly pulled out her phone and punched in the number, then waited for her father to answer.

"Hi, Dad," Jenny said, her voice quiet.

As they sped down the highway in the darkened car, Maddie could hear Mark bark out a question but couldn't quite make out the words.

"Yeah, I'm okay. ... Mom came and got me at the ferry. ...Yeah, I guess I'm coming back." She gave Maddie a mournful glance. "I'll call you tomorrow. ...Okay. Bye, Dad."

They drove in silence for a few minutes more and finally Jenny said, "I'm sorry. I'm sorry if you were worried and I'm sorry Dad was worried, but I really can't stay there. I want to come and stay with you."

"You don't even know where I'm living." As they drove through the village of Majestic, Maddie saw it through her daughter's eyes, the deserted main street illuminated intermittently by streetlights, and was surprised she hadn't already turned and fled.

"They don't want me. I swear they'd be happy if I left."

"We'll see in the morning." It was all Maddie trusted herself to say.

* * *

Jake stood at his front window, feeling trapped inside the house by the sleeping child upstairs. He had wanted to go with Maddie and just hoped she had found her daughter safe.

When he heard the knock on the door, his body tensed. He lunged for it, stopped with his hand on the knob to regain his composure, then pulled it open.

Maddie stood in a ring of light on the porch.

"Did you find her?"

"Yes. She's fine. Asleep on the couch."

He huffed out a breath, only now realizing how tense he had been. "Thanks for letting me know. I was worried."

She stood on the porch and stared up at the starry sky.

Why is she here? She seemed to have something on her mind, so he stayed as he was, leaning on the doorframe, hands plunged deep in his pockets to give her some space.

She turned toward him. "I wanted to thank you, for being there for me." She went up on her toes and kissed him on the cheek.

When she pulled away. the spot where her lips had touched burned in the cool night air. He wanted to take her in his arms and kiss her until her toes curled, wanted to make her understand what he was feeling—and would have, if he understood it himself. All he knew for sure was he wanted to see her again. Soon.

"Any time."

Later, hung like a web connecting them in the darkness. They held each other's eyes for a couple seconds more, then she smiled. His stomach rolled over and Jimbo jumped to attention, but she was already walking away and, with a wave, disappeared down the dark driveway.

Jake shook his head with a ghost of a smile. So, 'thanks' and a kiss on the cheek was all he would get tonight. Maturity was highly over-rated.

Chapter 26

The follow morning, Maddie slipped past the couch where her daughter was sleeping and went into the bathroom. She stopped in the darkroom on her way out and leafed through her growing pile of images.

Her new life. How would Jenny fit into all this? By the time acting camp finished and she could come to Fortune Bay, there would only be a month and a half of summer left before it was time to go. And in truth, Maddie didn't want to return to the city one minute sooner than necessary.

Jenny emerged from the cabin, rubbing her eyes like a child.

"Was the bathroom somewhere out here?"

Maddie pointed the way, then went in and made a pot of coffee, poured herself a cup and settled down on the porch. A few minutes later Jenny flopped down beside her on the couch, freshly scrubbed and apparently unfazed by her recent adventure.

"This is great Mom. What a view."

"It is great. I'm happy here." Maddie took a sip of her coffee. Her hand shook and she put down the cup. She wanted her daughter here so badly. "Except for missing you."

"I've missed you too," Jenny said, wiggling her hand through Maddie's arm to link elbows. "Dad's been pretty tough on me."

"Your dad can be tough, but from what I've heard, you've been tough on him too. I don't know if I would have let you do any of the things he objected to either." She wanted her daughter back, but they couldn't return to last winter's pattern of arguments and recriminations. Might as well clear up any fairy tales spinning in her head right now.

Jenny rested her head on Maddie's shoulder. "Yeah, but

at least I know you love me when you say it."

Maddie blinked back a tear and kissed her daughter's hair, straight and shiny and smelling like apricot shampoo. "I do. But your dad loves you too. He just has trouble showing it."

"I know, but I still want to come and live with you."

"What about your acting course? How is that going?"

"It's brilliant!" Jenny bounced up, turning sideways to face her. "They are talking about starting a Young Thespians group at the university next winter. I've met some new friends and we like to go out for coffee after class. That's what our fight was about. Dad has a fit if I go."

"I might feel the same way, you know. You are too young to be out on the streets alone late at night. And when did you start drinking coffee?"

"With Dad. All the kids do it. At first it tasted kind of gross but now I like it. Dad has this great cappuccino machine and we make lattes and things on the weekends." She sighed. "Or we did. He and Kate work a lot of weekends. At first we had fun, shopping and going out to dinner and stuff, but now it just seems we fight a lot." She sighed again, a hitch in her breath.

Maddie's heart ached to see her daughter unhappy, but maybe living with her father had been a good lesson. It had certainly helped guide their relationship back onto more stable ground.

"I'd love to have you here, but you have unfinished business in Seattle. First, you're committed to finishing the course. How long do you have left with that?" she asked, although she already knew the answer

"Only one week. Then can I come?"

"Second, you have to work it out with your father. You agreed to stay there for the summer, you know."

"He won't care." Jenny winced. "He thinks I'm a burden."

Her daughter's sad smile tugged at Maddie's heart. She put her arm around her shoulder and gave her a hug. "I never think you're a burden. I've missed you every day. I'd love to have you here with me. We'll work it out."

Maddie kissed the top of her head again, then stood up. "Okay. Let's go and get some breakfast."

* * *

When they walked into the café, Louise stopped pouring coffee in mid-stream and held up a hand. "Don't tell me, let me guess. Thelma and Louise. God, Maddie, does she ever look like you."

Maddie laughed and introduced Jenny to Louise.

Jenny grinned and climbed up on a stool. "Smells great in here. I'm starving."

Louise pointed to the glass-covered muffin display case. "The regular?"

"No, I think we'll go for the full deal today," Maddie answered, raising an eyebrow at Jenny for confirmation. They started with coffee and Maddie gasped when Jenny scooped two heaping teaspoons of sugar into hers, mentally toting up future dental bills and assigning them to Mark. After all, he got her hooked in the first place.

Louise slapped plates heaping with pancakes and sausage down in front of them, and Maddie and Jenny dug in, Jenny eyeing Louise's eclectic outfit: pink and orange paisley shorts and an orange Santana t-shirt.

"Where do you shop?" Jenny asked.

"Vintage. I know some great places in Seattle. I go over quite often. We'll go shopping sometime if you want."

As they drove back to the cabin, Jenny said, "She's great. Have you made any other cool friends here?"

"I've met lots of people," Maddie said as they got out of the car. "Come and look at my new pictures."

Jenny looked around the darkroom. "Great space." As a child, she'd spent her share of time in the cramped bathroom-darkroom at their Seattle apartment. When she was still too short to see into the sink, she stood on a stool, fascinated by the images that formed in the dark, liquid pools.

"It's working out well," Maddie said, pulling out a stack of proofs and setting them on the counter where the light streamed in through the open door.

Jenny moved though the pictures with a practiced eye, commenting, "nice contrast," or "cool shot" at the landscapes of the forest and lake, laughing at the ones of tall, exotic Louise dancing with short, formal Mr. Wilson at the Festival.

When she got to the picture of Sarah and Jake, nose to nose in profile, staring intently into each other's eyes, matching grins on their faces, she considered it for almost a minute. The next one was Jake at the logger sports, shirt off, muscles flexing, wielding an axe.

"Wow, Mom. He's hot."

Maddie laughed. "There were a lot of them there that day and most of them were hot."

The next picture was Jake again, leaning on the porch post, chewing on a piece of long grass, staring into the camera.

Jenny turned to her mother, photo in hand. "Who is this guy?"

Maddie blushed like the child under the scrutiny of her teenage mother. "He's my friend, my landlord, Jake. The guy I went on the date with."

"Mo-om." Jenny drew out the word as she studied the photo again. "When do I get to meet him?"

"Oh, you'll meet him." Maddie laughed, taking the photograph out of Jenny's hand and putting it back in the stack. And how would she introduce him then? As a friend? A boyfriend? Not just as her landlord. Not anymore.

She led Jenny back out onto the porch. "So. What have you decided?"

"I guess I have to go back," Jenny said reluctantly. "But I'll tell Dad I want to spend the rest of the summer here with you, and I will try to come back next weekend, right after I finish the course." She looked hopefully at Maddie for confirmation. "Okay?"

Maddie did a mental fist-pump, but she tried to sound calm. "Sounds like a plan."

A smile blossomed on Jenny's face. "Great. Now, can we go for a swim?"

Chapter 27

Jenny returned to Seattle on Sunday and when Mark phoned on Monday night, Maddie detected a change in his tone.

"Are you sure it's all right?" he asked stiffly. "I can keep her you know."

Maddie turned her gaze out the window to the whitecaps on the lake and slowly counted to three to put the brakes on her sharp retort. She sensed he had tried, and would have kept Jenny until the end of the summer if he had to, but was relieved nonetheless to have her taken off his hands.

And she missed Jenny terribly, so what was the point in putting them all through any more unhappiness? She could afford to be generous. Maybe at this point Mark and Jenny could still salvage something positive from their time together.

"Sure. I'm happy to have her here for the rest of the summer."

Mark sounded relieved and said he'd bring Jenny over the following Sunday afternoon.

The week flew by and Maddie tried to make a real dent in her work so she'd have time to spend with her daughter. On Friday morning, Frankie appeared at the cabin door and Maddie poured her a cup of coffee. This was new, having friends drop by, but not only could she handle it, she was secretly elated.

"So, I hear Jenny is coming for the rest of the summer."

Maddie was surprised. "How could you possibly...?" She closed her eyes, shook her head but couldn't help a smile. "Never mind."

Frankie laughed. "Small town life. You'll get used to it. Where are you going to put her?"

Maddie winced. "Upstairs?"

Frankie looked skeptically at the trap door in the ceiling. "U-huh?"

"I peeked up there when I first moved in and it's really not that bad. I think there's even a bed, although I should probably take another look at it before she comes."

They stared at the open staircase for another minute, then Frankie put down her cup and walked over to the foot of the stairs. "Let's do it."

"I guess I've been putting it off. I'm not a fan of spiders."

Frankie rolled her eyes. "I doubt Jenny is either."

"You're dying to see what's up there, aren't you?"

"You bet. I can't believe you've been here for what? —two months? —and haven't gone up."

Maddie dug two flashlights out of a kitchen drawer. "Two and a half. But it was cold then and would just have been another space to heat so I never went up."

With Frankie in the lead, they started up the narrow staircase.

"Besides," Maddie added when they reached the top, their heads brushing the trap door. "I did peek. It looked full of spider webs. And ghosts."

Frankie looked at her feigning horror. "And you're going to put your daughter up there?"

Maddie giggled nervously "I've kind of made friends with the ghost."

Frankie looked at her sharply. "You're serious."

"Jake says it's his Aunt Augusta."

"And you've seen her?"

"I've only heard her," Maddie admitted.

"Humph," Frankie said, clearly thinking it over. "Let's see if we can't rustle up a ghost."

They lifted the trap door above their heads, pushing it over onto the attic floor with a thud that raised a cloud of dust. Two more steps and their heads poked up into the attic through the opening in the floor.

The painted wood floor, now at eye level, was the same

size as the main room of the cabin, but the sharply sloping
attic walls made the room appear much smaller. A dim beam
of light forced its way through a small dirty window in the
gable wall above their heads, highlighting the swirling dust.
The air smelled dusty but slightly sweet, a smell Maddie had
come to associate with Augusta.

Teetering on the edge of the opening, Maddie went to
work on the latch on the window. It swung into the room from
a hinge on the top and hooked to a chain hanging from the
peaked roof.

Frankie began to work on the second window at the far
end. "It'll be fine for the summer," she said. "But I wouldn't
want to be up here in the winter."

Maddie reached up and pulled the string hanging from a
bare bulb in the center of the room and the dim light came to
life.

Frankie giggled. "Great color."

Maddie laughed. "Bubble-gum Pink. That's one mystery
solved."

Cartons tied with string were stacked around the opening
in the floor as if someone had lifted the trapdoor and shoved
them through, and beyond the boxes stood various pieces of
dusty furniture; an antique cradle, an upholstered rocking
chair with a badly torn seat, and a bike in the far corner in
front of an iron bed, still charming despite it's chipped white
paint.

Maddie studied the spider webs festooned on the rafters
and shook her head. "I don't know."

"This isn't too bad," Frankie said. "I wonder who the
boxes belong to."

"We never talked about me using the attic. Maybe I
should check with Jake or Stephanie."

"We won't throw anything out," Frankie said, opening a
box of hardcover books and reading off the titles. "*Girl of the
Limberlost, A Room with a View.*"

Maddie flipped open a cover and read the inscription

inside. "*Augusta Bonevue—1929.* They belonged to Jake's aunt. The ghost."

Frankie laughed. "Great. A literary ghost."

"There's a dresser up here too," Maddie said, brushing the top and sending up a cloud of dust. "I bet there's everything I'll need for Jenny."

Opening a drawer, she pulled out a wad of shredded paper. Frankie glanced up from perusing another carton of books. "Mouse nest."

Maddie dropped the paper, swallowing a shriek.

"Don't worry," Frankie added, "they've probably moved outside for the summer—and you'll be gone before they move back in."

Maddie flinched at the casual reminder of her departure.

Frankie opened another dresser drawer and pulled out an envelope. "Look. Pictures. Postcards and negatives."

She pulled out a handful of ancient black and white postcards, yellowed with age, of crumbling ruins and medieval streets and read the tiny print on the back. "*Italy.* Positively medieval."

"They must have belonged to Augusta. Jake said something about her travelling as a girl."

Frankie handed her the package. "These negatives were probably hers too."

Maddie held them up to the light streaming in through the open window, squinting at the tiny, transparent images. "Someone standing by a car, I think. They'd be fun to develop."

"I bet Stephanie would love to see them."

Maddie put them carefully back in the envelope and stashed it by the stairs. Her eyes swept over the jumble of furniture and boxes that cluttered the space. It might work for Jenny after all.

"Could you help me get some of this stuff downstairs? The bike could go in the back shed." She gave the mattress a sniff. "It's dusty, but otherwise not bad. Needs a good airing out before anyone sleeps on it though."

Together they wrestled the double mattress through the tiny opening in the floor and down the stairs. Out on the porch, Maddie took the broom to it, smacking it sharply and raising more dust. Then she left it there to freshen in the sunshine.

They swept and scrubbed, hauled and piled for the better part of the morning. In the end, the room was spare but clean, altogether adequate and possibly even charming for a teenage girl.

As the final touch. Maddie brought up the mirror from beside the front door.

"Thanks," she said as she surveyed their work. "I owe you."

"My pleasure." Frankie gave her a shoulder hug. "I can't wait to meet your daughter. I'm sorry I was away when she came before. Louise says she's great."

Maddie laughed. "Most of the time."

Frankie surveyed the room with obvious satisfaction, then she cupped her hand to her ear. "What's that I hear? My shower calling."

* * *

Jake dropped Sarah at his mother's and drove back to the cabin. The day was hot and sunny. Maybe he and Maddie would go for a swim. He couldn't stop thinking about their steamy darkroom kiss and wanted more. He'd heard Jenny was moving in soon. This was their window of opportunity and he intended to make the most of it.

A swim without Sarah and the dog offered a realm of possibilities.

As he came around the corner of the cabin he saw a mattress on the porch. He stuck his head into the kitchen and called Maddie's name. No answer. The *BUSY* sign was pinned to the darkroom door so he tapped.

Maddie's muffled voice came through the door. "Working in here. Be out in a minute."

The smell of brewing coffee drew him back into the cabin where he fixed himself a cup. Everything was the same, yet inexplicably different from when he had lived here. Now it smelled like lemons, but beneath that he could still smell that faint hint of spice. And he couldn't help noticing the cabin was a whole lot tidier than when he'd lived there.

He poked through the kitchen cupboards until he found the cookie tin. Children's Delight. He cleaned out the tin and continued to snoop. Maddie's sandals stood neatly by the door, her outdoor clothing hung on the hooks beside his old plaid jacket. His lips drew up in a smile as he remembered the morning after they met when she'd stumbled out onto the porch, half asleep, wearing his jacket, looking sexy as hell.

A nest of framed photographs, all of the same girl, sat on the old TV cabinet. He took a closer look. *Must be Jenny.* She had the same broad cheekbones and wide eyes as Maddie. And in one, where their faces were tight together filling the frame, the resemblance was unmistakable.

"Hello."

He looked up. Maddie stood in the doorway, backlit by the sun. Grinning, he held up the last cookie. "Thought I'd make myself at home."

She stepped inside. "Sure."

She hovered in the doorway. He used to think she wasn't glad to see him, but now he sensed her uneasiness stemmed from something else—like maybe she didn't want to admit what he knew they both felt. He wasn't ready to put a name to it either, just knew he couldn't resist the opportunity to come to see her again.

He stepped toward her and she pressed her lips together. He could feel the effort it took for her not to step back. He took another step. "What? No, 'Hi Jake. Nice to see you'?"

She smiled, humor pushing the uneasiness from her eyes. "Hi Jake. Nice to see you. What can I do for you?"

Interesting question. "I heard through the grapevine—that would be Louise—that Jenny's moving over."

Maddie inhaled sharply and smiled. "Yes. Tomorrow."

She stepped around him and perched on the arm of the living room chair. He took a seat on the couch.

Her dewy skin glistened, probably from being shut in the darkroom. He remembered that heat. How it unlocked the fragrance in her skin, releasing a smell like flowers in the sun. He shook his head to clear the memory and caught sight of the mattress airing out on the porch. "Where did you get that?"

"I hope it's okay—Frankie and I cleaned up the attic for Jenny. We didn't throw anything away."

"Sure it's okay. I haven't been up there in a while. Why don't I help take this mattress up? Or are you going to wrestle it up by yourself?"

She glared at him playfully, catching the reference to the wringer washer. "No, I wasn't going to do it alone. I would appreciate a hand."

They got the brute up—once almost losing Maddie over the edge of the staircase—squeezed it through the small opening in the ceiling and flopped it onto the bed frame.

"Whew," she said, and fell back on the mattress, arms flung wide.

Lying beneath him in short-shorts and tank top, burnished curls spreading softly around her face, she was almost irresistible. Her eyes flared with awareness and heat that hit him square in the chest, but beneath it he sensed an edge of caution, so he just held out a hand. For a nano-second she hesitated, then reached out and took it. With a jerk, he pulled her up and into his arms, planting a firm kiss on her lips.

"Payment for services." He grinned and let her go. She stepped back, as clear a message as if she'd held up a palm. Okay, he could respect that. He could take it slow.

To break the tension, he looked around the room. "Nice. Last time I was up here it was a mess."

"I hope Jenny likes it," Maddie said.

She had filled the old cradle with books. Jake reached

down to touch the spines. Then he spied the rocker. "Augusta's old rocker. I should fix this seat and take it to the farm. I could use more furniture." He sat down and rocked, making the floorboards creak.

Maddie's face turned ghostly white. She put a hand to her forehead and closed her eyes. She looked like she was going to pass out. He jumped up to grab her. "You okay?"

Her eyes opened, round with fright. "I've heard that before, the creaking. When I was downstairs during that storm last month. It sounded like a rocking chair, but I decided it must have just been the storm. Then the limb fell on the roof. It really freaked me out, but I never heard the creaking again."

Jake looked at the rocker. "Maybe I should leave it."

"No. Take it. Maybe Augusta will follow it. I can't put Jenny in a haunted attic." They both looked around the cheerful room, at the bright pink walls, the white antique furniture pleasingly arranged, and the sunlight streaming through the clean, open windows.

"I'll fix the seat," Jake said. "I think Augusta would be happy for Jenny to use this space. She always liked young people."

"Maybe you're right. All she ever seems to do now is move the recipe box around the kitchen. Maybe she's happy I'm here and using her things. But please, take the rocker anyway."

Jake picked up the rocker and together they maneuvered it through the trap door and started down the stairs. Halfway down, he stopped and frowned. "If you're going to use these steps every day I should knock up a railing."

"That would be great—if you have time."

He grinned. "No problem."

Chapter 28

Half an hour later, Jake had brought enough lumber from the kitchen reno to build the railing and set up sawhorses at the foot of the stairs. His kitchen might be going nowhere fast, but the railing went together quickly.

Maddie sat, perched on the steps, watching him work. More than once he caught himself thinking about her bare legs, right at eye level, instead of the board he was cutting.

She seemed relaxed now, telling him about the work she and Frankie had done the day before. "I found some negatives upstairs. Maybe they're Augusta's. I'll develop them when I get a chance and show you. Frankie thought your mom might like to see the pictures."

"She'd love that. They were very close." He glanced up, rewarded with a peek of cleavage as she leaned forward in excitement. He kept on working though, hoping he'd gotten his measurements straight with Maddie all arms and legs and wide eyes right above him.

He frowned and measured again.

* * *

Maddie watched Jake measure the same board for the third time. It must be a particularly tricky cut. She wasn't really helping, just sitting on the stairs enjoying the view, but occasionally he'd ask her to hold something.

As the temperature in the cabin rose, she fanned herself with a piece of cardboard. When Jake took off his shirt and hung it on a chair, her stomach took a hot rolling slide and the cardboard flew like a hummingbird's wings.

Finally, he stood back. "I think we're done."

"Ohhh." She couldn't keep the disappointment out of her voice.

Then he said, "Let's go for a swim."

She went from sinking to buoyant in two seconds flat, then skipped down the stairs and into the bedroom. "Great idea. I'll change."

"You won't need a bathing suit where we're going," he said, and chuckled as she swooshed the curtain closed.

Smiling to herself, she changed into her suit, pulling a shirt on over top.

When she opened the curtain, he was packing up his tools. The sight of him stopped her in her tracks. He'd put his shirt back on but left it hanging open, skin shining from the heat. Over cut-off shorts, his tool-belt was slung low on his hips. What was it about tool belts that made her body tingle in places she'd almost forgotten?

She tried to haul her thoughts back to more neutral ground. "Where are we going?"

"To the creek by the wildflower meadow. There's a pool there where we can swim."

He took off the tool belt and hung it over a chair, then held the door open for her. She grabbed her pocket camera and the keys out of her shoulder bag, then a couple of towels from the bathroom.

"We can take the Beast," she said, leading the way to the car.

Jake climbed into the passenger seat and slammed the door. Opened it and slammed it again. Then one more time before it finally caught.

She grinned as he cast a worried glance at the door. "It's probably closed now. But you better put on your seatbelt."

The Beast did not let her down. It started right up and almost purred as they rolled down the driveway.

She parked on the road by the wildflower meadow and followed Jake through the maple grove down to the creek. The undergrowth had filled in since their spring visit when the lilies were blooming, and now sword ferns stood full and lush, chest high, almost hiding the trail. Giant maple trees laced fingers overhead, filtering the sunlight through their dark summer-green leaves.

When they got to the creek, the water trickled over the rocks into a pool, still and deep. The fierce winter floodwaters, strong enough to uproot fully-grown trees and wash them away, had gouged a deep pool at a bend in the creek. Logs racing down at high water had caught on the rocks and when the water receded, the logs hung suspended until the next year's surge would set them free.

They left their shoes and shirts on a flat rock by the creek. Maddie picked up her little point-and-shoot camera and took a few shots, intending to come back later with her SLR to get some black and whites.

Jake dove into the pool, surfacing instantly and treading water, wiping his long hair out of his eyes. "Come in, it's perfect."

It felt as exotic as a jungle pool in South America, and Maddie found herself wondering, *is this my life, or is it a movie?*

Jake took a pair of clean strokes over to the rock and reached up to swipe a hand at her ankle.

"No," she shrieked, set down her camera and held her nose as she jumped over his head and into the water.

Nerve endings sparked as the water, cool as silk, enveloped her overheated body. She paddled around the pool, exploring hidden places under the rafters of logs where sunlight slanted in, laughing when Jake pulled her under.

He found a spot where he could just touch bottom and wrapped her in his arms. This was so far from any real-life experience she'd ever had that she barely noticed her reserve slip away. He had a way of doing that to her. Pulling down her walls.

He kissed her, long and deep, and she ran her hands over the slick muscles of his shoulders, fulfilling the fantasy that had plagued her all afternoon while she watched him work. She relaxed into the kiss, floating in the gentle current, trusting his arms to hold her up.

Trust was a heady new sensation for her, to relax and yield control to someone else. To him.

He ran his hands down her back, igniting the nerves as they passed until she was surprised the water didn't sizzle on her skin and steam around her. He angled his head and kissed her again, pulling her body tight against his.

Nose to nose in the water, he asked, "When can I see you again?"

She smiled, resting her elbows on his shoulders, tangling her fingers in his hair. "Anytime. You know where I live."

"Tomorrow night."

"No." She came back to reality with thud. "Not tomorrow. Jenny is arriving in the afternoon and I want to spend some time with her. Sorry."

"Okay, but soon." He kissed her again lightly, then let her go, swam to the edge and climbed out, reaching back to help her up the slippery bank, onto the rocky ledge.

* * *

Jake walked over to where their towels lay a few feet away, then looked back at Maddie, sitting in a pool of light on the rock. Her arms were wrapped around her knees and her hair hung in dripping ringlets. He picked up her small point-and-shoot camera from the ground at his feet.

"Can I take one?"

"Sure," she said, and talked him through the steps.

"Look at the water," he ordered, turning the tables and making her smile. She lay her head on her knee.

There was something ethereal about her, magic, a fairy resting by a forest pool. He couldn't put his finger on it, just knew he wanted time to figure her out.

He took a series of shots as he walked toward her, a frame with each step, surprised by the rush of power he felt. Through the camera, he could shape the world to his liking, find his own thoughts and feelings through the lens. Feelings that were heading deeper into dangerous territory every day. Heading toward love.

He knelt beside her, the camera inches from her face, until finally she protested. "Okay, enough." Laughing, she took the camera away from him.

He put his hands on either side of her face, drawing her in for one more kiss. Shadows shifted. Already the days were growing noticeably shorter and they were enshrouded in the shady blue light of late afternoon.

He rested his forehead against hers. "We could have dinner together."

Her eyes searched his face and he prayed she found what she was looking for.

"We could."

"If we stop at the farm I could pick up some chicken breasts to barbeque."

"What about Sarah?"

"She's at my mom's." And that's where she'd stay once he made a quick call.

Maddie went silent. They both knew what 'dinner' really meant. His heart stood still, the blood backing up in his veins until he felt like he would burst.

Then she smiled. "Okay. Let's go."

* * *

Her heart still pumping from the kiss, Maddie felt lightheaded, teetering on dangerous ground. She looked up at Jake in the changing light as he helped her to her feet on the rock.

She was sure he could read her thoughts, how she wanted to run her hands through his hair, over the hard planes of his shoulders and down his muscled torso to the waist of those shorts that hung on the blades of his hips.

The ball was rolling, had been gathering momentum for weeks. She couldn't stop it—didn't want to. He knew what was ahead as well as she did, but he seemed determined to go on. Lord knows she had tried to stay away from him—but he pulled her like a magnet, with that added zing of electricity thrown in that made her blood simmer and lowered her defenses.

When they got to the cabin, Jake said, "We forgot to pick up the chicken."

"We can eat later," she said. *Showtime.* And cripes, she was ready. He was everything she wanted, and when his arms came around her, she went into them willingly, hungrily returning his kisses, feeling his impatience where his hips burned into hers.

They stumbled across the room to the bedroom doorway, not wanting to break the seal of their lips. She devoured his face, his strong neck, ripping open his shirt in her impatience to feel his bare chest under her hands. He took hold of her hands and gently pulled them away, pressing a kiss on the back of each one.

"Slow down," he said, that damn beautiful dimple flashing. Then he carefully pulled the straps of her bathing suit off her shoulders caressing her collarbones in passing. "Do you know how long I've wanted to kiss your shoulders?"

"No?" she whispered.

"That hollow right here." His lips moved across her skin feather light, teasing, setting fires everywhere he touched. Her shoulder rose up to increase the pressure, encouraging, wanting. Her back arched and she pressed into the warm wall of his chest.

He undid the clasp at the back and the top fell away. His head dropped lower, and his clever mouth found her breast, letting out an animal groan that came straight from his groin.

The sound of his arousal speared Maddie into action. She thrust her hands under his shirt, running them over his ribs, his back and back to the waist of his shorts.

"Do you know how crazy you made me today?" she asked. "How much I wanted to do this?"

The rest of their clothes hit the floor an instant later and they fell together onto the bed.

Frantic and physical, fire consumed them and the frustration that had been building all summer exploded with an intensity that shook the foundations of the cabin.

Eventually they lay sated, in a heap on the bed, limbs entwined so neither could tell where one left off and the other began. She felt liquid with the release, and the relief of finally expressing her true feelings.

"Hungry now?" he asked, pulling her close, her head resting on his chest.

Maddie buried her head in the curve of his neck, so warm and solid. She wanted to stay there beside him forever. Through her haze of contentment, she realized *this* was what a normal relationship would be like. Warm nights of wonderful, rolling sex, followed by intimate, soothing, domestic chatter. Someone to share a life together.

"Starving," she said.

Chapter 29

By noon the next day, Maddie had been up and down the stairs to the attic a hundred times, tweaking and arranging Jenny's room. Now there was nothing to do but wait.

What if Mark and Kate wanted to come in? She flew around the cabin, sweeping, tidying, scrubbing—but the cabin was so tiny that she was soon tapping her fingertips on the counter again. She pulled down the cookie jar. *Empty.* A smile tugged at her lips. *Jake.*

Out came the cookie sheets, butter and flour. She reached for the recipe box, but the windowsill was empty. Her gaze swung up to the top cupboard shelf.

"Worried I'll eat too many cookies, Augusta?"

Truth was, she was addicted to Children's Delight with their old-fashioned flavor of peanut butter and spice. Hopefully Jenny would like them too. Jake and Sarah certainly did.

The memory of their intoxicating jungle swim and the amazing evening that followed sent a delightful shiver down her back. Best sex ever. She hadn't known it could be that way. That you could open up so completely to someone with no fear.

She looked across the room at the railing Jake had built. For Jenny. Such a sweet thing to do, and he hadn't even met her daughter yet. He had a caring soul. She could see that in the way he looked after Sarah. You could trust a guy like that.

She stopped halfway from the table to the stove, eyes wide, a tray of unbaked cookies in her hands, flour streaked across her face. Jake was the first man she had ever really trusted.

Unnerved by the realization, she opened the oven door and shoved the cookie tray inside. Then she leaned back against the warm stove. Trusting him flew against everything she had learned as a child, chipping away at her carefully erected walls.

Even with Mark, she had never let her defenses down, not all the way. Maybe that had been a major stumbling block in their relationship, but if so, all she could do at this point was learn from the experience. She saw now that trust was an essential ingredient in a successful relationship. She did trust Jake, she really did. And someday she might even trust him enough to tell him about Cindy.

Back at the counter, she plopped mounds of batter on another pan.

But trust was not all there was to it. Their lives would diverge at the end of the summer and nothing they could do would change that. Seattle was not the end of the world, but a long distance romance was just a recipe for a slow, painful death.

And come on, he was a healthy guy. They never said this was exclusive. For all she knew he could have another woman somewhere that he went out with sometimes.

She stopped and stared out the window at the lake. She could have accepted that before, but not now. Last night, in bed, he was all in. She knew he was, and so was she. For once, no walls. No games.

And this morning, when she'd developed the photographs he had taken of her yesterday at the creek, she could see the love in her eyes. Surely he'd seen it too.

Her eyes rolled up to look at the ceiling. "Oh, Augusta. What am I going to do?"

By one thirty, the cookies were cooling on the rack and the fragrant scent of cinnamon filled the kitchen. Maddie sat on the porch pretending to read, foot tapping on the floor. At the sound of every passing car, she jumped up and looked up the drive.

Finally, she took a kitchen chair out into the tiny yard and positioned it so she could see up the driveway. When she sat, the chair rocked on the uneven ground. She moved it. It rocked. She moved it again. Still rocking.

This is ridiculous.

As she carried the chair back into the house, engines roared overhead and a floatplane skimmed in over the lake.

Summer folk. She laughed at how local she sounded. Stepping back out onto the porch, she shaded her eyes against the bright sunlight and watched the airplane land out on the water, circle around and taxi back towards Frankie's dock.

Who does Frankie know with a plane? she wondered. Then suddenly she knew. *Jenny.*

Maddie sprinted along the path to Frankie's yard, around the house and down to the shore. Frankie came out onto the deck. "Does that belong to you?"

Maddie waved. "I guess it does." And she hurried down onto the dock.

* * *

Jenny watched the cabin on the shore get larger and larger as the floatplane skimmed in over the water. Finally, the plane set down with a bump, the force of deceleration pushing her back in her seat. The tiny figure of her mom waved from the end of the dock and Jenny's heart swelled until she thought it would explode.

Before they even came to a stop, she was tugging her seatbelt, her dad nagging, "Keep that belt on." But the pilot grinned at her as he climbed out to open her door.

And there was her mom. *OMG. Was Mom crying?*

Well, Jenny felt like crying herself. She'd missed her so much. Living with Dad was *nothing* like she had imagined. He was *such* a control freak. Her mom was a softy by comparison. She could tell he'd been trying to be nice this last week but it had still been agony, waiting for her sentence to end.

She leapt out of the plane and into her mom's arms, hugging her tightly.

Eventually, her mom pulled away. "How was the flight?"

"Awesome."

Mark and Kate climbed out of the plane and they each gave her mom a stiff hug. God, sometimes those two acted like automatons.

"I'm impressed," her mom said to her dad, looking at the airplane, her arm tight around Jenny's shoulder.

"Oh well, it's the company plane and it doesn't cost that much more for us all to fly over than to take the car on the ferry."

BS. He knew it was cool. He had only done it to impress her mom. But Mom only laughed. And she was right. Jenny was here and that was all that mattered.

"Would you like to come in for a cold drink?" Mom asked.

Her dad stiffened and shook his head. Kate glanced first at Frankie's place, then over to the cabin. Jenny held back a snort. Kate wouldn't be caught dead in either house. She was such a snob.

"We have to get this thing back," Dad said in that snotty voice he used for excuses. But she was glad he was going. It would just be awkward and besides, she wanted her mom all to herself.

While the pilot put Jenny's bags on the dock, her dad gave Mom an envelope. "For the rest of the summer," he mumbled. Probably money.

Then she was standing with one arm around her mom, the other hand waving as the plane taxied away, her goofy smile as big as her mom's.

* * *

From where he stood with Sarah on the shoreline path, Jake watched the floatplane land on the water, engines roaring, disturbing the peace. Maddie ran out onto Frankie's dock and Jake's eyebrows cranked up as the plane taxied in. A teenager climbed out and gave Maddie a hug. Had to be Jenny.

Then a couple got out and each hugged her again.

Jake's eyes narrowed. So, not just a city girl, but a rich city girl. Why then was she slumming in the cabin? Anger sparked in his chest, that defensive old feeling rearing its head. He wasn't going through that again.

"Let's go see Maddie," Sarah cried, starting back to the cabin.

Taking his daughter firmly by the hand, Jake pulled her in the opposite direction. "Not this time Sunshine. Grandma's waiting."

* * *

Maddie led Jenny up through the trap door and into the attic.

"Cool, a secret room," Jenny exclaimed. "So romantic, like in a story. I love the pink walls."

Maddie breathed a sigh of relief. Jenny seemed happy to be here. Exuberant even. Maybe the break had patched things up between them.

While Jenny unpacked her clothes into the clean dresser drawers, Maddie sat on the bed. Her cheeks flushed at the memory of Jake's hot eyes on her as she'd laid, arms flung wide, on that attic bed the day before. How had that even happened? At the time, she'd felt as if she'd been pushed, and it wasn't by Jake.

Her eyes narrowed. *Augusta.*

She'd have to tell Jenny about their ghost. It was only fair. But what if, once Jenny knew, she didn't want to stay?

"There's something you should know," she began nervously. "There might be a ghost."

"Awesome." Jenny flopped down on the bed beside her, looking around as if she expected the ghost to materialize on command. "Have you seen it?"

"No. I haven't," Maddie admitted, suddenly sorry she didn't have a more exciting story to tell. "But I've heard her. She moves things around."

"I hope I see her. Who it is?"

"Jake's Aunt Augusta."

"Jake? Our hot landlord?"

Maddie hit her with a pillow and laughed. "Yes, our hot landlord."

"When can I meet him?"

Good question.

"Soon."

* * *

Jenny settled into Fortune Bay like a cookie onto a bakery shelf. Much to Maddie's relief, their relationship remained significantly improved. Her daughter was still very much at that transitional age though—sometimes happy to be a girl and then, unexpectedly, the teeter-totter tipped and she became an independent young woman with plans of her own.

The first morning she joined Maddie for coffee and muffins at the café, Louise's sister Brandy waltzed in. From that moment on, the girls were inseparable and Brandy launched Jenny into the whirlwind teen world of Fortune Bay.

But Jenny's presence in Fortune Bay only served to remind Maddie of her life in Seattle, something she realized now she had almost pushed out of her mind. Sometimes, like when she was working, walking the roads and trails or in the darkroom, she'd forget for hours at a time that she was leaving. Then suddenly, thoughts of returning to the city in the fall would bear down on her like a thunderstorm and a wave of confusion would sweep in out of nowhere.

Of course she was going back to Seattle. That was the plan, and sticking to the plan was what kept her from falling off life's tightrope into the abyss, how she kept inching ever further away from her mother's trailer park life. She had a life in the city, commitments to Jenny. A job to go back to and the show to put up.

Don't I have a life here too, though? Friends and a community? And wasn't her new work centered on Fortune Bay?

And what about Jake?

Jake, she reminded herself, wasn't part of the Plan. In fact, he was counter to the Plan. A fly in the ointment. A spanner in the works.

The spice in the sauce.

Just a momentary diversion.

And if you believe that I have a bridge to sell you.

And where was he anyway? It had been almost a week and he hadn't even come by to meet Jenny. Maddie could take her to the farm, but for some reason she didn't feel entirely comfortable doing that. He always came to the cabin and, for reasons Maddie did not entirely understand, appeared to prefer to keep it that way.

Sometimes, when he disappeared like this, she thought she must have invented him, the funny, sexy, devastatingly handsome man who took her to dinner, to meet his family and who took her to bed. The fun-loving father who threw her off the dock right into the water. The sensitive listener who gave her his unquestioning support the night Jenny ran away.

But did she really need this kind of aggravation? A moody guy who came when it suited him and then vanished for no reason?

Then, in the darkroom, she saw the photographs: Jake, standing in the dappled light of the forest, muscles flexing as he climbed the spar pole at the Festival, caught with Sarah in a private moment. A disproportionate number of pictures in the pile were of him.

She shook her head. She had it bad.

And the look in her eye in the photograph he'd taken at the forest pool? Was it love? She sighed. If not that, then certainly lust.

So where was he now? She was dying to introduce him to Jenny, but she could be stubborn too.

She would wait him out.

Chapter 30

Maddie treated herself to a darkroom session that was just for fun and developed Augusta's negatives. Under the red glow of the safe light, in the clear liquid of the developing tray, the first image emerged like an apparition. In the close-up, a woman waved jauntily from the driver's side window of an old Ford with a split, front windscreen.

Seeing her wide-mouthed smile, Maddie smiled in response. "Hello Augusta, we finally meet."

The rest of the negatives proceeded like a silent film of Augusta's life on Majestic Lake; the tugboat towing the float-home down the lake, clearly recognizable as the cabin where Maddie lived today, and Augusta hamming it up on a slab of rock on the shore with her arms around a tall, handsome man. Her husband Sven?

And in yet another—Maddie peered more closely—Augusta appeared decidedly pregnant. Hadn't Jake said she had never had children?

Later that day, when the prints had dried, she put them in an envelope and walked the shoreline path to see Stephanie.

* * *

Stephanie looked up from weeding her vegetable bed, distracted by a shadow at the edge of the forest. It was Maddie. *Good.* Stephanie was more than a little curious about what was going on between Maddie and her eldest son. As usual, Jake hadn't said anything, but ever since the dance, Stephanie had been sure he had set his sights on this girl.

She raised her hand. "Hello."

Maddie stepped out into the sunshine.

"How nice to see you," Stephanie said. "Come in for tea. I'm ready for a break myself."

They walked through the vegetable patch and up to the

house. While Stephanie washed the garden soil off her hands and put on the kettle, Maddie hovered over a piece of silk stretched on a frame on the large, oak kitchen table. An intricate border design was sketched on the fabric.

"It's going to be lovely," Maddie said. "Like the jacket you made for Frankie."

"Silk painting is a new medium for me." Stephanie gestured to the large abstracts hanging on the walls. "A big change from oils."

"I noticed the paintings the day of the picnic. They're great. So bold."

"Thank you, dear. I've always painted, but it has only been in the past few years that I have been able to work this large. It has really loosened up my arm. And my style."

She led Maddie out onto the screen porch. "How is your work coming?"

"Quite well. At least, I have a lot of photographs, many I'm quite happy with. Tori, the gallery owner, seems to like the ones she's seen so far, but I still have a lot of work to do. Last time I was in the city I brought back all of my framing supplies. I have to make thirty frames." Maddie shook her head and blew out a breath. "I'm just glad Jenny is here now and can help me."

"I met your daughter at the store. Sweet child, but headstrong, I'd imagine."

Maddie laughed. "You've got that right. You know, I hated leaving her with her father but it might have been a good thing after all. She doesn't seem to think I am quite the wicked witch she thought I was when she first went to stay with him."

"A bit of distance can be beneficial at times."

"I have something for you," Maddie said, pulling the pack of pictures out of her bag. "I think they're of Augusta."

At the sight of the woman in the black and white images, Stephanie's heart softened. "Yes. That's Augusta."

She looked at the top photo for a moment, waves of memory rolling over her. Then she moved on to the next.

"And this is her husband Sven." She turned the pictures over and wrote their names lightly on the back in pencil in her bold loopy script.

She stopped at the one of Augusta standing proudly beside a fifties Chevy, hand on cocked hip, a smile on her face. "I remember that car. I must have ridden in it a hundred times when I was a child."

"Did you grow up here?"

"No. My family came out from Seattle to visit Augusta every summer though. She did love her cars, and kept them forever. Even when she and Sven lived in the float house down the lake, they kept a car in Majestic. She said it represented her freedom."

"Jake told me she didn't have any children. There is this one photograph though," Maddie shuffled through the pile of prints. "I thought she looked pregnant."

"She did have one child. The baby was stillborn, and then they had no more. Quite tragic." Stephanie picked up the photo and stared at it for a moment in silence. "Maybe that's why she was so great to me and my children. We were the family she couldn't have."

"There's a cradle in the attic at the cabin."

"Is it still there? Her husband made it. She always hoped they'd have another child, and even after he died, she hung onto that cradle. I would have used it for my own children when they were newborn, but Augusta couldn't bear to part with it. She was as sentimental as she was stubborn."

"It's funny," Maddie said picking up one of the photos. "I almost feel she's watching over me at the cabin."

Stephanie smiled. "I wouldn't be surprised. She watched over me, and later Jake. She always had a soft spot for Jake and he had one for her. Maybe she has one for you too."

Casually, Stephanie chose a cookie from the tea tray. "Have you seen Jake lately?"

Maddie blushed. "I haven't seen him since Jenny arrived."

Stephanie took a bite of the cookie. How much should

she interfere? Maddie deserved to know what she was getting into, and, for that matter, what she was losing if she didn't give Jake a chance.

"He's never been an easy man with his feelings," Stephanie said. "You can see the way he is with Sarah—fierce in his devotion, if a tad unyielding in his expectations." She laughed. "Luckily Sarah is equally stubborn. He won't steamroller her into anything she doesn't want to do. Much to his frustration."

After another sip of tea, she became serious again. "He tends to make rules for his behavior and then sticks to them, come hell or high water. Even when he's drowning because of them.

"He needs a strong woman who can hold her own and make her wants and needs known." She grew thoughtful. "That might have been part of the problem before."

Maddie blinked, eyes large.

Oh dear, Stephanie thought. *Too much information.*

She softened her voice. "He's honest and loyal. A good man and a good father. That's not always easy to find."

Maddie let out a mirthless laugh. "You've got that right."

When Maddie finally stood up to go, Stephanie tried to return the photos of Augusta but Maddie insisted she keep them. "I have copies. And anyway, they belong to you. I also found these in the attic." She pulled the postcards of Italy out of the bag.

Stephanie looked them over one by one. "Augusta travelled quite a bit before she came to Majestic." She gazed wistfully at the faded, old-world images. "I've never been further than Seattle myself, but someday, I'm going to Italy." She held the cards out to Maddie.

"Keep them. They're yours."

Stephanie smiled. "I'll put them on my dream wall," she said, and pinned the postcards to the cluttered corkboard in her kitchen.

* * *

As Maddie walked home along the shoreline path, she thought about what Stephanie had said. Had she been warning her about something? And what did she mean, *what happened before*? Was she suggesting Jake had somehow been at fault at the end of his marriage?

Maddie knew that every relationship breakdown had two sides. Hers certainly had. From this distance, she could admit that she never completely trusted Mark, never let down her walls, and he must have felt it. On his side, he tried to manipulate her, force her into a role she didn't want to play. Neither of them had been entirely honest nor entirely at fault. Probably the same was true in Jake's marriage—each partner had played a role in the breakup.

Jake's fierceness did not scare her though. Quite the opposite. Strongly protective, it wrapped around her like a shield. She felt nothing could go wrong when he was around.

She'd seen the other side of him too though—the indecision that haunted his eyes. She wasn't sure of the cause, although sometimes she thought it might have something to do with her.

Strange, because she was an open book. What you see is what you get. She straightened her shoulders. A woman with her life going according to her plan. Nothing confusing about that.

As she approached the cabin, a wave of pleasure washed over her as Jake's voice drifted around the corner of the building.

"Pump harder. It has to be harder."

Jenny giggled. "I can't keep it on, it must be enough."

"Let me try!" Sarah's high-pitched excitement overran them both.

Maddie rounded the corner and the tableau in the driveway made her heart falter. Sarah, Jake and Jenny huddled around the old bike, using the compressor from the back shed to pump up the tires.

Jenny hopped up on the bike and bounced a couple of

times, then took off, handlebars wobbling, down the lane.

"How do you steer on gravel?" she called back over her shoulder.

Jake sprinted after her down the driveway, placing a steady hand on the rear fender. Sarah clapped her hands as Jenny pedaled away and, seeing Maddie, ran over and gave her an excited hug around the waist. "We made it go."

"So I see." She dropped her hand to the little girl's shoulder, unsettled by how glad she was to see her again, although it hadn't even been a week.

Jenny pedaled triumphantly back with Jake jogging behind. "Look Mom, Jake found me a bike."

The paint was chipped and the bike only had three speeds, but seeing the tools and rags on the porch, Maddie realized Jake had done a tune-up right there in the driveway.

Their eyes met, Maddie with her hand on Sarah's shoulder and Jake steadying the back of Jenny's bike.

It would be perfect, but she knew better than to wish for things she couldn't have.

* * *

Jake saw the hesitation flit across Maddie's face. Maybe giving Jenny the bike had been the wrong thing to do. Maybe he was imposing. Maybe the old bike wasn't good enough.

"Thanks Jake," Maddie said.

She seemed a little distant. Suddenly all the scratches and dings in the paint of the twenty-year-old bicycle jumped out at him. "Maybe you wanted to buy her a new bike."

"Oh no," Maddie exclaimed. "There's no money in the budget for frills like that."

Frills? Now he was really confused. "What about the sea plane?"

Maddie waved her hand dismissively. "That was Jenny's dad. He has money."

Jake started to get the picture. Dad must be tight with the purse strings. The car – what did she call it? *the Beast* – was on its last legs. And Jenny didn't come across as a spoiled rich kid. She seemed genuinely happy with the rusty, second hand bike.

Maddie frowned in concern. "Is it really safe out there on the road? Jenny has never had a bike. Too much traffic in the city and cars parked on all the streets."

"It's not like that here, Mom. Jake brought me a helmet and I promise I'll wear it. All the kids here have bikes, until they get cars. Brandy has a bike but she's had to walk everywhere with me because I haven't had one."

Maddie looked questioningly at Jake. "I'm sure she'll be fine," he assured her. "Maybe not after dark, unless we can find her a light and make sure those reflectors work."

Maddie smiled at her daughter. "I give up. Put on that helmet and go and show Brandy."

In a flurry of thanks, Jenny wobbled off down the driveway.

"Thanks Jake," Maddie said. "And thank you too, Sarah."

Sarah went up on her tiptoes and twisted her hands together on top of her head. "Got any cookies?"

Maddie smiled. "As a matter of fact I do."

AUGUST

Chapter 31

Sarah marched out of the living room with Jake's black cowboy hat on her head, barely able to see over her armload of toys.

"Take them upstairs," Jake said. "Dump the toys in your room and throw the hat on my bed."

"Okay Daddy." She clumped up the stairs. "What are we going to give them to eat?"

Jake ran a hand down his face in frustration. Did he have to feed them too? He gathered up the clean laundry—there always seemed to be a pile of it on the couch—and threw it into the basket. Stuffing a giant panda under his arm, he picked up the basket and headed for the stairs.

Asking Maddie to come and give him advice about the kitchen had seemed like a good idea at the time, but she had never really been to the farm before and the visit was turning out to be anything but casual.

Without the veneer of toys and laundry, pizza boxes and cereal bowls, the living room did look neater, but he saw it with fresh eyes. No pictures on the wall, no rug on the floor, hardly even any furniture. *Pathetic.* He ran a wet rag over the sticky coffee table.

This was how they lived and they were doing just fine, thank you very much. He had no problem with her seeing the kitchen, it was a legitimate construction site, so she would expect there to be sawdust and rubble. The living room, however, was a decorating disaster.

He flicked the rag at the dust on top of the big-screen

television set in the corner and ground his teeth when he realized that a fine layer of plaster dust had managed to sift all over the living room too. *Well I don't have time to wash the damn floors.*

Sarah came back into the room babbling about cookies and drinks, but before they had time to talk, a knock sounded on the door. Jake took one final look around. They'd be okay—as long as she didn't go upstairs.

He stopped with his hand on the doorknob and took a deep breath. He looked back at Sarah who gave him a double-thumbs-up—their 'go for it' sign—then he opened the door.

* * *

Out on the porch, Maddie felt Jenny breathing in her ear.

"Spooky," Jenny whispered, just as Jake whooshed open the door. He looked sort of stressed—his eyes kind of bulging. Maddie thrust out the tin of brownies they'd brought.

It felt weird, more formal than when he dropped by the cabin. He had never invited her to his house before and, sensing his restraint, she had never dropped by. She understood, heaven knows she was pulling back on the reins of, well, whatever this thing was between them too, not trying to move it forward.

Now, though, he had asked for her help and she could at least look at the job. He had helped her so much in the past three months. And, to be honest, she was more than a little curious to see the inside of the farmhouse, both for its historic interest and to see how he and Sarah lived.

She stepped inside.

Like bachelors. The only furniture in the living room was a couch, a coffee table and a giant TV in the corner. Plaster dust coated the floor. No curtains, nothing to soften the walls.

But she wasn't there to criticize.

Sarah stood up on her tiptoes in excitement and asked if she wanted a Coke and cookies.

Maddie smiled. "Why don't you try our brownies?" She handed the tin to Sarah who took it directly to the living room coffee table.

Obviously where they eat. Then Sarah asked again if they wanted drinks and Maddie and Jenny both said sure. Sarah dragged Jake by the hand into the kitchen and the women followed because, after all, they were there to see the kitchen.

Jake had torn out the counters, removed the cupboard doors and ripped the flooring back to the subfloor. Holes peppered the plaster walls—the house had been built before drywall existed—and lights hung by bare wires from the ceiling in the middle of the room.

"Oh my gosh." Maddie's hand flew to her mouth. No wonder they didn't eat in the kitchen.

Behind her, Jenny giggled. "You do need help, don't you?"

Jake looked embarrassed. And overwhelmed. "I didn't have a problem with the demolition, but I haven't been able to get a handle on the new stuff."

"How long has it been like this?"

"A couple of months. I keep chipping away at it...but I don't know how to start putting it back together."

He took her on a detailed tour of the room, pointing out where the old cupboards had been and where he planned to put new ones, where the walls were down to studs and he intended to put more windows, where new appliances would go once he figured out what kind to get.

All the while Sarah and Jenny were assembling a tray, reaching into the remaining cupboards through open fronts and down into drawers through counter-less tops.

Maddie shook her head in confusion. She wasn't sure where to start either.

Jake led them back into the living room. "Colleen brought over a load of decorating magazines. Said I should take a look at them." He reached behind the leather couch and brought out a carton of magazines. "I looked, but I don't know what I'm looking for."

The three females pounced on the stack of magazines,

eating the brownies and tearing out pictures, all talking to Jake at once.

He kept nodding, his eyes glazed, obviously still bewildered, until Maddie said, "Have you got any thumb tacks?" When Jake returned with the tacks, she pulled a piece of plywood into the living room and began attaching pictures to the plywood, circling possibilities for the kitchen in each one.

Maddie and Jenny left two hours later and Jake carried the plywood into the kitchen where he started writing up a list of supplies. "I think that went pretty smoothly."

Sarah nodded. "I think so. Good brownies."

* * *

Jake pounded another tiny finishing nail into the kitchen trim. Ever since Maddie's first visit, he'd been working full out on the kitchen. Sean and their old friend Blue had both helped quite a bit and together they'd gotten a lot accomplished during the summer layoff.

Asking Maddie to help with the planning had been a brainwave. He'd taken her to town on two shopping trips, for counter tops and appliances, knobs and trim, and he'd managed to sneak in a couple of lunches that almost qualified as dates.

Other than that, with both girls around every day, all they'd managed were stolen moments alone. The stealth built excitement into every encounter until he felt as horny as a teenager, ready to explode.

Summer's end was sneaking up on them, and his agitation grew sharper every day. He felt increasingly sure it could work out though, that they could be a family.

Fortune Bay obviously agreed with Maddie; her frosty edges had thawed and she smiled all the time now. She'd made friends here and so had Jenny. Fortune Bay had become her home. Surely she saw that. What was so damned important in Seattle that she had to go back?

The worst part was that Sarah would miss her when she

left. Maddie often came by now at lunch, and Sarah would run out of the house with a book in her hand and climb up on the new, white wicker love seat beside her. Maddie loved reading to Sarah, something Jake rarely found the time to do. He would watch them, heads bent close over the book, laughing together over the story and wonder what happened to following the rules, keeping the women he saw away from his daughter.

And he'd wonder why this couldn't be.

But if he was truthful, that wasn't the worst part. He had fallen in love with this woman—and she was leaving. He ran his hand roughly through his hair. He didn't know if he could go through it again.

He'd let down his guard and she had gotten past all the rules and into his heart as no woman had in the years since Sarah's mother had gone.

He was in big trouble if Maddie left too. Time to do something about it to make sure that didn't happen.

* * *

Maddie let herself in through the front door of the farmhouse. "Knock, knock."

She dropped her sunhat onto the living room chair and smiled, eyes widening, as Jake swung her around and planted a firm kiss on her lips. She could see the heat in his eyes, but then Sarah—her timing impeccable as always—ran up to greet her.

Coming over like this was asking for trouble, but on the days she didn't, she felt restless and edgy. Then the next day, like an addict, she'd give in and come again.

Jake took her hand, entwining her fingers lightly with his, and led her back into the kitchen.

"Wow," she said, "Great job on the molding."

Every day the reno grew closer to completion. Jake and Sean had set in a new window, no small feat in two-foot thick walls of solid log, and painted the trim a creamy white. They'd installed a mottled, charcoal gray countertop and the stainless-steel appliances were in cartons in the living room. As soon as the electrician and plumber were finished, they'd roll them into place.

"What did you bring today?" Sarah asked, dragging a chair over to the counter to inspect the packages Maddie set there.

"Chicken wings with barbeque sauce and potato salad."

"Thanks. Again." Jake said.

"That's what friends are for," she said lightly, denying the furious beat of her heart. A voice from the living room announced another guest.

"Sean," Sarah squealed, hopping off the chair and running to meet him. "We have wings!"

"Wings, eh? Then let's see you fly." He scooped her up and flew her back airplane-style into the kitchen where he set her down, laughing, on the floor.

Sliding an arm around Maddie's waist, he planted a friendly kiss on her cheek and wiggled his eyebrows like Groucho Marx. "I love a woman with wings," he said as he grabbed a piece of chicken from the carton. This man oozed charm. Maddie couldn't figure out why some woman hadn't snapped him up years ago.

She piled the paper plates and napkins onto a tray, added a big jug of water, and Jake carried it out to the new, white wicker garden furniture on the veranda that she had helped him pick out on one of their shopping expeditions. Now, in high summer, when the sun beat down mercilessly every day, the shady refuge was their favorite lunch spot.

The trees of the old orchard beside the farmhouse hung heavy with apples and pears. Last week, she and Jenny had picked cherries, juicy and sweet, straight off the tree. That was one of the few good experiences she remembered from her childhood in the Chelan Valley, one she was happy to share with Jenny.

Sometimes they all met on Frankie's dock in the late afternoon for a swim. A couple of times the casual gathering had extended into the evening with a fire on the beach and a potluck supper. It had been the best summer of her life and Maddie was afraid to let herself think about leaving.

Sean reached for the last wing a split second before his brother. "So, when do we get to see these famous photographs?" he asked.

"You'll all have to come to my show," Maddie said, trying to put a positive spin on it. She and Jake never talked about the show. The pictures yes. The show, never.

"I think the people of Fortune Bay deserve a sneak peak," Sean said. "Like an advanced preview at the movies." He sat back and let the idea percolate.

"I guess it could work," she said slowly. She sent Jake a questioning glance.

His often-dark countenance had been considerably lighter in recent weeks and a smile would light up his face when she came into the room. But now a gamut of emotion flickered across his face. Maddie thought she recognized love, and an underlying fear.

She ached for this man in the dead of the night. She even ached for him in the daylight. And she knew he wanted her just as much. Other people had casual affairs all the time. Why couldn't they?

Because this isn't casual. Like a deep plunge in a cold lake, she came up gasping for air. She loved him and wanted this life with him, more than she had ever wanted anything before, but she still couldn't figure out how to meld their lives together.

Chapter 32

Maddie set up her computer on the kitchen table, got a glass of lemonade and settled down to resize the photographs of Seattle for her website. It was too easy to ignore the practical side of her business plan when the darkroom work was so much fun, when the weather was so beautiful day after day and when there were friends to visit along the shore.

To say nothing of Jake. With both girls around all the time, they hadn't found a chance for another "dinner" date, and stolen kisses were all they could manage. Which was probably just as well because try as she might to dismiss Colleen's cautionary words at the picnic, they still echoed in her mind.

Jake needed to stay in Fortune Bay with Sarah. That was a deal breaker, and she couldn't blame him. She would have loved to have given Jenny the same childhood he was giving Sarah, but it was too late for that now. Jenny was already talking about getting back to the city. She had enjoyed the summer break and her new friends, but her life was still tied up in Seattle with her high school friends. With only one year until graduation, it did not make sense to uproot her now and make her start over again somewhere new.

But the bottom line was that even if she and Jake could work out the logistics, he deserved a real home and family. And regardless of how she longed for the same thing herself, she wasn't sure what she could promise since she was still struggling with the concept.

On the table, her cell phone erupted in a shrill jarring ring. She snatched it up.

"Hi Mad." At the saccharine sound of her mother's voice, a sick cocktail of anxiety flooded her system. She recognized the tone. Cindy had been drinking. Never a surprise, the question always was, how much. As a child she'd learned how to judge her mother's level of drunkenness when she'd walked through the door after school every day.

She rested her forehead on her fingertips. "Hi, Mom," she said, her voice low.

"Now Mad, what have I told you? I can't have a grown woman calling me that." A quick intake of breath over the line—the draw of a cigarette.

Okay, she'd play the game. Anything to move this along. "Hi, Cindy. What's up?"

"You must be doing okay to afford a summer at the lake."

"What do you want Mom?" It had to be money. It always was.

"Cindy, Cindy." The sound of another drag. "Can't a mother visit her only daughter?"

Her skin grew clammy. "Where are you?"

"Right here, at the store in Fortune Bay."

Maddie leapt to her feet.

"I took the bus from Bremerton. The nice lady who works here let me use her phone."

Maddie grabbed her purse and was out the door, heart racing, stomach churning, already in damage control mode. "Stay right where you are. Don't talk to anyone."

How many times had she done this before? She learned early on that in these situations it was best to get her mother away quickly. Before she did any serious damage.

Her only hope was that no one she cared about had seen Cindy.

She barked a hoarse laugh. In Fortune Bay? Impossible.

She drove the Beast like a madwoman into town, pulled up at the store and tore inside. Fiona looked up and pointed to the café.

Cindy's too-loud laugh reverberated through the open arch. Maddie's heart sank and she clutched the arched opening. Then steeling herself, she went into the lion's den.

Her mother was perched on a stool at the counter, skinny

legs sticking out of tight short-shorts, her loosening belly sagging below her skimpy T-shirt. Her makeup was downright scary. A huge beat-up bag hung on her shoulder. Thank God she didn't have any luggage.

She was talking to Stephanie's neighbor Bob Foster, smirking and patting her straw-blonde hair like a fading actress well past her expiry date.

Louise poured some coffee into Cindy's cup and when she saw Maddie in the doorway, she raised her eyebrows and sent Maddie a look.

Maddie winced as if shot through the heart. Not *the look*. Not from Louise.

Cindy registered Maddie's presence at the door and leaned heavily on the counter, looking past Foster. "Nice to see you, honey."

Maddie clenched her teeth and tried to swallow past the lump in her throat but couldn't force out any words.

Cindy struggled to get off the stool.

"Let me help you," Foster said with a gentlemanly gesture he would undoubtedly offer to any woman, not only the ones too drunk to stand by themselves.

"Why thank you," Cindy gushed, leaning against him, rubbing her breasts on his arm in a clearly provocative way.

"Let's go Mom," Maddie said between clenched teeth as she took her mother's arm and tried to hurry her out of the café.

"Maddie—" Louise began.

"It's okay," she said, and kept walking.

"I've told you not to call me Mom," Cindy said in a stage whisper as she minced through the store on her sky-high platform sandals. "I don't want them to think I'm old enough to have a daughter your age."

Maddie grasped her arm tightly as Cindy wove dangerously through the displays in the store, then held the door open as her mother went through.

Cindy turned in the doorway and waved to Fiona. "Thanks

Hon. See ya' later."

Maddie hustled her down the steps. *Not if I can help it.*

The stale aroma of liquor and cigarettes followed Cindy into the car, sending Maddie reeling back to sick, dark times. She gritted her teeth and shook off the memories. Best to get right to the point.

Her clammy hands gripped the steering wheel. "What do you want Mom? I don't have any money."

"I don't want your money." Cindy tried for indignant but all Maddie heard was the drag of alcohol on each word. "Can't a mother visit her daughter?"

Shit. Funny how she only cursed when her mother was around.

"Now dear, it's only a visit."

Maddie had hoped she wouldn't have to take Cindy to the cabin. Her home was her refuge; she didn't want to contaminate it.

Her shoulders dropped and she touched her head to the steering wheel. There was no other choice. She had to get out of the parking lot before anyone else saw them. She turned the key in the ignition. "One night, Mom. Just one night."

She drove mechanically back to the cabin, not really seeing the road. What would she do about Jenny? She couldn't meet Cindy. Not like this. Maybe some other time when hopefully Cindy was in better shape.

As if that time would ever come.

Maybe they would never meet. Would that be so terrible? She had talked to Jenny about Cindy in Seattle. Surely that was enough. But she had to get word to Jenny to stay at Brandy's for the night, then she'd have a chance to get Cindy out first thing in the morning.

Her mother chattered on brightly about her life in Seattle and the new boyfriend who might be 'the one'. Apparently he was waiting in Bremerton, an hour away.

Thank God for small mercies. That would have been so much worse.

Maddie didn't want to know about her mother's life or her mother's men. She had heard it all a hundred times before. Cindy was so trusting. She never learned. Every man was 'the one', until the night he took off out the trailer door with all their money, never to be seen again.

When they pulled up behind the cabin, Cindy said, "Ohhh... Not at all what I was expecting."

Maddie closed her eyes, face tight.

Cindy quickly backtracked. "I mean, it's real cute and everything. I just thought you'd have something bigger. Fancier. Mark always had lots of money."

"I'm not married to Mark any more Mom, and he doesn't give me any money."

"I told you not to call me 'Mom'," Cindy murmured as they got out of the car and climbed the steps to the porch.

Cindy poked around the kitchen, touching Maddie's things.

Maddie's eyes swiveled toward the pictures of Jenny on the TV. She walked over briskly, swept them into her arms and took them into the bedroom where she squeezed them into her underwear drawer. Cindy didn't seem to notice.

"You'll have to sleep on the couch," Maddie said, rubbing a palm over her forehead where a headache was beginning to brew. Bedtime was still hours away. Hours of torture, watching her mother degenerate from overly talkative to maudlin and slurring her words until finally, thankfully, when she'd drunk enough of whatever was in that bag of hers, she would pass out.

The couch would be fine. She wouldn't remember anything in the morning anyway. Maddie just hoped they could skip the belligerent stage.

She called Jenny when Cindy went to the bathroom, making up an excuse about going out with Frankie that night. Fortunately, Jenny was happy to stay at Brandy's, would go straight to work at the store at ten the next morning and be home mid-afternoon. Perfect.

Cindy settled at the kitchen table, chattering about her life, her man and their 'holiday' on the peninsula. He was a salesman, but sales hadn't been good. It was the economy; things would pick up. *Yada, yada, yada.*

It had been years since they had spent this much time together, in the same room, but nothing had changed. The torture was the same. Eventually numbness set in.

Cindy stubbed her cigarettes into one of Augusta's pretty china saucers. Maddie prayed the ash wouldn't leave a mark.

Although she tried, she couldn't block out the sound of her mother's voice. She could picture all too clearly the squalid rooms where Cindy lived with her current flame, where they spent their days drinking their money away. How some days he would drag himself out to make a few bucks anyway he could, or Cindy would go and stand in the welfare line. She was a pro at that. She'd done worse when Maddie was young, bringing men home for money. For all Maddie knew, she still did.

Maddie could picture the scene—they'd needed money, then Cindy had a brainwave, she would find her daughter. She had that rich husband. Surely she owed her mother something for all those years Cindy had taken care of her.

Because that was how Cindy remembered it, even though, in reality, Maddie had been the one who held things together from the time she was old enough to make a peanut butter sandwich. If they were lucky enough to have peanut butter. Sometimes it was a ketchup sandwich, when they were lucky enough to have bread.

Cindy's voice droned on.

When Maddie got a bit older, she learned to go through her mother's purse when Cindy had safely passed out on the couch. She would take some of the money—not all of it though, because if Cindy caught on there'd be hell to pay—and walk along the highway to the gas station where she could buy a few things to keep herself going.

"Hungry Mom?"

Cindy sat at the kitchen table, chain smoking, her eyes darting around the room. "No thanks dear, but I might have a little drink to calm my nerves."

"I don't have anything to drink Mom. Why don't you have coffee?" Maddie filled Augusta's electric percolator with water and put coffee in the basket.

"That's okay." Cindy reached into her voluminous bag and pulled out a twenty-six-ounce bottle of gin. "I have a brand new bottle here. Got a glass?"

Maddie clenched her teeth and slapped a glass on the table. She might as well, otherwise her mother would just drink it straight from the bottle.

She glanced at the clock. Four o'clock. Still hours to go. She took the frying pan off the wall, the eggs out of the fridge, and opened a can of beans. Anything to soak up the alcohol.

She made some toast to go with the eggs and by the time she put the plates on the table, Cindy was pouring herself a second gin, straight up.

"I'm not hungry..."

"Eat," Maddie said, and to encourage her, she tried to force down some food herself, although her stomach was a churning acid pit and she worried she wouldn't keep anything down. Cindy nibbled on some toast and dabbed it into the yolk and beans. Maddie just hoped it was enough.

Cindy didn't ask about Jenny and although Maddie had worked hard to keep them apart, it still hurt. She reminded herself it was better this way. Her mother continued to talk, the story as familiar as a recurring nightmare, one Maddie could never escape.

Finally, she couldn't take it anymore. "I've got to get some air." She stalked out the front door and onto the porch, inhaled deeply and sank onto the couch.

The porch lost its usual calming effect when misery, in the form of Cindy, followed her out the door. Her mother set her glass and bottle on the railing and settled on the couch beside her, not missing a beat of her story.

Maddie scarcely registered the words, but noticed the tone had twisted into a self-pitying whine. *Phase two.* She knew the steps of Cindy's ritual descent into drunkenness by heart.

This is not my life, a voice cried out in her head. But it *was* her life. Always had been. Some of her earliest memories were of guiding Cindy home after an evening of huddling quietly in a corner while her mother and her "friend" bounced around on the couch.

At the time she didn't know what they were doing, but now it turned her stomach to think a mother would put a child through that. Looking back, she thought her mother must have taken her along for insurance, to make sure she made it home.

But she wasn't a child any more, although that was exactly how she felt whenever her mother was around. She was a grown woman, she reminded herself, with a child of her own to protect. She had to break Cindy's hold if she was going to survive.

She tried to remember what she'd read in magazines about interventions. They were usually a group effort, but she'd have to deal with this alone. All she could remember was—*Don't accuse.* Keep your comments about how *you* feel.

When her mother took a break to pour herself another drink, Maddie began. "Cindy, I'm worried about your drinking."

Her mother stopped. With excessive care, she turned to her daughter. "Mine' your own business. Sis has nothin' to do with you."

"It does, though, Mom, because I care about you."

"If you cared so much you'd keep in touch. You'd send me some money from that rich husband of yours."

Maddie looked away. Her jaw tightened and she rubbed her hand over her chin and down her throat. Then she tried again. "I'm worried you'll ruin your health."

Cindy laughed harshly and took another sip. "You're worried I'll get sick and you'll have to take care of me. You've always just thought 'bout yourself. You never cared about the family."

The family? What family? There was no family. But there was no use arguing with Cindy now. She'd fallen into her own distorted version of the past, one where Maddie was at fault. And somehow Cindy's accusations managed to pluck a guilty chord deep inside her because Maddie had always wondered if she *was* at fault for never being able to stop Cindy's drinking. For not stopping her from ruining their lives.

Night fell around them like a blanket, but Maddie didn't turn on the lights. Cindy's words slurred to incomprehensible murmurs and when her chin dropped onto her chest, Maddie steered her into the house and onto the couch, where her mother immediately sank into oblivion.

The cabin was warm, but Maddie took the soft quilt off her bed and covered her mother, then stared down at her while she slept. Cindy looked old and broken, her skin ashen, her features sunken.

A tear escaped and ran down Maddie's cheek but she rubbed it away. She wasn't sure who she was crying for, her mother or herself. Either way, it wouldn't change anything.

Unplugging the coffee pot, she made herself a cup of chamomile tea. The house reeked of cigarettes so she opened the windows wide and went out to sit on the porch, breathing deep the clean night air.

Maddie put down her tea and turned her hand over to look at the tattoo on her wrist. When she'd first run away at sixteen, she'd fallen in with a bunch of kids in Seattle who had given her a place to sleep. One of the boys worked in a tattoo parlor, and he snuck her in one night and gave her the tattoo. She'd chosen a chain that started on the pulse point of her wrist, wrapped most of the way around and then, as it curved up her inner arm, the links began to dissolve and, like an Escher drawing, slowly morphed into flying birds. It expressed perfectly how she felt in those heady days—breaking free of the chains, getting away from her mother, finally flying free.

She hadn't escaped though. Not really. Not fully. Cindy was her mother and would always be part of her life. She was fooling herself if she thought she had a chance of escape, of a different life, of a future with Jake.

She stood up and walked down to the lake where she sat on the big rock and stared at the dancing reflection of stars on the water. Lonely times stretched ahead once Jenny was gone for good, but at least alone she would have control of her life.

And she would be alone. She rested her forehead on her fingertips. Why would anyone want her? Jake thought he did, but he didn't really know her. She'd never learned the first thing about relationships. How to let someone in, how to share her life, how to trust him not to leave in the night.

The only thing she'd learned from watching her mother was that you couldn't trust men. That even the good ones let you down.

No, she'd stick to her plan. Her and Jenny, all the way. She wouldn't risk losing this life she'd built. Not for anyone. Not even Jake.

That way, no one had to get hurt.

Chapter 33

Maddie had never been more grateful to see the faint glow of dawn in the sky. The first bus out of town left at eight, so at seven o'clock she made a fresh pot of coffee in the old electric percolator and woke her mother.

Cindy was a wreck, although probably no worse than any other morning of her adult life. Black mascara stuck to the wrinkled pouches under her eyes. She objected strongly and coarsely to being woken, to being "pushed around," to the coffee—although she inhaled two strong cups—and to generally everything.

But Maddie was clear in her own mind—Cindy had to go.

"I don't feel very well this morning," Cindy whined. "I think I got the flu."

Heard that before. "Sorry Mom, you have to go. I have work to do. I'll take you to the bus."

"Okay, okay," her mother said. "I'll just go freshen up."

Then she locked herself in the bathroom.

Maddie paced the porch for half an hour, knocking on the bathroom door and calling her mother's name. But then the shower would come on or the toilet would flush and Cindy wouldn't answer. The smell of tobacco smoke drifted out and Maddie knew her mother was sitting in there, smoking cigarettes, waiting her out so they would miss the bus.

Every few minutes Cindy called out in a weak voice. "I'm not feeling very well," or, "Just a few minutes." Once she said, "Maybe I should stay."

It was the same old story. Every time Cindy wanted to get out of doing something, she said she had the flu.

Maddie wracked her brain for a strategy short of breaking down the door and dragging her mother out, and slowly an idea took shape. It was the only way. She whirled around and went into the cabin.

In the bedroom she pulled the curtain closed behind her, knelt on the floor by the dresser and stealthily opened the bottom drawer. Reaching into the back corner, she took out the money sock.

Money was the carrot at the end of the stick. She couldn't really afford it, her nest egg was almost gone, but there was no other way. Cindy was digging in for the long haul and Maddie desperately needed to get her on the bus today, so she peeled five twenties off the roll and quietly put the sock back into the drawer.

When she opened the curtains to the kitchen, Cindy was sitting at the table, pouring straight gin into a glass. "Hair of the dog," she said, unconcerned to be caught drinking at eight in the morning.

Maddie waved the money in front of her eyes. "You've got to go Mom. If you get on the bus and don't come back, I'll give you this. It's all I can spare." Cindy's eyes narrowed and she opened her mouth to speak. "No Mom, I mean it."

"That's no way to talk to your mo—"

"In the car, Mom. Now." Maddie grabbed her purse and held open the door.

Cindy made a production of gathering up her things, a delaying tactic that allowed her to finish her drink, but finally she minced outside and climbed into the car.

Maddie parked at the far end of the General Store parking lot where the bus turned around. They had missed the first bus and would have to wait for the next one. That was cutting it close with running into Jenny when she came to the store for her shift at ten, but it should work. She put on some music so they wouldn't have to talk. Cindy got out of the car, but Maddie didn't try to stop her, just turned her head away and looked out the driver's side window.

And saw Colleen's car pull in across the parking lot.

Colleen got out of the car, opened the rear door and leaned into the back seat to adjust the buckle on her son's car seat. Maddie's eyes flashed to Cindy, who was pulling the bottle of gin out of her purse. She looked back at Colleen, who hadn't seen them yet.

Maddie jumped out of the car, her only thought to get Cindy back in the car. She ran around to the passenger side and threw open the door. She grabbed Cindy's arm, trying to hide the bottle, but Cindy was surprisingly fast.

Colleen turned around, her eyes widening as she saw Cindy raise the humongous bottle and take a swig. Then her eyes jumped to Maddie and her jaw dropped.

Maddie wished the ground would open and swallow her up. Her, Cindy, the whole mess. She stuffed her mother back in the car and saw Colleen frantically punching numbers into her cell phone, glancing at them every few seconds across the empty lot.

Maddie jumped into the Beast and floored it, tearing out of the lot, leaving Colleen in a swirling cloud of dust. She drove like a maniac, following the bus route to Majestic. They had no chance of catching up to the first bus, but she had to get Cindy out of Fortune Bay.

Her eyes blurred with tears as she took the corners of the winding road. Fiona and Louise were one thing, but Colleen was even worse. She had influence with Jake and this would give her all the ammunition she needed.

Maddie pushed back a sob as the enormity of the damage Cindy's visit had caused sank in.

She was finished in Fortune Bay.

* * *

Two hours later, Cindy caught the next bus out of Majestic. Maddie gave her the money as she pushed her up the stairs and into the bus.

When it pulled away and she was sure Cindy was gone, Maddie drove back to the cabin. In a daze she climbed into bed, wrapped herself in a cocoon of blankets and fell into a deep sleep.

It was mid-afternoon when she crawled out of bed, still

hardly able to breathe, or think. Her head felt stuffed with quilt batting and even the air felt oppressive. Looking out the window, she wasn't surprised to see rainclouds hanging low over the lake.

She shuffled into the kitchen, numb and deflated, like she'd been the one on an all-night bender. Her body ached and she wanted nothing more than to crawl back into her cave and nurse her wounds. Jenny would be home any minute though. She had to pull herself together.

What was she going to say to her friends? What was she going to do next?

She'd cut their stay short. She couldn't bear to become a pariah in the eyes of her new friends. Did she have enough photographs for the show? It would have to be enough.

Why did Colleen of all people have to drive into the parking lot? Jake was bound to find out about Cindy now, in glorious detail, and when he did, Maddie was sure she'd never see him again. Even though he hadn't actually met her mother, she was sure Cindy had ruined that relationship too.

Maddie re-heated the coffee and took a cup out onto the porch, hoping the breeze off the lake would clear her head. Inhaling deeply, she blew it all out, trying to visualize the pain and memories going with it. It was an exercise she'd read about in a magazine, and after the requisite five repetitions, she did feel a bit calmer.

Jenny and Brandy arrived in a flurry on their bikes.

"Mom. Can I go out again? We're having movie night at Nadine's—hey, you don't look very good."

"I think I've got the flu." She winced when heard her mother's words come out of her mouth, was furious with herself for repeating them and angry at her mother for making her to lie to her daughter. "No. That's not true."

Jenny looked at her curiously.

"My mother was here."

Jenny's eyes widened. "Really? Is she coming back? Can I meet her?"

"I don't think so. Not this time." There would be time later to tell Jenny that they were going back to the city early. She forced a smile. "Go to Nadine's and have fun."

Jenny accepted her story without question. Grabbing her pajamas and a bag of cherries from the fridge, she raced out the door.

Maddie got another cup of coffee and continued to sit. The cup was warm between her hands and from her spot on the couch, she watched the rain slowly make its way down the lake. The hills became a watercolor blur as the squall progressed, washing away everything stained and dirty in its path.

Spirit crept up on the porch and hopped lightly onto the couch beside her. She didn't know if the cat sensed the approaching rain or her own melancholy mood, but Maddie stroked her back in a rhythm that seemed to soothe them both. As she picked the thorns and burrs out of Spirit's long white fur, numbness, an old friend, began to take hold, shielding her broken heart.

Later—she wasn't sure how much time had passed—she heard voices in the driveway. Female voices. She threw off the blanket and rubbed her hands over her face, although not quite sure what good it did short of making her feel slightly more alert. She pushed her unruly hair back from her face just as Frankie and Louise came around the corner of the cabin.

"Hey there." Frankie climbed the steps. She gave Maddie a hug. "Heard you had a rough day."

Maddie's eyes filled with tears. She was afraid of what she would see in Frankie's face, dreading *the look*. When Frankie pulled back to face her, however, she saw only concern in her friend's warm brown eyes.

That was Frankie. Louise wouldn't hold back.

"How are you doing? Jeeze, your old lady's a piece of work."

For a moment Maddie didn't know what to say, then she

shook her head. What had she been thinking? It wouldn't faze Louise. "She caught me off guard. I hadn't even told her where I was staying."

"How did she track you down?" Frankie asked, sitting next to her on the couch.

"My ex-husband told her." She sat up straighter and looked them both in the eye. "Anyway, I'm glad you came by, although I would have come to say goodbye before I left."

"Goodbye?" Frankie asked. "Where are you going?"

"Back to the city."

"Why?" Louise asked.

"Well, my mother was here." Surely that was self-explanatory?

Frankie squinted as if trying to understand. "We know. What has that got to do with you leaving?"

Maddie let out a jagged breath. "Oh come on. Soon it will be all over town."

"Well, yeah. Probably already is," Louise allowed. "But everybody likes you. They won't care."

Maddie shook her head. "You don't understand. It's happened before. Over and over. She's ruined every friendship I've ever had."

"Every family has problems you know," Frankie said softly. "It doesn't reflect on you."

"It *always* reflects on me," Maddie said, unable to hide the bitterness in her voice. "Growing up, I always had to hide it— the fact that my mother was a drunk. I could never bring other kids home. Never had any friends. No nice clothes, often no clean clothes. Not until I was old enough to wash them myself."

She remembered standing in the shower fully dressed, scrubbing her clothes with a bar of soap, tears of humiliation burning in her eyes. She sniffed and swiped her nose with the sleeve of her sweatshirt.

"She was always drinking, always drunk. So many men in and out of her life. Our life. They all left eventually. I was usually glad."

Frankie put an arm around her shoulder. "That must have been hard."

Maddie stuck out her jaw. "I learned to take care of myself. To trust no one but myself. As long as I do that, Jenny and I are okay. Jenny has to come first. I just have to stick to the plan."

Louise propped a hip on the railing. "What plan?"

"I always have a plan. It's how I keep on track. Right now, number one is to get Jenny through school and out into the world. Next is to get my career up and running. Get my website up, take the photographs for the show, and don't go broke in the process."

"And what about Jake?" Louise asked. Maddie looked at her in surprise. Louise shrugged and glanced at Frankie for backup. "Hey, we've got eyes."

Maddie pulled herself up. Not good to give herself away like that. "I don't think we'll be seeing each other anymore. I'm sure he's heard..." She thought of Colleen and shuddered. "Anyway, it wouldn't have worked. Summer's almost over. I'll be going soon anyway."

"Give him a chance," Louise said softly.

Maddie pressed her lips together to hold back the tears, not trusting herself to speak. She shook her head. Jake had never been part of the plan.

Chapter 34

Stephanie wondered if she should tell Jake what she saw in the parking lot that morning. In the end she decided, better her than Colleen.

She had been walking from the Post Office to the store when she saw her daughter in the parking lot, punching a number into her phone. As Stephanie approached, she saw Maddie at the far end of the lot, panic etched on her face, pushing a woman clutching a liquor bottle into her car. At eight in the morning. Then Maddie peeled away in a cloud of dust.

Stephanie walked up behind Colleen who was watching Maddie drive away as she spoke into her phone, and heard her say, "You won't believe it. A big bottle of gin. Call me."

Stephanie tapped her daughter on the shoulder and Colleen spun around.

"There you are." Colleen closed her phone with a snap, her eyes bright. "I was trying to call you."

"Why?" Stephanie's eyes followed Maddie's car as it disappeared in the direction of Majestic.

"Maddie had a visitor. Some old lush, drinking straight from the bottle right here in the parking lot."

Stephanie looked thoughtfully at her daughter. "I saw. How difficult it must be for her."

Colleen blushed. "I'm just worried about Jake. That's all."

"Jake's a grown man. He can take care of himself."

Fiona had called the night before, out of concern, to fill Stephanie in. They, and a small circle of friends, tried to look out for the women in the village.

This morning Stephanie had come to town to see what she could do to help. Growing up, she had some experience with alcoholism, saw first-hand the damage it could do. Her uncle was a drunk—that's what they called alcoholics in those days—and she had always been uneasy about the conspiracy of silence surrounding his drinking. How the family blamed him for his weakness but excused his actions because he was drunk.

His children, her cousins, were often withdrawn and never spoke of what happened at home. And it didn't stop there. The damage followed them into adulthood, the effects noticeable in their own families to this day.

As a child, she found the atmosphere at family gatherings confusing. Once she understood what was going on, she promised herself she would never again be part of a circle of silence at the cost of the children involved.

It explained a lot about Maddie though. Her grim earnestness. Her obvious discomfort in large gatherings, be it strangers, family or friends. The wall she had built around herself that barely hid her vulnerability.

Stephanie hoped Jake knew what he was getting into. And hoped he could handle it if he did.

* * *

A knock echoed on the cabin door. Maddie dried her hands on a tea towel and glanced out the window. When she saw Jake was standing on the porch, anxiety coiled like a snake in her stomach. She hadn't seen him since her mother's visit, and now he was here. On the porch. Giving her no sign whether he knew or not.

Once he heard, she didn't think she would see him again. Ever. So he must not know.

She opened the door but then just stood there. She didn't know what to say.

Apparently he didn't either. They stared into each other's eyes through the screen, her heart beat slowing, her breathing shallow. What did he know? She couldn't very well ask, *did you hear my drunk of a mother was in town?*

"How are you?" Jake asked, his eyes searching her face.

Her heart sank. He knew. What could she say? *Not fine,*

but not completely in pieces either. In fact, maybe even a little stronger than before. "Fine."

"I heard your mother was here."

She smiled stiffly. "I don't want to talk about my mother. But now you know. Now you must see why this can't really go anywhere."

"That's not true." Opening the door, he stepped inside and took her in his arms.

She stiffened. She wanted to surrender, knew how good it would feel. How loving him could wash everything else away and, for a moment, she would believe it could be only them.

But that would be an illusion. She'd never forget how Mark had changed when he found out about her past. With Jake, there was so much more to lose. More love meant more pain when it ended. Better to end it now.

He kissed her tenderly "I want you to stay with me, forever."

She let out a shuddering sigh. "I can't." The dam broke and tears streamed down her face. "Don't you see? There is no forever. Nothing has changed. I can't stay. I never could."

He stepped back, fumbled a white handkerchief out of his pocket and wiped her tears.

"I could never give you what you need," she said, trying to pull herself together. They had to finish this, now. She'd never be able to do it again.

"You can. You're all I need. Jenny can go to school here. We'll get married and live—"

"It won't work. I have to do what's right for Jenny and me. Surely you of all people can understand. We should have kept our distance. It's so much harder now. You don't know my mother—"

"I don't give a damn about your mother. It's you I love."

"I know you think you mean it, but you don't understand. Anyway, it's not really about her. It's about me."

"What do you mean? You're perfect."

"I'm damaged." She almost shouted the words, then

struggled to get control of her voice. "You want a family—a real family. All I know about family is what I learned on TV, and even I know that's not reality." She couldn't ruin his life like that.

"You can stay –"

"I can't, not now."

At the bleak look on his face, her conviction weakened, cracking the wall around her heart. She really wanted to stay. "Maybe I'll come back."

His face twisted in pain. She shrank back.

"Maybe?" He spat out the word. "You say that now, but you won't."

"I could. I want to."

He stepped back out onto the porch. "I can't do this. Not again."

Through her tears, she watched him storm away.

Chapter 35

A week passed, and Maddie did not see Jake again. She felt responsibility for the disaster. They never should have made love. That warm communion, those loving moments, she should never have let it go that far. Now she would always know what she was missing.

She'd tried to hide her tears when Jenny came home the next morning, but Jenny had known right away. She'd put a maternal arm around her mother's shoulders and said, "Aw, Mom. I told you not to let him break your heart."

After that, Maddie threw herself into her work, but keeping busy didn't stop the ache, the emptiness in her heart. As her hand went up and rubbed the spot, she realized why poets called the heart the organ of love. It really did hurt when it broke.

He was never part of the plan.

She lifted her hand to her forehead, trying to remember the once so important points of the plan. Number one was raising Jenny in as normal a home as she could possibly manage. Well, her smart, beautiful daughter was almost an adult. Jenny was her own person and while Maddie couldn't take credit for all Jenny had turned out to be, she hadn't ruined her daughter's life either. *So check that off as a job on track.*

That had always been the main thing, but what else? Her burgeoning career was also in there somewhere. Oh hell, surely there was more. She had to go back to her job—for a little while at least—but it was only a job. She needed the money, so if Eileen would take her back she'd go, but it was nothing to plan her life around.

In frustration she pushed thoughts of the plan aside and went out to the makeshift workbench behind the cabin where she and Jenny had been taking turns working on the frames. In the soft balmy air of the late summer afternoon, she worked gluing and clamping the pieces of molding together. Repetitive assembly-line work, it soothed her nerves.

It had been dry for weeks and the maple leaves were beginning to turn orange-gold. As the nights lengthened and the heat of the sun began to wane, the temperature of the lake dropped a few degrees turning swimming into an invigorating plunge. Blackberry vines curled around the corner of the shed, deep purple berries the size of her thumb scenting the air, sweetly enticing until you hit one of the killer thorns that ran along the canes.

Frankie appeared in the driveway and Maddie saw her brow wrinkle in concern as she assessed Maddie's mood.

Maddie herself would give it a five out of ten. She'd survive.

In the past week, she'd developed a rationale for what had happened with Jake: a summer affair that couldn't possibly have worked out. They had different needs, different plans. It happened. She'd get over it, someday, she hoped.

That's what she'd told Frankie and Louise on the dark porch two nights after the heartbreaking scene. Although she'd managed to hold back the tears, they hadn't been fooled. They had been treating her like an invalid ever since and it was starting to get old.

"Thought you might want to go blackberry picking and help me make some jam," Frankie said. "You can take some jars."

She didn't say "back to the city". They were all trying not to mention her impending departure. She didn't need a reminder that her time here was running out.

"Sure," she said, faking enthusiasm. But as they loaded pails into the back of the Beast and headed out to Frankie's 'secret spot', she felt her spirits begin to rise.

Frankie's spot turned out to be a goldmine and they were back in her kitchen, knee deep in pails of blackberries, when

Louise arrived. She pulled a stool up to the island and plucked a juicy berry from a large bowl on the counter, looking it over appraisingly.

"Where did you get these? They are so much bigger than the dried-up ones that grow around the store."

Frankie gave Maddie a wink. "Our secret."

Louise laughed. "I don't really care. I just want some of the jam." She turned to Maddie who was stirring the pot on the stove, waiting for it to boil. "I talked to Ms. Bowden, she handles the bookings at the Hall. She said we could have the show there next week, as long as we clear out before the dance on the long weekend."

Maddie had not forgotten their tentative plan for a preview of her work, however recently she'd been having second thoughts. "I don't know. I actually shouldn't show them anywhere before the show at the gallery in Seattle. It's in the contract."

Louise sighed, clearly disappointed. "People are asking about it. They assumed they'd get a chance to see them."

Very few people from Fortune Bay went to Seattle even once a year, so Maddie did not expect anyone to come to the show—except for Louise and Frankie, who had promised they'd try.

"Could we hang a few here?" Frankie asked.

Maddie thought for a moment. "I don't see why not."

"And if a few people dropped in, they couldn't help but see them."

Louise kept the ball rolling. "I could make some appetizers on Saturday."

Maddie shot her a look and she shrugged with a grin. "I guess I could bake some cookies," Maddie said.

"We should have coffee and lemonade," Frankie added as she spooned the fragrant magenta jam into sterilized jars.

By the time the jar lids started to pop, their plans were well underway.

* * *

Maddie needed some nails and picture wire, so she stopped at the hardware store in Majestic.

She was at the nail bins when Jake came in through the big glass doors. Even with the glare of sun behind him, she recognized his silhouette. And she would never mistake the walk.

Her heart constricted. She couldn't breathe. She'd been on tenterhooks for the past week expecting to run into him everywhere she went. Now she had.

He stopped dead when he saw her, jammed his hands in his pockets and frowned. No smile for her anymore. Maddie bit her lip—hard—and walked up to him.

"Hi Jake."

Silence. Then he replied, "I guess you're leaving soon."

Ouch, straight to the jugular.

"Next week."

The painful silence threatened to smother her. "How is the kitchen coming?"

"Fine," he said, a muscle jumping in his jaw.

Another pause, and she tried again. "I'm showing my photographs at Frankie's on Saturday. I was hoping I would run into you"—*liar*— "so I could invite you to come."

He glared, looked away, shifted to the other foot. "I'm busy on Saturday."

She was bleeding inside. That was as many stabs to the chest as she could take. She tried to smile. "Well I hope you can make it. I would like to say good-bye to Sarah too.

He didn't respond.

"Good-bye Jake."

He nodded and walked away.

* * *

It broke Stephanie's heart to see her son in so much pain. She couldn't believe Maddie was taking this calmly either. She'd watched them together over the past few weeks and although Maddie still had that slightly distant air about her, Stephanie had seen how she melted when Jake touched her.

And once, when he'd turned away, how she closed her eyes, pressed her lips together and took a deep breath. What it meant, Stephanie didn't know, but she felt she had to try one last time to help them save what they had.

Word was out that Maddie was having a show of her photographs at Frankie's house tomorrow, so Stephanie loaded a plate with chocolate chip cookies and headed down the shoreline path.

As she suspected, lights were blazing at the lakeside house. The front door was standing open and Stephanie let herself in. Maddie and Louise were hanging photographs in the living room and Stephanie took a moment to look at the pictures they had already hung. They were stunning, the composition, the use of lights and darks.

"Oh Maddie, they're lovely," Stephanie said. "I'm so glad you're giving everyone a chance to see them."

Maddie was facing away from her and stopped working. Stephanie could see her shoulders rise and fall with a deep sigh. Then she turned around. "Thank you."

Stephanie held out the cookies and smiled. "I brought these for tomorrow, but I don't think there's any reason you couldn't have one now."

Maddie looked at the cookies as if she didn't know what they were, then shook herself and said, "No thank you." Excusing herself, she went out onto the back deck and a moment later, Stephanie heard her banging nails into the cedar siding.

Louise raised her eyebrows and inclined her head after Maddie, so Stephanie followed her outside.

"I'm sorry you're leaving."

"That was always the plan." Maddie pounded another nail into the wall.

"I know, but you and Jake seemed to have really hit it off in the past few weeks..."

"Well, I have to go back." Maddie stopped hammering, but she did not look at Stephanie.

"I'd love to see you give it a chance."

At this, Maddie turned to face her and Stephanie could see the tears in her eyes. "I can't give him what he needs. You saw my mother. Can you imagine my childhood? Probably not." She let out a hoarse laugh, then bent over and dug for nails in the sack at her feet. "Whatever you're thinking, make it ten times worse. I am not like you all. I'm not what he wants. He needs a family and I don't even know what a normal family is."

She went back to swinging the hammer, missing as many times as she hit.

Stephanie said, "That's not true. I've seen you with Jenny and Sarah. You're a great mother. Anyway, there is no such thing as a 'normal family'. We all just do the best we can."

"Yeah, well, that's easy for you to say." Maddie took a shuddering breath and turned back to Stephanie. "I'm sorry. I don't mean to be rude, but you don't know what you're talking about."

"Maybe not," Stephanie said, saddened by the pain she saw in Maddie's eyes.

* * *

Maddie worked with Frankie and Louise late into the night, stripping Frankie's paintings off the walls in her large living room and hanging Maddie's black and white photographs closely, side by side, above the furniture and out onto the deck, trying not to think about the world she was leaving that was staring out of the pictures at every turn.

Some were framed and some were not but even so, she felt a melancholy thrill to see her work, her summer, laid out like that: the views of the lake, the nature studies and, of course, the people, her neighbors and friends whom she would dearly miss.

The next day the town came out in full force and, judging from the excited comments, everyone loved the work. By noon the steady trickle turned into a stream that continued all afternoon.

She teared up when Sean hugged her, and said a stoic good-by.

Stephanie brought Sarah who accepted a cookie with her best party manners and took Maddie's hand, demanding the grand tour. She knew, though, that something was wrong, and asked, "Are you coming back? Will I ever see you again?" To which Maddie could only reply, "I don't know, honey. I hope so." It broke Maddie's heart to say goodbye.

When they were leaving, Stephanie took her hand, looked deep into her eyes and said, "Come back, dear. Come back soon."

After that, Maddie tried to keep a welcoming smile on her face, but she watched the door all afternoon. Her hopes crested and crashed each time someone arrived, both hoping and fearing Jake would walk through the door. By the end of the day, she was exhausted, but it was probably better this way. She didn't think she could handle seeing him again.

Finally, late in the afternoon after everyone cleared out and Jenny and Brandy had gone to the cabin, the three women sank into the chairs on the deck.

"Thank you." Maddie said. "That was a lot of work."

"They loved the photographs," Frankie said.

"They did, didn't they?" Maddie said. "It gave me a chill to see the pictures up on the wall like that."

"Thanks for giving me the one of me in the café," Louise said. "I love it. I'll put it up in the café while I'm working there."

"While you're there? Are you thinking of leaving?" Maddie asked.

"One day," Louise answered vaguely. "I can't be a cook in a diner forever." Then she smiled. "Maybe someday I'll open my own café."

"I love my photograph, too," Frankie said, picking up the matted photo of the scene of the lake, called *Silence*. "I'll get it framed and hang it in the living room."

"I'll give you both frames," Maddie said. "I've made a

bundle, as you may have noticed. It's the least I can do after how much you two have helped me. Not only with the show, with—everything." She gulped some air. "I'll miss you both."

"We'll miss you, too." Frankie's voice was soft

"If we're going to get all teary anyway, how about the real info on what happened with Jake," Louise said, as she refilled her glass.

Maddie shook her head sadly. "It just didn't work out. I can't stay—he knew that from the beginning—and I know he will never leave Fortune Bay. This is such a wonderful place for Sarah to grow up, I wouldn't ask him to leave."

Silence descended on the deck.

Louise raised her glass in a toast. "Love sucks." The three friends could all drink to that.

* * *

Across the road at the farmhouse Jake toasted the single life too, alone with the last half of a bottle of scotch.

SEPTEMBER

Chapter 36

Two days later, Maddie finished packing and was ready to go. The Beast couldn't hold all of her and Jenny's things, plus the frames, so Louise offered to bring the rest of the frames over in a few weeks.

Jenny was excited to get back to the city and was already waiting in the car when Maddie did her final sweep. The cabin looked just as it had when she had arrived: clean, impersonal, sad.

She would miss Frankie and Louise. Without their twilight meetings, life wouldn't be the same. She left the map of the peninsula she'd brought from Seattle up on the wall. She wouldn't need it now.

Augusta's carved recipe box was the hardest thing to leave behind. Maddie had copied out her favorite recipes, but not the recipe for Children's Delight. She wouldn't be making them anymore. Too many memories.

She hung a framed photo of Augusta up on the wall. In it, she had stuck her head out the driver's side window of her old car, maybe a fifties Chevy, and was grinning as if her whole life was before her and everything was wonderful. Maddie straightened the frame and said softly, "I'll miss you."

She lingered at the door, an envelope in her hand. A warm breeze brushed by, carrying the smell of sweet spice. A voice whispered, "Leave it."

Maddie nodded, set the envelope beside the key on the table and gently closed the door.

Chapter 37

Maddie returned to work at the gallery right after Labor Day and a few days later took her pile of proofs to Tori. She had enlarged thirty-five and needed help to whittle them down to thirty. Then she still had to mat and frame the chosen images and was glad she had finished making the sleek black frames while she was in Fortune Bay.

She tried to maintain a cool, professional façade while she and Tori went through the pile, fighting the waves of longing washing over her. She missed the warmth of the sun in the rocks by the shore, the energy of the wind that lashed the tall firs, and the honey-sweet friendship on Frankie's deck at sunset. Hardest of all to see were the pictures of the man and his daughter who had started to feel like family.

Tori snapped her fingers, breaking Maddie's trance, and gave the picture in her hand a tug. Maddie held onto the photo of Jake and Sarah for another second, then let it go.

"What happened with that?" Tori asked.

"It didn't work out. Too complicated. We needed different things."

Tori raised her eyebrows.

Maddie shook her head dismissively. "He had issues." She sighed. "I guess I did too."

Tori gave her a gentle nudge. "Coward. What do you expect? He's a man and that is always complicated. It's the nature of the beast."

She cocked her head at an angle and studied the picture of the man and his daughter. "Well, this one's a keeper. Don't give up so easily. There's always another way. The question is, what do *you* want." She raised her eyebrows.

It felt more like a challenge than a question, and Maddie groaned. "I don't know. I'd love to go back, but it's not practical."

Tori grinned. "Life is short. Don't deny yourself pleasure when it comes knocking on your door."

* * *

Maddie stopped at Mark's house on the way home to pick up the rest of Jenny's things.

"I'm glad I had the chance to connect with Jenny this summer," Mark said when Maddie stood at the door, ready to leave. "She's a great kid. You've done a good job."

Maddie was stunned by the compliment. As stunned as if he'd hit her on the head with a two by four.

"It's much harder than I thought to keep track of a teenager," he said. "I can't imagine what it was like for you when she was small. I'm sorry I wasn't more help."

Maddie swallowed hard. His apology brought tears to her eyes. "Thank you. That means a lot. And I'm sorry too for my part in it all. I know I was never very..." She didn't know what to say. Open? Accepting? Trusting? "I did try my best."

"I know," he said. "And I could have tried harder too." He cleared his throat. "I'd like to see Jenny next Saturday, if she'll come."

Maddie put a hand on his arm. "Why don't you give her a call."

He smiled and, for the first time in years, she caught a glimpse of the man she used to know.

As Maddie packed Jenny's things into the backseat of the Beast, she realized that Mark wasn't the only one to praise her for how she'd raised Jenny. Louise had said the same thing, and it was true, she'd raised a lovely child. She was a good mother.

She stopped on the sidewalk as the words sunk in. She was nothing like her mother. Nothing at all.

This short conversation with Mark had gone a long way toward easing the residue left by negative comments he had made during their marriage. The badgering, the blame. In fact, she realized, he had treated her much the same way her mother did.

She sat in the car for a moment before driving away, staggered that she'd never made the connection before. Could it be a coincidence? Or was that what she thought she deserved? Obviously it had been, because she'd run from her mother right into Mark's arms.

Learned behavior. Repeated cycles. Until now they had only been words in magazines, part of the baggage that children of alcoholic parents carried with them. She had never thought it applied to her, but now she saw it did.

The last thing she wanted to do was pass this attitude on to her daughter. It was time to break the cycle.

* * *

Two weeks later, Maddie was neck deep in the mammoth job of framing the thirty prints for the show. She had cobbled together a workbench by setting an old door on a pair of night tables, and had tucked it under the sloping ceiling in a corner of the living room. There she set up a framing assembly line: frames, glass, mats, cardboard backing and a tin of brads, the tiny nails that held the whole thing together.

The work was repetitively mind numbing, yet she couldn't let her attention wander or the picture would end up crooked in the mat or she'd find a piece of dust trapped under the glass when she was done. She could have used some help but Jenny was out with her friends. In her last year of high school, she was trying out her wings.

It was inevitable and Maddie knew she might as well get used to it. Soon Jenny would be all grown up and gone for good and Maddie would be alone.

She carefully picked up the next print by the edges, whisked off the protective onionskin and winced as Jake and Sarah stared up at her. She would be glad when the show was over and reminders of Fortune Bay were not all over the apartment, ambushing her at every turn.

Now, though, there was nothing to do except tape the print to the mat board, drop it onto the glass in the frame, cover it with cardboard and tap in the brads. Then she put it on the floor with the others, but facing the wall. She didn't want it blindsiding her every time she walked in the living room.

That was her last frame. Only half of the frames had fit into the Beast when they'd returned to the city, but Louise should be arriving any minute with the rest.

She missed her friends, that much she could admit. She had no real friends in the city, except for Tori, who was fast becoming a friend. It had never mattered to her before, but then, she had never known real friendship before. Had, in fact, avoided that kind of intimacy. Over the summer, however, her new friends had become closer than family. She had grown to enjoy the gentle teasing and easy comradery, the comfort of knowing someone had your back.

Now back in the city, the old ache had returned and she recognized it as loneliness, something only the company of true friends could ease.

Straightening up from her workbench, she rubbed her lower back and looked out the open window. Below her an autumn dusk settled on the residential street. More than a month had passed since she'd left Fortune Bay, but she could imagine the view from the cabin as the golden glow on the mountain gave way to an early dusk.

Maddie snapped out of her reverie when Louise's yellow Jeep pulled up below, snagging a lucky parking spot right in front of the house.

Running down the two flights of stairs and out the front door, she whooped with joy as she threw herself into Louise's arms. Together they carried the frames from the car up to the apartment.

"I love this neighborhood," Louise exclaimed later when, after Jenny came home, they all walked to the cluster of restaurants on a nearby busy street.

"It has its benefits," Maddie agreed.

"I'd like to live in the city for a while," Louise said, checking out the window of a second hand store on the corner.

Maddie tried to see her old neighborhood through Louise's eyes but what she used to find charming now seemed tarnished. She used to love the mix of cultures and styles—but now the neighborhood seemed crowded and dingy and hard. Hard pavement, hard people and hard brick buildings. She longed for the lake, the forest and the gentle serenity of the cabin instead.

They ate at her favorite South Asian restaurant and once they were settled at their table with lassis and naan, Maddie broke the silence. "How is—everyone?"

"Everyone is fine. Frankie's back at work, Stephanie sends her love and some fig jam."

Maddie bit her lip in silence.

Jenny rolled her eyes. "Come on Mom, we know who you're really asking about."

"I haven't seen much of Jake," Louise said softly, "although Sarah seems to be at Stephanie's a lot. I don't really know how they're doing."

Maddie nodded. It would have to be enough.

"What are you going to wear to the show?" Louise asked, clearly changing the subject.

"I have no idea. A simple black dress?"

"No way. You're the star. You have to shine."

"I can't afford to shine."

"I know a place with 'Previously Loved' dresses. Some are completely covered in sequins. I'm thinking red. We'll go tomorrow."

* * *

Louise's visit ended much too soon. She promised to come for the opening, so Maddie focused on that and, with only one month to go, threw herself into the final preparations.

It worked to distract her for a while, but a week before the opening she stood alone at the window again, watching the streetlights below blink on one by one and the people hurry home.

What she was doing here?

You know where you really want to be, a voice whispered in her head. *Why are you afraid to say it?*

The vision of the cabin was so clear in her mind, but something held her back. The crabs of Frankie's tarot reading were still pulling her back into the murky pond. Childhood memories that told her she'd never belong. She closed her eyes. Would she ever be free of her past?

She seemed to have managed to blow a future with the man she loved—whose mother had almost begged her to stay— mostly because she hadn't been able to get past her own mother's influence. And now she may have missed her chance.

Coward. Tori's words came back to her. *Don't give up so easily.*

Maddie had told her that she and Jake wanted different things, but that wasn't true. They wanted the same thing—a home and family in Fortune Bay. She was just afraid to try.

Afraid to make the leap.

The time had come to face her demons.

Jenny's footsteps pounded on the stairs and she burst through the door. "I'm home."

Maddie turned to face her.

"Mom, what's wrong?"

She forced a reassuring smile. "I think it's time to visit your grandmother."

Chapter 38

Jenny was clearly excited about the visit, in distinct contrast to Maddie's trepidation. They decided to go after school the following day, late enough, Maddie thought, that Cindy would probably be up, but not so late that she'd be too drunk or, heaven forbid, entertaining.

She tried to warn Jenny. "She's an alcoholic. Sick. She might be drunk. The place will be a mess. It might smell bad. I called though, so hopefully she'll remember we're coming."

"Oh come on," Jenny protested. "She'll remember."

"It's bad Jenny. I can't be sure she will."

"Then why are we going."

Good question. "She's my mother, good or bad, and I've been thinking a lot about her since she came to Fortune Bay last summer. She didn't look well. She needs us. We are her family, she is your grandmother, and you are old enough to know the truth. The truth can't hurt you if you face it square on. It's only when it sneaks up on you that it can ruin your life."

Impressive speech. Let's hope it's true.

Her mother had moved again. She wasn't with the same man anymore, but Maddie wasn't sure she was living alone. The Beast pulled up before a row of faded two-story houses cowering under a maze of overpasses on the edge of downtown. Even in daylight, the dingy street was washed with grey. Flags and drooping sheets hung in the windows in lieu of drapes. Swallowing hard, Maddie's eyes searched the tipsy front porches for Cindy's number.

Her mother had sounded curious, almost worried over the phone, as if Maddie might ask her for something she wasn't prepared to give. The mention of Jenny did not seem to ring a bell, and for a moment Maddie had wondered if she shouldn't leave well enough alone. But she had a demon to face, and Jenny deserved to know the truth.

One lonely oak tree stood in the tiny front yard, the leaves crunching underfoot as they made their way to the stairs. Jenny held Maddie's arm in a viselike grip, her daughter's enthusiasm paling as the reality of her grandmother's life became clear. Maddie tried to hold herself tall and still to give Jenny a shot of much needed courage, but as she climbed the stairs, her wobbly knees refused to cooperate.

The front door stood open a crack and Maddie wondered if it was for them. She took Jenny's hand and they stepped inside.

Cindy's first-floor room was on the right just inside the front door. *Thank God.* She couldn't have climbed the darkened staircase if her life depended on it. Dread crept up her back on spidery legs as she knocked on Cindy's door.

A voice sounded faintly from within. "Come in."

Maddie turned the knob and the door swung open.

The stale smell of full ashtrays rolled out over her first as she stepped inside, then the sour stench of empty beer bottles hit her hard. She ushered Jenny inside but left the door open behind them.

Glancing quickly around the room, she saw that Cindy was alone, and had, in her way, tidied up. Bottles overflowed a cardboard box in the corner and the coffee table, although sticky and stained, was clear. The bed was a sea of blankets and a window was open, facing a brick wall next door.

Maddie blew out a breath she hadn't known she was holding. One minute in and she was still standing.

Her mother was sprawled on the couch, her ashtray and a tall glass on a side table within easy reach.

"Hi Mad," she said. She struggled to get up but lost her train of thought before she made it to her feet. Her eyes drifted to Jenny.

"Hi Grandma." Jenny's pinched voice was almost inaudible.

"Hi honey. Call me Cindy. I'm too young to be a grandmother." She cackled faintly and reached for her glass.

Maddie took her daughter's clammy hand in her own. "Nice place Mom." She tried hard to sound sincere.

"I like it." Cindy's eyes drifted away again.

"Why don't I make some coffee?" Maddie asked, mostly to break the sticky silence.

Cindy brightened and pointed to the kitchenette in the corner. "Sure, there's instant in the can by the sink." She sunk back into her seat and lit another cigarette.

Jenny was velcroed to Maddie's side as she walked across the room to the kitchenette. A week's worth of dirty dishes was piled in the sink and spilled across the counter. Bright orange mac and cheese had hardened in one pot.

Cindy waved her hand in their general direction. "I haven't had a chance to do the dishes."

"No problem." Maddie filled the electric kettle and plugged it in. She lifted the dishes out of the sink and started running hot water, squirting in soap from a bottle under the sink. She found a torn but clean dishrag in a drawer and threw the used one in the trash. She washed two cups from the cupboard and spooned instant coffee into each.

"Want some Ma?"

"No thanks Hon, I have a drink here."

Jenny stood like a mannequin, rooted in place. Maddie found an unused dishtowel and tossed it to her. Jenny's hand shot out and she caught it by reflex.

Maddie washed and Jenny dried, and by the time the kettle boiled they had the tiny kitchen in some semblance of order. Maddie took the dishrag and wiped the torn vinyl seats of the two kitchen chairs. There was no milk, so she added cold water to cool down their coffee quickly, then they perched on the chairs and drank the foul brew.

No one said anything of importance. That wasn't the point of the visit.

Maddie took a good look around. The place was

adequate, better than sometimes. There was food, mostly tins, in the cupboard. Her mother probably wasn't eating much anyway.

"You living alone here Mom?"

"Ya. I'm taking a break from men."

And how long will that last?

Cindy muttered something else that Maddie didn't catch, but she let it go.

Her mother had bags under her eyes and her skin had a yellowish tinge. Smoking and drinking and poor nutrition were taking their toll, but Maddie knew there was no point in trying to change her. She'd gone that route too many times before. Cindy was set in her ways. Satisfied, in her own mind, with her life. If she had a roof over her head and a bottle on the counter, that was all she wanted. It was terrible what alcoholism could do to a person, but Maddie had learned long ago she couldn't force her mother to change.

Jenny looked around in mild panic at the mess in the rest of the one room apartment, then at her mother, the whites of her eyes wide.

Maddie shook her head. "This is all we can do, for now," she said softly.

When they finished their coffee, Maddie washed out their cups and left a few bills on the counter. She gave her startled mother a kiss on the cheek and, twenty minutes after they entered, she and Jenny walked out of the house.

Maddie took a deep breath. The city air smelled sweet by contrast. Her shoulders relaxed. She'd done it, looked the demon in the face and was still in one piece. Her back straightened. Better than one piece. She'd taken control of her past.

She looked carefully at Jenny. Her daughter's eyes were wide. Maddie recognized shell shock when she saw it.

"So, that was your grandmother."

Jenny shook her head. "I never knew."

"I didn't want you to know." She took a deep breath.

"Sooner or later though, you had to find out."

They walked down the street to the car in silence. Jenny glanced back at the house as they drove away. "I'm glad we went. She's family, and she needs our help."

A proud tear came to Maddie's eye. She reached over and patted Jenny's hand. "I'm glad too. She's a sick woman. She might not always want our help, and she certainly won't let us to tell her what to do, but we can keep an eye on her and do what we can."

Jenny nodded. "Next time we'll take new dish cloths—and some duct tape."

* * *

Back at the apartment, Maddie felt strangely energized. Clear-headed. Free of a weight that had sapped her energy for, well, forever. She was free to focus on *her* life.

Framed photographs leaned against every square inch of wall space around the apartment, but the familiar faces and scenes seemed oddly out of place in this urban setting. Her gaze landed on the face of the mother bear and she felt the same spark of connection now that she felt the first time their eyes met through the lens.

We're not so different, you and me. Just caught in the wrong place at the wrong time and wanting nothing more than to head back where we belong.

But she had reasons for coming back to the city and she'd see them through. Starting tomorrow with hanging the show.

* * *

Maddie carried the first load of pictures up the stairs to the Edge. Tori had painted the walls a pale silver-grey to set off the black frames and crisp white mats. Soon the photographs circled the room on the gallery floor, leaning against the walls. Finished and framed, each photograph now stood out as an individual piece of art.

Tori stepped back and took a good look. "They look great."

Maddie folded her arms tightly across her chest to contain

her excitement.

Tori stepped up to the one of Jake and Sarah. "Have you decided what you're going to do?"

"It's not my decision to make."

Tori put her hand on Maddie's arm. "Don't give up so easily. Your life is always your decision."

When Maddie got home, the apartment felt empty and strangely forlorn. Her babies were gone. *This is what it will feel like when Jenny leaves home.*

She had taken a week off, despite Eileen's disapproval, and as she paced the small living room, she went over the week's schedule in her mind.

Monday, she and Tori would hang and tweak the show. Then Tuesday night was Art Walk and the opening party. Thankfully, that was Tori's department.

Eileen had grumbled, but Maddie had pushed and gotten the weekend off too. She wanted to do something special with Jenny, maybe take her somewhere nice for dinner.

But then what? She dropped into the chair by the window, closed her eyes and took a deep breath.

She wanted to go back—*really* wanted to go back. But mostly, she wanted to see Jake.

Once admitted, relief filled her lungs. But at the same time, a warm wash of misery rushed over her. How could she have thought of that wonderful opportunity for love as a complication? It had been the opportunity of a lifetime and she had blown it. Who's to say it wouldn't have worked out?

She wasn't the same person who went to Fortune Bay six months ago. She had changed; made real friends, wrestled a wringer washer into submission, stared wild animals straight in the eye and she had the pictures to prove it.

The lessons of Frankie's solstice tarot reading still churned in her mind. Since then, a few things had become clear. She had taken the staff and silenced the old demons that held her back—and gained strength in the doing. She finally stepped outside that circle of swords and could see that her mother's condition didn't define her. Cindy couldn't ruin her life. Only she could do that.

And she almost had. Hopefully, it wasn't too late.

She sat forward in her chair, hands resting on her thighs. She knew what was in the two full cups too. Love and Happiness. What she did with them was her choice. She could let them spill out onto the dry ground like the others on the card, or pick them up and carry them to the castle. Once there, she would find her knight and use the staff to whack that shiny helmet right off his stubborn head.

She was boiling for action, but she needed a new plan.

She sat back in her chair, frowning thoughtfully. Okay then, what did she want?

I want to go home. The words sent a shiver through her heart. In four short months, Fortune Bay had become her home and the people there had become family. Because what was family except the people you lived with, who loved you and knew you and would not let you down? Who accepted you for who you were, even when they knew your secrets.

Yes, I want to go home. And for the first time in her life, she knew exactly where that was.

Starting this weekend. She'd been refusing Frankie's invitations, afraid that seeing Jake would be too painful. But that had to change.

The walls that protected them while Jenny was growing up now kept out the very people she wanted *in* her life. She would go back to Fortune Bay and, if necessary, she would live there alone, like Augusta. But at least she'd be close to her friends.

The reasons she came back to Seattle were still valid and first she would do everything necessary to see Jenny on her way. But then she was going back to Fortune Bay, with or without Jake Murphy.

She had the power, she just had to use it. Checking her watch, she picked up the phone.

"What's up?" Frankie asked when she heard Maddie's

voice.

"Is your invitation still open?"

"Always. What did you have in mind?"

"I want to come over for the weekend. Can Jenny and I stay with you?"

"That would be awesome."

Maddie grinned to herself at the "awesome". Frankie was back at work at the high school.

"And you're coming to the opening? I don't think I can face it alone."

"We sure are. You'll knock 'em dead."

When she got off the phone, her blood fizzed and sparkled like champagne in her veins. She went into the tiny kitchen and got out a mixing bowl and baking sheets. An hour later, when Jenny came through the door, Maddie had streaks of flour on her cheeks, the air smelled like sugar and spice and cookies were cooling on the rack.

Jenny sniffed the air and grinned. "Children's Delight?"

"You bet. Turns out I know the recipe by heart. We're going back."

OCTOBER

Chapter 39

Maddie and Jenny arrived at the gallery half an hour before the show was to start. "Now Showing" screamed her name from the poster on the front door and her nerves danced a jig as they climbed the stairs.

"This is it," she said to Jenny. She had wanted this, had worked for it, but now that it was show time, she would have rather been anywhere else.

What if no one comes?

Of course people would come. It was *Art Walk.* There would be people and she couldn't hide because *she* was the center of attention tonight. Everyone would want to talk to *her.* The frogs in her stomach started jumping into the gurgling acid pond. She pressed her hand to her middle, feeling the sequins on the *previously-loved* sheath Louise had found for her.

"I hope they make it," she murmured. "I hope someone comes. I hope I sell something." Her voice rose with every new thought. "This is going to be a disaster."

Jenny laughed. "No, Mom. It's going to be great."

When they reached the top of the stairs, Maddie walked into the middle of the room and slowly turned around. Familiar faces and vistas shone from the walls. Her stomach muscles relaxed, her shoulders dropped and her heart rate slowed. They were good. She might just pull it off.

"Want a drink?" Tori asked at her shoulder. "The bar is setting up in the corner."

"No thank you."

"Probably just as well. You have a big night ahead of you," Tori said, heading off to field a question from the caterers.

Maddie could see from the clock in Tori's office that the patrons would start arriving in ten minutes. She clenched her clammy hands together. *If anyone came.*

She'd sunk everything she had, money, time, energy—her heart—into this show and it could all go belly up. Tonight. In eight minutes.

Her throat constricted so tightly that her head began to swim. She stumbled into the tiny washroom in the corridor, locked herself in, put her hands on the cool porcelain rim of the sink and waited for the nausea to pass.

The minutes ticked by as she eyed herself in the mirror. She'd talked Louise down from an all red dress to black with red slashes, and of course the crimson heels Louise had insisted on to finish the outfit. Maddie loved the shoes, even if the stilettos were a challenge. Sparkly earrings hung from her ears and for the finishing touch, she pulled a Cherry Bomb lipstick out of her clutch and painted it on, smacking her lips at her image in the mirror.

A knock sounded on the door. Jenny called, "Mom? People are starting to arrive."

Giving herself a brave smile in the mirror, she unlocked the door and stepped into the gallery as the first Art Walk visitors emerged from the stairway. Tori took her arm and gave it a squeeze.

"Here is the artist now," she said, passing Maddie off to an eager middle-aged couple.

The evening unfolded in a blur of people. Handsome young waiters in black pants and white shirts, their sleeves rolled up to the forearm, threaded their way through the growing crowd with trays hors d'oeuvres. Dramatic spotlights blasted down from tracks on the ceiling, highlighting the work on the walls, sparking off wine glasses in the hands of the guests and raising the temperature in the room.

Sending up a prayer of thanks for Tori's client list, Maddie plastered a smile on her face for the hundredth time and greeted another potential customer. The woman, big hoops in her ears and black kohl ringing her eyes, shook Maddie's hand, not letting go. Maddie pushed down the spit of panic that constriction always spurred—it wasn't the first time tonight—and smiled modestly, answering her questions as she had all evening. *No, they weren't digital. Yes, she did the darkroom work herself. Yes, she could do weddings.*

Slowly, she relaxed. She was handling it, although as the evening wore on, she wanted nothing more than to take off the damn high heels and slip on her sneakers. She exchanged smiles with Tori across the room, then saw Jenny leading her dad and Kate around the gallery, talking about the photographs like a trained professional. Before they left, they cornered Maddie for air kisses.

"Fabulous Maddie," Mark said, doing a terrible job of hiding his surprise. She smiled, going for regal, and graciously accepted their praise. That moment was worth all the anxiety so far.

Red stickers indicating sales lined up on the walls below the photographs. In the noise and confusion, she wondered what the people actually saw. The magnificence of the coastal forests, the lake and the mountains were obvious, but did they catch the sense of community she'd tried to portray? The strength of the people who live there? The pioneers who had opened up the area and the hard-core loggers doing what they did best?

The photo that garnered the most attention was the sepia headshot of the mother bear.

"Did you really face it alone?" they asked, and she was glad she had told the story so many times at the Fortune Bay café that tonight she could tell it with finesse.

She continued to schmooze until finally, out of the corner of her eye, she saw Frankie and Louise emerge from the staircase. Jenny hurried over to give them hugs and as they walked toward her Maddie's eyes misted over.

Louise gave her a whopping kiss on the cheek. "Sorry we're so late; we caught the six o'clock ferry after work."

"You're not late; things are finally quieting down a bit. It was crazy right at seven. Now we can talk." She shepherded them to the refreshment table and put glasses of wine in their hands.

Louise's head swiveled right and left. "It's so weird to get here and find these familiar faces on the walls." She pointed to one shot. "That's me! I feel like a star. I have to look around."

Frankie went with her, Louise checking out the crazy fashions many of the Art Walk patrons wore. It was great to see them, but Maddie had secretly hoped that Jake would come too. All evening she had been checking the entrance, hoping and fearing he would emerge at the top of the stairs. But he would have taken the same ferry as Frankie and Louise and would have been here by now. Her friends would have told her.

So, apparently it was up to her. She didn't know how she would handle it when she saw Jake in Fortune Bay.

* * *

The next morning, Frankie and Louise left to catch an early ferry. Maddie was excited to be going back to Fortune Bay for the weekend, but anxiety buzzed through her like an electric current, overshadowing her excitement about the show. She tidied up the kitchen, wiped the counters again, then recognized her old cleaning habit creeping back and threw the cloth in the sink.

"I am *not* that woman anymore," she said. There was no one there to hear her declaration, but it bolstered her confidence nonetheless.

She would go to see Tori, that's what she'd do, see what the final sales count was last night. Then she'd come home and pack for the weekend. Maybe she and Jenny would even leave for Fortune Bay tonight.

She parked the Beast in front of the Edge, jogged up the

stairs to the gallery and stopped in the doorway. It was early, for a gallery, but already someone was there.

He came.

His back was to her as he stared at an enlargement of the photo of Sarah with the candy apple; the photo they had developed in the dark room together; the photo Maddie had left for him on the kitchen table at the cabin with the note, *I will never forget you.*

Even from the back he looked gorgeous, his dark hair curling over the collar of the turtleneck he wore under his leather jacket. Blood pounded in her ears and her heart twisted in her chest, oozing warm goo that spread all through her insides.

Look at me, she thought, and as if he could feel her eyes on him, he turned. His eyes burned, electric blue, fusing a link between them. She couldn't move, pinned by the intensity of his stare. Then he started across the room toward her.

His cheeks were hollower than she remembered but the raw vulnerability that had been on his face at their last meeting in Majestic was gone.

She reached out and he grasped her hand tightly. A current of warmth rushed through her.

"They're perfect," he said, glancing around the room. "I knew you could see it."

"I always loved Fortune Bay."

"Thank you for the picture." He indicated the larger version on the wall that he had been studying when she arrived. "It helped. I didn't think so at first, but it did." They stood locked together in a silent vignette.

"I've missed you," he said, his voice deep. "I need you to come back."

She lifted her fingers to his lips. He kissed them and she smiled, but held them in place.

"Before you say anything more, there is someone I want you to meet."

* * *

Maddie's slippery hands almost slid off the steering wheel when she made the last turn onto her mother's street. Jake hadn't spoken in the car and she had no idea what his reaction to Cindy would be. Meeting her might ruin everything, however, she had to get this hurdle out of the way. No more living in Cindy's shadow. She refused to give her mother that power anymore.

Jake had insisted on buying a few pastries from the shop next to the Edge to take. Maddie tried to explain that Cindy wouldn't eat any, then decided that at least it would give them something to do.

She phoned, but Cindy didn't answer. Not really a surprise. It was still early, before noon. Cindy could still be in bed. Hopefully, alone.

Maddie led Jake up the rickety front steps and into the dark hallway where they stood in front of Cindy's door. Maddie couldn't move, couldn't knock. This was a bad idea. A *really* bad idea. Tears formed in her eyes as she glanced at Jake. She didn't want to lose him, not when she had just gotten him back.

"Is this her door?" he asked.

She nodded mutely.

He knocked. There was a rustle inside, a shuffle of slippers on the floor and the door opened a crack. Cindy took one look at Jake and her eyes widened in fear. Maddie stepped quickly in front of him.

"It's just me, Mom."

Cindy put her hand on her chest. She opened the door and stepped back. "You gave me a fright. I thought it was the cops. Not that I've got any reason to think they'd be coming here, just, you know..."

Maddie stepped inside and quickly looked around. Thank goodness, her mother was alone. Cindy pulled her battered housecoat closed and tightened the sash, eyeing Jake with a gleam in her eye.

"I called Mom, but you didn't answer."

"I was probably out," Cindy said. Obviously not true, but Maddie let it pass. Cindy continued staring at Jake as if he was a prime cut of meat and she was a starving dog.

"This is my friend Jake. From Fortune Bay."

Jake took Cindy's hand in both of his. "Nice to meet Maddie's mother."

Maddie was afraid her mother would climb Jake's leg in another minute so she thrust the box of pastries at her. "We brought these for breakfast Mom, chocolate croissants. Why don't I make some coffee to go with them?"

In confusion Cindy took the box and followed her to the kitchen where Maddie put on the kettle and searched for clean dishes. The kitchen was in more or less the same condition as when she'd come with Jenny. On the edge of the counter stood a bottle of gin, two-thirds gone.

Maddie didn't try to do all the dishes this time, just enough to get through the ritual coffee and pastries. She cleared off the table and wiped it clean, then wiped the chair seats for good measure. Jake held out a chair for Cindy who took it, although her eyes kept returning longingly to the gin bottle on the counter.

Maddie tried to hurry the process along. She couldn't wait to get him out of there. And although Jake seemed quite relaxed, she couldn't look him in the eye. Now he'd seen it, not the worst but enough to let him know where she'd come from and what he was in for if he stuck with her for the long haul.

Finally, it was time to go and, as they stood at the doorway Jake shook Cindy's hand. "It was nice to meet you. I want to marry your daughter."

Maddie's head jerked around so fast she could have gotten whiplash. This was the last thing she expected him to say.

"Oh, honey, you got yourself a looker," Cindy said. Jake laughed and bent down and kissed her cheek.

Maddie couldn't take her eyes off Jake. He still wanted

her. He'd met the dragon and hadn't run. She knew she had a big goofy smile on her face, but she didn't care.

He took her arm as they walked down the steps and once they were on the sidewalk, she turned to him, serious once more. "Are you sure?"

He smiled. "Sure I want to marry you? Yes."

"Even now that you've met my mother?"

"Yes."

"This is my family. This is how I grew up. I don't have any idea how to make a real family."

"Sure you do. I've seen you with the girls. You're a wonderful mother. And hopefully, someday, we'll have a child of our own."

She threw her arms around his neck. He felt sturdy and sure and, best of all, hers. This was good, better than good, but there were still a few logistics she had to get clear.

"I am coming back this weekend, but I can't just move back. Not yet."

"That's okay. We'll work it out. I know you have your own life and I won't try to tell you what to do. But consider this." He reached into his jacket pocket and pulled out an envelope with her name written on the front in Stephanie's looping script.

Maddie took the envelope and pulled out a letter, but before she could read it, he hurried on.

"She's offering you the cabin." His voice dropped huskily. "Or you can stay with me. Whatever you want. I love you Maddie. I'm in. We'll to do it however you want."

Maddie's heart expanded to fill her chest until she could feel every beat. "I still have to get Jenny through school. That's only one more year, a few months really, but I have to be here for her until then. But I'll try to come to Fortune Bay for every holiday. Jenny likes it there too. And we would love to use the cabin. Maybe some local handyman will lay in a load of firewood for us. I hear it gets cold in the winter." Her lips curved into a smile.

"Then what?" he asked, taking her hands again and running a row of soft kisses along her knuckles that somehow connected with her belly and turned her brain to mush.

She shook her head. Couldn't let it distract her. She had to finish. "I love you too Jake, and once Jenny is finished school, I'm coming back. I belong with you in Fortune Bay."

He swept her into his arms and Maddie fell into the reassuring strength, felt the sweet warmth of his lips. He smelt of sunshine and autumn leaves. The city disappeared and she was back at the lake with the man she loved. Her nervousness vanished. She could trust him. Forever.

He kissed her there on the street until her legs felt like melted candle wax. When he finally released her, she leaned against a lamppost while he searched his pockets again. This time he pulled out a small, square jeweler's box. "I'd planned to wait for a more romantic setting..."

She opened the box and her breath came back in a whoosh when she saw the ring inside, a circle of tiny rubies surrounding one central diamond. The facets caught the light and reflected back a rainbow of color.

"Beautiful," she whispered.

"It's a family ring." Jake took it out and slipped it on her finger. "Aunt Augusta's. It reminded me of you."

Putting her hands on his shoulders, she went up on her toes as he pulled her in for a searing kiss. A kiss that felt like coming home.

* * * * * * *

I hope you enjoyed Maddie and Jake's story in **Summer of Fortune***.* To read the first chapter of the next book in the series, **The Good Neighbor,** Frankie and Sean's story, go to my website, ***www.JudithHudsonAuthor.com***

While you're there, you can also join my Readers Group and I'll send you a free eCopy* of the prequel novella of the series, **Lake of Dreams***, background on all the Fortune Bay books and news of new releases.*

*On my website, **search "how to read eBooks without an ereader"** *for instructions for how to read eBooks on your tablet, phone or computer.*

I love hearing from readers. ☺ *You can always contact me at Judy@JudithHudsonAuthor.com.*

Thank you for your support.

Judith Hudson

P.S.: You'll find the recipe for Children's Delight Cookies on my website too. ☺

The Fortune Bay Series
Available on Amazon as eBook and paperback.

Lake of Dreams
Get this free prequel e-novella when
you sign up for my readers group at
bit.ly/freeFB-e-book

Summer of Fortune
Book One
Maddie wasn't looking for romance. Could a summer of
freedom change her life forever?

The Good Neighbor
Book Two
Sean hates to see Frankie and her father estranged. He'd give
anything to know where his own daughter is.

Home for Christmas
Book Three
Blue's carried a torch for Louise his whole life, but this time
he's not sure he can wait around to pick up the pieces.

Family Matters
A Sequel Novella
Things are at a low ebb for Frankie and Sean. Be sure to read
The Good Neighbor and *Home for Christmas* first!

Starting Over
Book Four
After a horrific motorcycle accident, Marshall's life seems to
be over—until Lily knocks on his door.

Starlight and Tinsel
A Christmas Novella
Star finally gets her chance to shine in this Christmas novella.

Also by Judith Hudson
Writing as J.M. Hudson

The Rocky and Bernadette Mystery Series

Temple of the Jaguar
A Mayan Murder Mystery
A travel cozy mystery. A travel writer and a
photographer's first job together in the Yucatan quickly
unravels when a body is discovered in the crocodile lagoon.

I want to thank my legion of beta readers who encouraged me throughout the process of writing this book. I have always appreciated, and in many cases implemented, your comments and ideas to improve the story.

I particularly want to thank those valiant souls who read this manuscript more than once; Jenny Watson, Kama Aldersey, and anyone else I may have forgotten. Jo-Ann Terpstra who is always on call for formatting advice, as well as my friend and terrifically supportive editor Stephanie Webb, who has been a great sounding board for story ideas since the beginning.

My family has stuck by me through it all. Early on; my son Frank saw the Cindy's potential as a main character, my daughter Rosey has also read the manuscript many times and always offered great feedback in addition to designing the beautiful covers for this series, and my long suffering husband Reid who, with his usual good grace, put up with me during the years I've been working on this series and this book.

Thank you all.

Judy Hudson

Summer of Fortune is a work of fiction. Names, characters, places and incidents are the product of the imagination of the author or are used fictitiously. Any resemblance to actual events, locales or persons, living or dead, is entirely coincidental.

Published by Tall Trees Books, June 2016
Cover designed by Rosey Hudson